Praise

"Weepingly funn[...]"

"Lovely, delightful, funny." —BUZZFEED

"Vibrant and bright." —BUSTLE

"Beautifully told." —HYPABLE

★ "A soulful and hilarious debut." —BOOKLIST, starred review

★ "Effervescent." —PUBLISHERS WEEKLY, starred review

★ "Universal." —SCHOOL LIBRARY JOURNAL, starred review

★ "This deserves a place on every shelf, though it will not stay there long."
—VOYA, starred review

"Eye-opening, hilarious, and sometimes heartbreaking." —SHELF AWARENESS

"An earnest, funny, and emotional story." —BOOK RIOT

"Charmed my socks off."
—DAVID ARNOLD,
NEW YORK TIMES BESTSELLING AUTHOR OF
KIDS OF APPETITE AND MOSQUITOLAND

"Incredibly timely, honest, and moving."
—SANDHYA MENON,
NEW YORK TIMES BESTSELLING AUTHOR OF
WHEN DIMPLE MET RISHI

Also by Gloria Chao

Our Wayward Fate

American Panda

Gloria Chao

Simon Pulse
New York London Toronto Sydney New Delhi

SIMON PULSE

An imprint of Simon & Schuster Children's Publishing Division

1230 Avenue of the Americas, New York, New York 10020

First Simon Pulse paperback edition July 2019

Text copyright © 2018 by Gloria Chao

Cover photographs of wall and items on table copyright © 2019 by Getty Images

All other cover photographs copyright © 2019 by Image Source/Glasshouse Images

Also available in a Simon Pulse hardcover edition.

For information about special discounts for bulk purchases, please contact Simon & Schuster
Special Sales at 1-866-506-1949 or business@simonandschuster.com.

The Simon & Schuster Speakers Bureau can bring authors to your live event. For more
information or to book an event contact the Simon & Schuster Speakers Bureau
at 1-866-248-3049 or visit our website at www.simonspeakers.com.

Cover designed by Sarah Creech

Interior designed by Tom Daly

The text of this book was set in Adobe Caslon Pro.

Manufactured in the United States of America

2 4 6 8 10 9 7 5 3 1

The Library of Congress has cataloged the hardcover edition as follows:

Names: Chao, Gloria, author.

Title: American panda / by Gloria Chao.

Description: First Simon Pulse hardcover edition. | New York : Simon Pulse, 2018. |
Summary: A freshman at MIT, seventeen-year-old Mei Lu tries to live up to her
Taiwanese parents' expectations, but no amount of tradition, obligation, or guilt
prevent her from hiding several truths—that she is squeamish with germs
and cannot become a doctor, she prefers dancing to biology, she decides to
reconnect with her estranged older brother, and she is dating a Japanese boy.

Identifiers: LCCN 2017014314 (print) | LCCN 2017045891 (eBook) |
ISBN 9781481499125 (eBook) | ISBN 9781481499101 (hardcover)

Subjects: | CYAC: Taiwanese Americans—Fiction. | Family life—Fiction. |
Massachusetts Institute of Technology—Fiction.

Classification: LCC PZ7.1.C4825 (eBook) |
LCC PZ7.1.C4825 Am 2018 (print) | DDC [Fic]—dc23

LC record available at https://lccn.loc.gov/2017014314

ISBN 9781481499118 (pbk)

For Anthony, always, for believing in my words, for helping me find my inner *měi*, for giving me the world

And for anyone who's ever felt like they didn't belong

Author's Note about the Mandarin Words

In this book, I used the pinyin system for the Mandarin words because it is the most widely known Romanization system. For pronunciation: the marks above the vowels represent four tones, with the lines indicating the pitch contour of the voice.

A straight line (ā), the first tone, is high and level, monotone.

Second tone (á) rises in pitch.

Third tone (ǎ) dips, then rises.

Fourth (à) starts high and drops, producing a sharp sound.

For some of the Mandarin phrases, I chose to depict the tones as the words are pronounced in conversation in my family's accent. There may be some discrepancy with other accents and dialects.

CHAPTER 1

Stinky Tofu

The stench of the restaurant's specialty walloped my senses as soon as I entered. Even with seventeen years of practice, I didn't have a fighting chance against a dish named *stinky tofu*. I gagged.

My mother sniffed and smiled. "Smells like home."

Mmm. Who doesn't love the scent of athlete's foot with lunch? I held a fist to my face, desperately inhaling the pomegranate scent of my hand sanitizer.

She swatted my hand down. "Don't touch your face, Mei. Give yourself pimples for no reason. There are no ugly women. Only lazy women."

In my head, I counted to ten in English, then Mandarin. Two more hours, three tops.

Mrs. Pan, a family friend who used to drive me to Chinese school, came over to our table to say hello, which apparently required grabbing my chin to inspect my face. My instinct to be deferential (heightened by my mother's side-eye) warred with my desire to shake off Mrs. Pan's bacteria-covered hands. When she finished her inspection and let go, I fought the urge to cover my now-sticky chin in pomegranate antiseptic, my trusty little sidekick.

"I can't believe this is little Mei," Mrs. Pan squeaked. "You got pretty! And look how big your nose is! That's promising."

I pasted on a well-rehearsed smile but couldn't keep said nose from scrunching. I like my nose just fine, thank you very much, but years of "compliments" about its large size had made me insecure.

Mrs. Pan misinterpreted my embarrassment for confusion and explained, "It's a Chinese superstition—having a big nose means you will have lots of money."

Yes, because people will pay me to see my clown nose?

"*Aiyah*," my mother said, using the Chinese word of exasperation that, for her, preceded every faux brag. "I do hope Mei makes money in the future, not for her sake, but mine. She just started at MIT this week, premed of course, and her tuition is driving me to an early grave. Ah, if she hadn't skipped a grade, I would have had one more year to save up money. Sometimes I feel her intelligence is a curse."

2

I probably should've been embarrassed, but this was the only form of praise I ever heard. I replayed my mother's words in my head, letting the undertones of pride embrace me. Then, in anticipation of the round of my-child's-brain-is-bigger-than-your-child's that usually followed, I held my breath. Like if I breathed too loudly, I might miss it.

But Mrs. Pan went in another direction. A much worse, infinitely more embarrassing direction.

"Is Mei single?" she asked my mother as if I'd disappeared. "My firstborn son, Hanwei, is the sweetest, smartest boy, and he just might be interested in Mei!"

This was a first for me, probably sparked by my entrance to college, which to some Asian mothers meant releasing the hounds—husband-hunting season had begun. Never mind that I was only seventeen and had been forbidden to date until a week ago.

Mrs. Pan flashed a picture, always at the ready. The corners were dog-eared from frequent trips in and out of her pocket. I smiled, but it wasn't because I thought Hanwei was cute. I could never date the boy who once peed on my foot. Sure, we were six at the time and in a car, but to me he would always be the boy who couldn't control his bladder. And to him I was the carsick girl who had to carry a vomit bag—aka a recycled Ziploc my mother washed out by hand after each upchuck, too stingy to dip into the mountain of new ones in the garage. God, I might need a Ziploc right now at the thought of Pee-Boy and me together.

"Mei has lots of suitors," my mother said. A lie. "Nice seeing you. Enjoy your meal."

Perceiving her matchmaking to be a bust, Mrs. Pan turned off the charm and voiced what was really on her mind. "How did you get both of your children to be doctors? Especially your firstborn, Xing. He was always so *tiáopí* as a child, always getting other kids, even my *guāi* Hanwei, to do the worst things, like watch the R movies or play those violent video games."

To avoid acknowledging my brother's existence, my mother covered her face with a menu and declared she was so hungry she could die—a common Chinese saying. Mrs. Pan hovered a minute, hoping to break through my mother's defenses, but the situation was too awkward for even her to bear.

As Mrs. Pan left, my mother leaned over and whispered, "Hanwei isn't good enough for you, Mei. He went to Northeastern! *And* I heard from Mrs. Ahn who heard from Mrs. Tian—Remember Mrs. Tian? Her son went to Princeton—that after Hanwei graduated, he threw his college degree away to pursue music."

I wondered how he had pulled that off. How did he get his way when his mother dreamed of Dr. Hanwei Pan saving the world, a surgeon despite his nubbin bladder?

"I bet you Hanwei's nose is tiny—a peanut," my mother continued. "He's now begging for money in exchange for guitar lessons."

"You mean he's teaching music? Like many other normal people?"

"Not normal. Last resort. Soon he'll be just like Ying-Na."

Poor Ying-Na. The Taiwanese-American cautionary tale of a girl who chose happiness over honoring her parents and was cut off financially and emotionally. Now she was the *pìgu* of every rumor, all created to support other parents' warnings. *Ying-Na decided to major in English and now lives in a refrigerator box. Ying-Na had an American boyfriend and he stole all her money. Ying-Na had one sip of alcohol and flunked out of college.* And for my mother, *Ying-Na veered off her parents' career track and now takes off her clothes for quarters.*

"I'm so glad you will be a doc-tor," my mother continued, her pride overemphasizing each syllable. "Doctors always have a job. Never have to worry. So stable, so secure. And so respectable. That's why we're so happy to pay your tuition."

I ducked my head in fear of her seeing the truth in my eyes—that bacteria-ridden patients made my skin crawl and biology put me to . . . zzzz. But unless I wanted to be Ying-Na 2.0, I didn't have a choice.

The waiter set down three Wet-Naps, which my mother immediately swept into her purse. Then our drinks: soy milk for my mother and a plum smoothie for my father, who was still out looking for elusive street parking.

As the waiter handed me my papaya smoothie, my mother poked my breast. "These are still so small, like mosquito bites."

Due to rumors of a papaya-eating aboriginal village in China that churned out big-breasted women, my mother had been forcing mushy pink fruit down my throat since I hit puberty. Spoiler: It didn't work.

My B-cup breasts were too small for my "no-ugly-women" mother and the rest of my size-eight frame too big. She wished I was a classic Chinese beauty who would "fall over when the wind blows," but I had missed the "skinny" gene on her side and instead inherited from my dad, whose college nickname was *Lu Pàng*, or Fat Lu. I preferred not to look like a chopstick with two cantaloupes for breasts, but I was in the minority.

As if on cue, my mother's inspection traveled to my waist, which she pinched. "You're getting fat. Have you been exercising?"

It had to be a trap. If I admitted how much time I'd spent sneaking away to dance classes, she'd scold me for (1) not studying enough and (2) "throwing away" good money. I pressed my lips into a hard line, choosing silence. *It's because she loves you,* I reminded myself. Right before they disowned my brother, they had stopped criticizing his negative attitude, his laziness, his weight. . . . It had been the last step before cutting him out. Reprimands meant they still cared . . . right?

"You need to be careful, Mei. No man wants a panda—lazy, round, and silly. All *yuán gǔn gǔn.*"

"Pandas are cute."

"Do you think the concubines won the emperor's attention by being *cute*? Be a cat. They know how to *sājiāo* and get the man's attention. They're *nián rén* without being clingy—the perfect rice. Not too sticky, not too independent."

"Apt example, Mǎmá. People declaw cats, essentially cutting off their 'fingers,' and our ancestors used to break women's feet to bind them into three-inch monstrosities. Except that was to keep them from running away." I just couldn't help it.

She slapped the air with her open palm. "So disrespectful! How will you ever get a man?" She cleared her throat. "Actually, I have this friend—remember Mrs. Huang? Her son is interested in meeting you. Eugene is Taiwanese, a senior at Harvard, and will be a good husband. He's applying to medical schools now." She began pawing at my blunt bangs as if she were Edward Scissorhands. "We'll have to clean up this mess before you meet him. Really, Mei, why you insist on having these? Just to give me a heart attack?"

I had gotten bangs to hide the off-center mole on my fore-head. The one that was so close to smack-dab-in-the-middle that my mother's Buddhist friends were always commenting on how I had *just* missed out on it being in the center. Too bad, so unlucky, because *that* would have made it less embarrassing. After the hundredth friend had touched the mole without permission, leaving it sticky and violated, I had taken matters (and the scissors) into my own hands. And I haven't looked back, not even when my mother said, *Why you want the hairstyle of Japanese schoolchildren?*

I batted her hand away, then scooted my chair farther for good measure. "Yeah, Mămá, I can't wait to meet this guy who needs his mom to get a girlfriend."

"Wonderful! We'll set up a date for next week!" Sarcasm didn't translate.

"I was joking, Mămá."

She accompanied her signature tongue cluck with her signature phrase. "I'm your *mŭqīn*," she declared, using the formal, distant version of "mother" that implied authority.

This was becoming a pain in my *pìgu*. I tried to shut it down. "According to you, no boys were allowed in high school. And I'm only seventeen; I should be a high school senior."

"But you're not. College is the best time to find a husband. American girls peak in junior high, high school with looks, but you will peak now. You hated that you got your period so much later than the other girls"—I covered my face to hide from any patrons who might have overheard—"but like I told you then, it's a good thing. All my older friends with *mean-o-pause*—they look okay one day, then wrinkly the next. Like those *suānméi* your bǎbá loves." She shuddered, probably from picturing faces on my dad's prunes like I was. Then she straightened her spine. "I still have my period," she said in a tone that others would reserve for *I just got a promotion.* "And you'll have yours many, many years after your peers sag. It's genetics."

Well, we rough-roaded it, but we managed to turn off course, away from preapproved Ivy League husbands. I just wish it didn't have to involve my period. Or hers.

"Wait, what was I saying?" Guess I spoke too soon. "Oh right. Mei, take advantage of your youth while you can. And I chose Eugene *precisely* because you're still so young. He is a good boy. Won't try anything. Other boys will try to trick you into having the sex, and you're too young to know how to handle that. As your *mǔqīn*, I'm going to tell you the truth. It doesn't feel good for women. It's only to make babies, which you are not ready for quite yet. But soon. With Eugene."

Since I was about to toss my fortune cookies, I played my trump card. "Maybe we'll see what Bǎbá has to say about this when he gets here."

Her mouth snapped shut, knowing my father, who still saw

me as a five-year-old, would fly into a chopstick-throwing rage at the thought of me dating. She excused herself to the bathroom, most likely to touch up her makeup. Clarification: to powder and reapply mascara; her eyeliner and lipstick were tattooed on.

My ears perked up at the sound of English amid the sea of Mandarin. Across the restaurant, a group of students was leaving their table.

A familiar face. Well, a familiar outline of hair—he was still too far away to be more than a blurry shape. Because of my near-sightedness and my mother's tenet that "no woman is attractive in glasses," I recognized people by silhouette and motion. At orientation, his head had bobbed above the sea of freshmen, and I had been attracted to his spiky anime hair. It had taken me half an hour to work up the courage to smile at him, but he'd been too busy laughing with the perky blonde beside him to notice shy, not-blond me. My heart had lurched, and then I had traveled back in time to first grade. Wooden desk. Chalkboard overhead. And six-year-old me looking from one classmate to another, wishing I didn't look so different.

Oh God, I was totally staring. Probably because I could see him clearer now that he was only a few yards away, and, well, I'm just happy I didn't drool. His face was all sharp angles and smooth skin, and he was that kind of lean muscular build—you know, nerd hot. Exactly my kind of poison.

His eyes caught mine, then shifted down to my MIT shirt. While I was deer-in-headlights frozen at having been caught gawking, he said something to his friends (never had I wanted superhearing so bad), then weaved between chairs to my corner (!!!). I popped a hip-level wave, then regretted it immediately.

He slid into the seat across from me, his knees bumping the table. "You look familiar. Did we meet at orientation?"

"No, but I'm Mei." I stuck a sweaty palm out.

He took it and didn't say *ew*. "Darren. Nice to meet you. Are you a fan of Chow Chow? I've never had Taiwanese food before."

"Did you like it?"

When his head bobbed up and down emphatically, I smiled, excited to have one more person in on the secret. There weren't enough Taiwanese restaurants on this side of the world, and braised pork rice and oyster pancakes were much too delicious to be so scarce.

"It was amazing"—the right side of his lip quirked up—"although that stinky tofu smell does take some getting used to. Sorry if you're a fan."

I shook my head. "Never tried it. I've already gotten enough of a taste through my nose. You know, smelling is a large part of tasting, so in a way, we've all 'tasted' dog poop and garbage." What a charmer. Maybe Hanwei was my soul mate after all.

But Darren wasn't ruffled by my unladylike words. "Well, stinky tofu isn't that far off, but I'm way more likely to try that than poop. In fact, I'm kind of curious about it—like, I want to try it *because* it smells so bad but it's still food. Funny how that works, you know?" He raised an eyebrow. "You've never been tempted? Not even one bite?"

"Ehhh, I'm good. I learned early not to trust my parents' food preferences. Because of them, child-me thought stinky tofu was normal and Chili's was the culinary master that invented fettuccine Alfredo." I'd never admitted this to anyone before—it was too embarrassing—but instead of pity or judgment, there was . . . something else . . . on his face. Empathy? Dare I say, interest?

"You must've been a cute little kid," he said. I expected him to be embarrassed by his words, but he was leaning back in his chair, a small smile on his lips, completely comfortable.

I wished I could be that self-assured, but since I was just me—*not* comfortable and completely awkward—I continued rambling. "Not according to my mother. I always talked with my mouth full, spoke when I shouldn't, and said rude things." I wondered if stinky tofu would taste better than my foot tasted right about now.

He shrugged. "Honesty is sometimes misconstrued as rudeness, which is probably why it's so rare." Suddenly he snapped, then pointed a finger at me. "That's where I know you from! You were the one who came to that girl's defense at orientation."

Aiyah. How much had he heard? Even though I knew exactly which girl he was talking about, I furrowed my eyebrows at him as if I didn't. Like I saved people daily.

"When the international student didn't get that joke," he clarified. "How MIT is like sex without a condom; you're glad you got in but—"

"—sorry you came," we said in unison.

Darren finished recounting, and I breathed a sigh of relief.

After I had chastised everyone for laughing at her—which had been a spur-of-the-moment decision fueled by my own experiences as the *pìgu* of the joke—I had told the girl, in an attempt to make her feel less alone, about that time in elementary school when I had brought my stuffed goat, Horny, to show-and-tell.

Darren leaned closer as he said, "I thought it was really nice of you to stand up for her."

"Thanks." I brought my eyes up to meet his and tried not to be too obvious about sneaking a deeper whiff of his scent. It was fresh, like spring, with a sprinkling of that distinct guy smell (the good kind).

He ticked his chin up at the plum smoothie and soy milk beside me. "Meeting some friends?"

"Sort of." I coughed into my fist. I couldn't lie now after his comment about honesty. I coughed again. "My parents." I shrugged, like I was so cool I was totally down hanging with them.

"Are they still in town from moving you in?"

I shook my head. "They live close by, in the suburbs."

"I wish my parents were closer. They're in Southern California. Orange County."

Instead of trying to make sense of the confusing mix of envy and sympathy fomented by his words, I simply nodded.

My mother exited the bathroom, her makeup the same as before, as far as I could tell. Ten rapid steps brought her to the table, and she stuck a hand out with a polite, "Hello, I'm Mrs. Lu."

"Nice to meet you. I'm Darren."

"Darren . . . ?" She waved her hand in a circle.

"Takahashi."

Her lips pursed to the side, then returned to a demure smile as she stepped to the left to clear him an exit path. "Nice to meet you. Have a great day."

If he was bothered by the send-off, he didn't let it show. I, for the record, was very much bothered but also knew it could have been worse. My mother not asking for his SAT scores or views on divorce was an improvement over her past record.

"Mei, it was a pleasure meeting you. I hope I see you around campus." He winked, making me freeze.

I managed another hip-level wave before he was out of sight.

My mother folded herself into the seat and placed her hands on the table, one over the other. My radar *ping*ed—I was going to hate the next ten minutes.

"He's Japanese, Mei."

"And?"

"They murdered our family. Orphaned my mother." Her voice caught as it always did whenever she spoke of the war.

"*He* didn't kill them. Please, don't make a thing of this. He saw my MIT shirt and came over to introduce himself. He probably won't remember me in a week." I hoped that last part was a lie.

My mother raised an eyebrow. "I saw how he was looking at you. You know the rules. No Japanese boys."

Or white, black, or Hispanic. Only Taiwanese, and a doctor to boot. I had been so excited about finally being allowed to date that I had overlooked the restrictions. Until now.

"I already found your husband, Mei. Eugene Huang. *Dr. Eugene Huang. Búyào tuō kùzi fàngpì*"—that is, *Don't take your pants off to fart*, the Chinese idiom my family used for, *Don't waste your time doing something extraneous*. In this case, dating.

"Oh my God, Mămá." I dropped my head in my hands, the flush from my cheeks warming my palms.

My mother fetched the dreaded comb from her purse. It looked like a normal, innocent comb, but I knew it was made from a dead cow's foot. "Do you have a headache? Come here. Let me *guā yi guā* your neck."

The cuteness of the Chinese phrase is deceiving—it means *to scrape away*, as in skin and blood, not toxins as the ancient healers once believed (and my mother still believes). I shuddered thinking about her sanding my neck until it looked like I had measles.

I did, in fact, have a bit of a headache, as any seventeen-year-old would upon hearing that her mother had already picked out her future husband. But I wasn't letting that bacteria-covered hoof near me.

I knew from experience not to fight this one with logic, which only instigated tongue clicks and guilt, my mother's number one weapon. *You dishonor your ancestors. Our medicine has been around longer. How can you, a future doctor, not understand that the practice of* guāshā *lets out bad energy?*

Instead, I pasted a smile on my face and lied. "I feel great. Don't bother with the cow's hoof. *Búyào tuō kùzi fàngpì*, right?"

My mother smiled and the tension waned. Nothing like using

her own wisdom to lighten the mood. Sometimes I just had to whip out my Mandarin. I pulled another trick out of my *xiùzi.* "I saw on Facebook that Amberly Ahn has a new boyfriend."

My mother bit the hook. Gossiping was harder for her to turn down than a soup dumpling is for me. "Ah, thank goodness."

As she chatted on and on about all the horrible things Amberly and her mother have done—*Mrs. Ahn betrayed me, wanting Eugene for Amberly. Hunh! As if Mrs. Huang would want Amberly's tiny hips instead of your child-bearing form*—I felt a (very odd) sense of security wrap around me, a blanket of comfort. Even though some—okay, most—of the things she was saying were gross, even though I didn't really want to meet Eugene, there was some kind of twisted pride in there.

And Chow Chow was my second home, my Taiwanese home away from my Taiwanese home. I knew its calligraphy wallpaper and ceiling lanterns as well as the plastic wrap covering my parents' furniture.

My father strolled in and sat sans words. Upon his arrival, the waiter brought over our favorite appetizer: "open-mouth" dumplings with steam pouring out the sides. Fitting, since I was sitting with my mouth open and some drool spilling out. My mother clucked her tongue at me and my jaw snapped shut.

As I was about to dig in, my father cleared his throat—a thundering noise that always made me sit up straight and lower my eyes. "Mei, a few words." He paused for effect. "MIT is your first step to a good life. Work hard, get good grades, get into a good medical school, and make us proud. Don't worry, we will be watching every step of the way. We will see you here, at Chow Chow, every Saturday, to check in." A decree, not a request.

My mother gave me the eyeball, and I knew she was telecommunicating, *You also need to marry Dr. Eugene Huang and pump out a litter of Taiwanese babies.*

I wanted to enjoy my newfound freedom and cut the umbilical cord, but with these words I realized it would never be severed, only stretched.

When my parents raised their soy milk and plum smoothie in the air, I needed a moment before I could lift my pink mush in return.

VOICEMAIL FROM MY MOTHER

Remember Amberly Ahn? She had eyelid surgery and it turned out great. We should think about doing that for you. Maybe we can tattoo your makeup on at the same time. Remember, there are no ugly women, only lazy women. Repeat that three times every morning.

And don't forget, "měi" means "beautiful" in Chinese. Live up to the name I chose for you.

Oh, and it's your mǔqīn.

CHAPTER 2

BB-Hate

When I opened the door to my usually empty dorm room, a gorgeous girl with olive skin and wavy hair (that I was immediately jealous of) was rearranging the furniture.

Guess she was the replacement for Leslie, who MIT's roommate-pairing algorithm had originally thought to be The One for me. But they hadn't accounted for Taiwanese politics. Upon seeing my chopstick-straight hair and black-as-bean-paste eyes, Leslie had asked, before I even knew her name, "Where're you from?"

Given her similar hair and eyes, her question had startled the words right out of me. I was used to being asked this, but not by other Asians, at least not in that tone. I gave her the answer I gave everyone: "Massachusetts."

She shook her head at me, annoyed, same as everyone else. I rubbed my eyes in case her Chinese-ness was somehow a hallucination.

Nope.

Instead of asking all the questions flooding my brain—*Why does it matter? Well, where are* you *from? What the hell is your name?*—I said, "I'm Taiwanese," hoping to move past the awkwardness so we could start the lifelong friendship promised me by books and movies.

"Thank God," she said. "I was worried you were from China."

Well, that was weird. And a first. "If I were, then would we not be friends?"

She furrowed her eyebrows at me for a second. Then the realization dawned on her face and she sighed, not bothering to hide her exasperation and perhaps even exaggerating it. "That means your parents aren't native."

When I stuck my chin out, silently asking what she was talking about, she clarified. "Your family came to Taiwan in 1949, during the Communist Revolution." A statement, not a question. Then she said the sentence that would haunt me for years to come. "Your family killed my family."

I gaped. Just stood there with my eyes wide, mouth open— completely incapacitated by the bomb she'd just set off. Finally, I managed to squeak out, "I don't know what you're talking about."

"Figures. Learn your own history. When your people"—she

practically spat the word—"invaded our home, you massacred us—my grandpa—for no reason."

"I—I'm sorry," I stuttered, so overwhelmed by the venom in her voice, as if I had personally wielded a gun in that war.

"And you all covered it up like they always do." She repacked the T-shirt she had just unpacked. "You don't get to call yourself Taiwanese. You're not. And you're not Chinese either, since your grandparents fled from there. You don't belong anywhere."

I was used to being shunned by others for my different-tinted skin, different-shaped eyes, and my parents' difficulty with *l*s and *r*s, but this was completely new. I guess to Leslie, we weren't the same either. Shortly thereafter, her bed was empty, a constant reminder of how much I didn't belong.

So even though the new roommate intimidated me with the confidence exuding from every cell of her long, lean, stupidly perfect body, there was no way this could go any worse.

I paused at the door and waved, a nervous grin on my face.

She wiped her hand on her tank top—what was on there?— and stuck it out to me. "Nicolette."

"I'm Mei." My hand remained by my side. There was an awkward pause as she dropped her arm and returned to moving her desk. I didn't want to address the germ-conscious elephant in the room, so I didn't say anything.

With a smirk, she said, "You're already better than my last roommate, Chatty Patty." I wondered what Nicolette would have called her if her name had been Gwendolyn. "She wanted to be BFFs"— Nicolette rolled her eyes—"and none of that will be happening, got it?" She dumped shiny new polka-dot sheets, which were as cute as she was, onto the bed. I cringed at my garage-sale floral bedspread that screamed, *I once belonged to an old lady.*

"Thanks to her, I'm stuck with you and you're stuck with me now, k? Sorry to change your single into a double." She emptied her suitcase on the bed but made no move to put anything away. "Oh, and just a heads-up—I'm gone most nights, so don't ever wait up for me."

I shrugged, not sure what else to do.

She nodded. "This is gonna work out great."

Maybe we were matched up because even the computer knew I'd be too scared to talk to her, just like she wanted. My age alone suggested I was a maladjusted, socially awkward introvert.

Or maybe the computer just sucked.

I felt foolish. I had never been able to show anyone what was really beneath my skin—why had I believed the roommate-pairing algorithm could find the one person to unlock my secrets? Oh for two now.

"See ya, Mei." Nicolette brushed out of the room, and I had a feeling those would be the last words between us for a long time.

• • •

Laughter streamed down the hallway and in through my open door, filling my ears and taunting me. I practiced a friendly smile in the mirror (it was fake and a little creepy), straightened my clothes (still wrinkled and smelled like stale drawer), then slunk down the hall with as much confidence as a *Bachelor* contestant.

Don't mention your age, I reminded myself. There was a strange (and often detrimental) human need for the familiar, and that extended to age. In high school, after multiple negative reactions to my being younger—which included some form of slapping an "immature" label on me like a huge *I* on my forehead—I started avoiding the topic, even awkwardly so, making the situation worse than if I had just answered them. *Why won't you tell me your age?* they would ask, worried I was a weirdo, and then, when I didn't respond, they'd ignore me for the rest of the time because, you know, I *was* a weirdo.

Maybe college was different, but why risk it? MIT did have their fair share of young phenoms, but I didn't want to be lumped in with them. I just wanted to be Mei, whoever that was.

The laughter embraced me as I walked into the common room, and my hope soared and straightened my spine. My plastic smile turned genuine as I looked from one pair of bright eyes to another.

Seven students of various ages, races, and genders were spread among the four tattered sofas, separate but together. Almost everyone was wearing apparel featuring TIM the MIT Beaver, and for once I fit in.

"Hi! I'm Mei," I yelled—well, I thought I yelled. The actual scratchy sound that came out was lost among the chatter. I waved—large, dorky, and in a huge awkward circle in front of me. Not wanting to see their reaction, I lowered my eyes and folded myself into the corner of the closest armchair, the one with the multicolored stains splashed across the pilly fabric. I tried not to think about the parade of people who'd probably had sex there through the years.

The cute girl in the I ♡ MY BEAVER T-shirt leaned over and

filled me in. "We're having a debate: C-3PO versus BB-8."

"What's a BB-8?" I asked without thinking.

They all stared at me as if I had just asked, *What's pi?*

I thought about adding *just kidding*, but I didn't have a chance. One girl started laughing immediately. Her neighbor swatted her elbow and hissed, "C'mon, Valerie," but she just laughed louder.

Suddenly I was six years old again, wearing traditional Chinese garb complete with knotted closures, trying to hold my shaky chin in the air as I was laughed out of the school picture line. Forever the outcast, even at this school of nerdy outcasts.

One boy turned to me. "Don't pay any attention to her."

Beaver Lover leaned in again. "BB-8," she repeated, as if that was all I needed. When she saw my blank stare, her wide eyes mirrored mine. "*Star Wars?* Have you never seen *Star Wars?* How is that . . . ? But you're at MIT. . . ." She shook her head as if she finally heard what she was saying. "Sorry. I mean, that's totally fine. I was just a little surprised."

I forced my gaze to meet the rest of theirs as I explained, "I don't watch many movies." Only a few, snuck in during the rare moments my parents were out of the house. I went for the most scandalous ones I could find on TV. *American Pie. Grease.* Tiny acts of rebellion, done mostly to try to prevent incidents like these.

The Caucasian boy across from me nodded along. "Were you sheltered because of your Asian upbringing?"

I squirmed, not liking where this was going. He was completely right, and it seemed he was trying to understand, but something felt off. I shrugged.

"Did your parents, like, make you play an instrument? And you had to go to Harvard or MIT? Practice SATs every weekend? My ex was Korean. We had to date in secret." He looked down his nose at the rest of us, as if his past made him cool.

I may not have taken practice SATs every weekend, but I did have to take it three times until I got a perfect score. And I played the piano. But I didn't want to reduce my parents to shallow stereotypes. They may have done versions of what he was implying, but not in the same tone. Since it was all too hard to explain, I simply said, "It wasn't quite like that."

A boisterous student in an MIT CREW cap swept in with leftover Bertucci's pizza from the Student Center. As everyone swarmed the free food, I ducked out. The only thing I knew for sure was that no one there remembered my name.

Not wanting to return to my room since it didn't feel like home, especially not with Nicolette's lacy push-up bras and Untameable nail polish everywhere, I tiptoed around the dorm, secretly hoping to bump into someone. Maybe a potential friend.

On the floor below mine, I walked past the library, then saw them. Double doors, shut, unwelcoming, the opposite of the library's open glass doors on the other side of the hall. I was drawn to the mystery, the secrets behind the metal.

They creaked, signaling their long disuse, and for a moment I worried I would get in trouble. But they weren't locked. I inched forward into the darkness, then emerged into an expansive room lit by floor-to-ceiling windows.

The dusty tables pushed into the corner and the tray-size

tunnel in the wall told me this was Burton Conner's now-defunct dining hall—the Porter Room, I recalled from the dorm booklet that had arrived with my acceptance letter. (Nerd alert: Of course I had read it cover to cover.)

The emptiness and extra-shiny floors called to me. Something stirred deep in my soul, the mix of excitement and awe that happened when you felt like the stars were aligning even though you didn't believe in fate.

I kicked off my shoes, one flick of the ankle, then another, and the second my socks met the floor, my movements morphed. I was always a dancer—that was a part of me, not something that could be separated—and alone in this vast space, I stopped holding back.

My pointed feet slid across the linoleum as if they were already intimately acquainted. My curved, extended arms swept through the air, and I leaped, spun, and *pas-de-chat*-ed my way to the other side of the room.

I had found my safe space. It was worth having to disinfect these socks now. And it was worth having to withstand the disapproving Mămá Lu in my head with her pinched lips and hands on her hips. *Dancing instead of studying, Mei? Each step is a stomp on my heart.* God, she was always so dramatic. I pushed her out and focused on the breeze through my hair, the swishing of my feet, the energy flowing from my fingertips to my toes.

Even though I was exerting myself, my breathing was easier here. Natural. It was the one place I could express myself, be completely me. If only I could find another who spoke dance.

VOICEMAILS FROM MY MOTHER

12:01 p.m.: Mei! Why aren't you picking up? Where are you?

12:08 p.m.: Maybe you're in class. Good girl. It's your mǔqīn.

1:34 p.m.: Mei? How come you're still away? I saw on the news a girl was kidnapped right out of her dorm room. Call me when you get this!

2:10 p.m.: You need to give me your schedule so I know when you're in class and when I need to worry because you don't pick up.

3:27 p.m.: Mei! Are you in trouble? Eating drugs? Pregnant? KIDNAPPED? Call me!!

CHAPTER 3

Liquid Nitrogen

I had started dancing at age six under my parents' coercion as a tactic to make me stand out on college applications. Because, horror of horrors, perfect Kimberly Chen—who was captain of the debate team, an academic decathlon champ, and salutatorian—"only got into NYU" since she was "too much like every other Asian out there." So dance was to be my "in" to the "top" colleges.

At my first class, as soon as the beat hit, I fell in love. Dance was the one place I truly belonged, where age, race, looks, and intelligence didn't matter. I had pretended to continue dancing for my parents' sakes—partly to earn brownie points but mostly because I was scared if they knew just how much I loved it, they would take it away. *Dancers don't make money, Mei.*

But they took it away anyway. Once MIT notified me on March 14th (Pi Day!) that I had been accepted, my parents cut me off from my only mode of expression. *Dance has served its purpose,* my mother had said. *Why you need expensive shoes and classes? Just* dòng yi dòng—*move here, more there—around the house. Walking in place costs no money and is also exercise* (said by the person who was chopstick-thin without trying).

I had to sneak dance in from then on, just like so many other things. Non-Chinese food. Romance books. Even now, away from home, I felt the need to hide. Because I couldn't escape them. They were always with me, overhead, scolding me and trying to steer me onto the one right track for my life.

And right now I was sneaking in one more thing: teaching dance. The local dance studio's ad had popped up all over campus, greeting me everywhere I turned, asking me if I knew of a Chinese dance instructor for their workshop sponsored by China Adoption Agency, the nonprofit organization whose mission was to help adoptive, non-Asian parents educate their Chinese children about their heritage.

Even though a sliver of me felt that these children should be kept in the dark about their often-harsh culture, every time I saw the flyer, I couldn't help thinking, *Yes, I know a Chinese dance instructor who just miiight be interested.* I pictured what styles I would teach. Picked out music. Choreographed combinations. And then, two days before the workshop, I finally called. I had reasoned that by then they had probably already found someone, so I wasn't *really* disobeying my parents. And the fact that they hadn't and begged me to help . . . well, I was being a good person by offering my assistance. So how could my parents be mad about that?

A little Chinese girl age five or six dressed in a pale-pink leotard and matching tights walked into the studio. Her steps were shy and she was holding her mother's hand, but she was eager enough to lead the way. With each step, her leather ballet shoes crinkled with newness.

I breathed a sigh of relief. The studio owner had told me over the phone that she wasn't sure anyone would show up given the late notice.

"Sweetie, can you introduce yourself?" the mother said.

"I'm Rose. Like the flower." She pointed to a plastic rose charm on her bracelet.

"I'm Mei," I said, but she wasn't paying attention.

She reached out a hesitant finger and touched my purple ballet skirt as if it were Cinderella's slipper. As she gazed up at me with huge watery eyes, she asked, "Are you a princess?"

I'd never felt like a princess before—just the ugly stepsister. I shook my head no.

She touched my skirt again. "You *look* like a princess."

"If I'm a princess, you're a princess." I grabbed an extra skirt from my bag, made a mental note to wash it as soon as I returned home, then wrapped it around Rose's waist, five times instead of the usual three.

Rose twirled right, then left, watching with unbelieving eyes as the billowy fabric danced with her. Her mother took this as a sign to leave.

I lowered myself to the floor and extended my legs to both sides. "We have to warm up so we don't get hurt."

Rose joined me, her flexible young legs shooting into a perfect split. She lay forward on her belly, her head toward me, and said, "You're Chinese, like me." She pointed a stubby finger at herself.

Except you're really American, I couldn't help but think. I hated the touch of envy that shot into my throat like bile. She would never have to deal with child-of-immigrant guilt.

I managed a smile. "We're going to learn some Chinese dance today. Are you ready?"

Rose sat up and bobbed her head. A hair loosened from her bun.

I started my playlist, and the studio exploded with the crashing of cymbals and the twanging of the Chinese lute. Something inside me shifted, and my fingertips tingled with the need to dance. It was as if a key had been turned, and my alter ego switched off.

This was home.

I grinned at Rose genuinely and lost myself in the music, timing my head shakes and wrist turns to each bell chime and drum beat. The Dunhuang style was my favorite because of the rich history, the movements originating from paintings of gods discovered in ancient caves in the Gansu province.

I raised my arms in a *U* shape, my hands forming tails like a serif font. Rose imitated, keeping pace with me as I quickened my head bobbles to match the beat. As the music crescendoed to its climax, I spun and Rose followed, twirling in a tornado of giggles.

Next a Dai song flowed from the speakers: smooth, sultry, and slow. I started to show Rose the peacock hands that the Yùe Nán aboriginal tribe was known for, but she was too busy galloping around the studio to notice me. Her Dunhuang head shakes were accompanied by a few creations of her own—kung-fu kicks, jelly legs, even some air slaps—and my instinct was to rein her in. But why? Wasn't she just being creative?

My old dance teacher popped into my head. That old flamingo—all legs, pointy mouth, and always too much pink rouge. I hated her and the castanets that would click her disapproval, just like my mother's tongue. I used to try to add hip-hop to Chinese dance until she clacked it out of me.

I held back and watched Rose stomp, clap, and sway, only periodically following the music. My innocent little rule breaker. She wasn't straddling two cultures, stuck; she was a smooth blend.

I joined her, dancing Dai, Xinjiang, hip-hop, whatever I was inspired to do. And for that brief stretch of time, I felt as carefree as Rose looked. I already knew that from then on I would forever be mixing styles and music in the Porter Room—only smooth blends.

When class ended, Rose's mother ran in from her seat by the window, clapping frantically. With tears in her eyes, she covered her daughter in hugs and kisses.

"Thank you, Mei," she said between pecks.

"Thanks, Mei!" Rose echoed from underneath her mother's arms.

She pulled at her bow until the skirt came loose, but I held my hand out in protest. "No, Rose. You keep it. You're a princess, remember?"

Her mother pushed it into my hand. "Oh no, we really couldn't. Rose, sweetie, we'll get you one for your birthday. Any color you want!"

"Red! Like a rose! Like me!"

She ran to me and wrapped her chubby little arms halfway around my waist, and I let her. I wanted to scoop her up and waltz her around the room. Swing her in the air and hear her laugh. When she danced, I didn't care what germs she harbored.

With one last squeal, she was out the door.

Oblivious to the balloon of glee in my chest, Donna, the studio owner, apologized for attracting only one student. I shook my head, and even though the words did my feelings no justice, I thanked her for this opportunity.

When she asked if I was interested in teaching a regular class, I answered "absolutely" without thinking, continuing to nod as she launched into possible class times and dance styles. And my head just kept going and going until I was committed to teaching adult hip-hop and children's Chinese dance on Sundays, to start in a few weeks.

Donna left, offering me the studio space to prepare choreography for my upcoming classes, but I was too overwhelmed to do anything but sprawl on the floor, faceup, like I was about to make a snow angel. All I could think was how Rose would love the ribbons and fans I had at home. I chuckled, picturing all the creative ways she would use the props.

Owning a dance studio had been my fantasy when I was young, naive, and full of dreams. Ever since I was one of Miss Daisy's pre-prima ballerinas. My imagination took off—a dance school offering styles from all cultures, demand so high there was a waiting list, money in my bank account, my parents beaming proudly nearby.

The image of them brought me back to reality. I sat up, the excitement draining out my pointed toes. Even if my business was wildly successful and featured Chinese dance, they still wouldn't be proud.

Suddenly I realized the weight of my earlier blunder—if my mom found out I was teaching dance instead of devoting every second to studying, I might as well move into Ying-Na's refrigerator box now. I had to back out. What had I been thinking? My insides felt cold, not because of the impending embarrassment at reneging (which yes, sucked), but more because I wouldn't get to teach dance. No more Rose. No more pre-prima-ballerina dreams.

As I stared at the cracks on the wall, I tried to imagine a Harvard Medical School acceptance letter. Instead of feeling excited like I should have been, dread washed over me. How could someone like me be happy in that life? But I had to make it work.

My two options were clear. And they both ended in misery.

* * *

I eventually managed to drag myself off the floor.

Five missed calls.

When I heard the voicemails, I almost dropped my water bottle.

Then I ran the entire way back to Burton Conner.

Flashing lights, an MIT campus police officer, and a tiny Asian woman crying out front.

Oh. My. God.

My jog turned into a sprint despite my fatigued muscles from my workout.

I could hear my mother telling the officer between sobs that I was so young, only seventeen, and he should have kept a better eye on me. She was so distraught that only half her words were audible.

Despite wanting to crawl into a hole, I yelled, "Mămá! I'm here! Everything's okay!"

My mother ran up to me and I started to wrap my arms around her, but she shook me instead. "Where've you been? You gave me a heart attack! I paid sixty dollars to take a cab here!" She didn't drive in the city, too scared of Boston's traffic, one-way streets, and aggressive drivers.

The officer's eyes darted back and forth between my mom and me. "Miss, your mother here said you've been unaccounted for. For the past forty-eight hours."

Before I could respond—not that I knew how—my mother bowed and said, "Thank you, Officer. You found her. So smart, so skilled. I'll be sure to call and tell your boss what a great job you're doing." She bowed every few steps as we scrambled into Burton Conner.

Once we were inside, my mother swatted my arm. "Don't scare me like that again!"

"I'm sorry!" I paused for a moment before saying, "Maybe now, in retrospect, you can see that you overreacted a tad?"

"Mei, I worry about you because I'm your *mǔqīn*. It's been . . . hard." Her voice trailed off, but I could see in her face that she had been worrying about me since I left home. In fact, now that I was looking more carefully, she had a few new lines around her eyes and mouth. She couldn't be happy about that.

The exasperation that had been swimming through my system evaporated. I dug through my bag and handed her a printed copy of my schedule. "I'm sorry it's been hard. Thanks for worrying about me, but next time try to wait a little longer before freaking out and calling the police, okay? I'm careful and you don't have to worry so much. It's not good for you." I wished I could say more— tell her I loved her and worried about her too, that I thought her high blood pressure was a result of her constant panicking and that I wished I could take it away—but the words merely bubbled in my throat before dying.

She studied the piece of paper like it was a cheat sheet for an upcoming exam. "Where were you just now?" Her eyes raked over my spandex pants and gym bag.

Cue the guilt sweat. "I was at my PE class," I lied, a little too smoothly for my own comfort. "We have to take physical education as part of our curriculum." At least that part was true, but there were no dance classes. I had signed up for yoga, and MIT's version was basically napping with strangers.

She pointed to my schedule. "That's not on here."

"Well, I'll put it on there for you, but you can't know where I am *every* second. . . . I mean, I have other things that come up too, without warning. Like my study group." The lies came out easily, and the shame rained down. Would the heavens open so my ancestors could smite me?

"Okay, you're right. Study group is important. I'll be better. Well . . . I'll try." She squeezed her tiny *pìgu* onto the ledge by the entrance and clutched her giant purse in front of her. "You go study now. I'll wait for Bǎbá to pick me up. Save money."

I glanced at my watch. He wouldn't be done with work for hours. "Why don't we go do something? I don't have any more lectures today. And I'm all caught up with assignments and readings," I added quickly.

My mother glanced back at my paper schedule and nodded as if confirming she had indeed memorized it correctly. "Okay. What do you have in mind?"

I racked my brain. We couldn't spend any money. Couldn't do anything adventurous or dangerous or weird. "Can I show you around MIT?"

Her face lit up. She had wanted to attend some of the parents' events during orientation week, but my father couldn't get off work and I knew she had held back because she was insecure about her English and rarely talked to strangers in the foreign tongue (the exception being when she thought I was kidnapped, apparently).

With the rare flicker of excitement in my mother's eyes, my grin grew so wide my lips felt strained against my gums, and they remained this way as we walked past the dome-shaped Kresge Auditorium and into the Student Center.

"This is—" I started, but my mother left my side to inspect the students making ice cream at a table in the lobby. She clutched her purse in front of her as she leaned toward them, peering curiously at the thick gloves on the boy's hands. Her eyes ping-ponged between the gloves and me as she silently asked me what was going on.

"They're making ice cream with liquid nitrogen," I said.

The boy grabbed the liquid nitrogen canister and poured carefully into the metal bowl. Fog bubbled up and flowed out like dry ice contacting water. Double, double toil and trouble. Was there anything cooler than seeing molecules shift before your eyes?

My mother took a step closer, but I reached out and gently pulled her back by the elbow. "Be careful," I whispered. "The vapor coming off is so cold it could burn you. Don't touch the table either."

Her eyes crinkled, pride dancing with curiosity in the folds of her crow's feet. My heart soared into my throat, making my breath hitch.

"Did you learn that in your classes?" she whispered to me.

I managed a nod even though I wasn't sure where I'd learned it. High school? 5.111? Deductive reasoning? I didn't care. I just stared at my mom's face.

The boy dished some creamy goodness out and pushed the paper bowls across the table to us. "It's strawberry." He turned to my mother. "It should be creamier than normal ice cream because the liquid nitrogen freezes it so much faster than conventional methods. Fewer ice crystals this way."

I hesitated before grabbing mine, but my mother's tongue didn't cluck before she coated it in ice cream. In fact, she wasn't even looking at me. Her mouth still full, she nodded at the boy to signal her appreciation. "Mmm." She retrieved a tissue from the giant stack in her purse and dabbed, then flashed him a thumbs-up. Was I hallucinating?

Ice cream in hand, we resumed touring the campus. We walked through MIT's iconic Killian Court and, as usual, a horde of East Asian tourists milled about, squatting into kung-fu horse stances here and there to capture the perfect photo. I had learned within my first week that they were as much a fixture on campus as the courtyard itself.

My mother chuckled. "Look at their *mǎbù*—pretty good, right? And all for a photo." She thought for a second. "Well, I guess if it makes you look better it's worth it."

I wanted a photo of this moment. So badly I would *mǎbù* to get it, just to have proof of my mother giggling with me over dessert, no criticisms spilling out between sentences—only strawberry liquid nitrogen ice cream.

I wanted to come up with something witty to knock her socks off, make her laugh in that genuine, high-pitched way that was as rare as imperial green jade. But . . . there was nothing. Nothing she would understand anyway. I poked around my brain for some Chinese *chéngyǔ*, an idiom or cautionary tale that somehow related, but . . . nothing.

"Do you like the ice cream?" I asked instead.

"It's like *bàobīng* but softer. And sweeter."

I had no idea if that was a good thing or not. Chinese desserts were typically not very sweet—all red beans, mung beans, or the rare fruit. "So you like it?"

"It's like cake, but liquid." I wondered if my mom didn't want to admit it was delicious because she was scared I'd eat it all the time, or if this was yet another instance of us being on different wavelengths. We were usually on opposite ends—radio waves and gamma rays.

She barely paused before diving into her next thought, which was related only to her. "You know, Mrs. Ahn is the worst chef. She tried to make *bàobīng* at home once. It was all ice pebbles drowning in milk soup. Disgusting."

I chuckled, picturing the gross red bean Popsicles Mrs. Ahn used to force on me. I always had to thank her profusely, then find a way to flush them down the toilet. She probably thought I had irritable bowel syndrome. And that I loved her Popsicles so much I couldn't stop eating them even while doing my business.

"I tell her, stop trying to make such hard things. Even her *dànchǎofàn* is bad. Who can't make egg fried rice?"

Me, I thought, but I didn't want to remind my mother that I would be a bad wife for Eugene Huang because I couldn't cook.

At the MIT Coop, my mother tried on twenty different MIT MOM shirts until she found The One that accentuated her figure. I snapped a photo (no *mǎbù* needed), just managing to catch the hint of pride at the edge of her eyes.

"Imagine everyone's faces when I walk into Chow Chow wearing this," she said to herself, but loud enough that I heard. "Mrs. Pan will be so jealous!"

I laughed despite myself and thought I could soar no higher, but then she paid, ripped the tag off, and wore the shirt out.

On our way back to Burton Conner, my mother's bright pink MIT shirt lighting our way, I stopped at the parabolic benches, two concave stone parabolas spaced a few feet apart. Since the benches matched the rest of MIT's funky eclectic architecture, their unique sound properties were a secret from most passersby.

I positioned my mom at the focal point of one of the parabolas, her front to the concrete seats.

"What's this?" she asked. Her words, traveling as sound waves, hit the bench, concentrated, and shot back to us, amplified. Her jaw dropped as her hand flew up to cover her open mouth.

"*Giǎ xiláng*," she whispered in amazement, so softly I wouldn't have been able to discern her words had we not been in the whispering gallery. She didn't speak Taiwanese often—only to my father when they wanted to talk about Xing and me without our knowing what they were saying—and it caught me off guard.

Suddenly I was happy and sad at the same time, like oil and water in my brain. Where had this side of my mother been my whole life? Had she appeared now because I was in college? Or had she been there all along, but I had been too busy or selfish to spend time with her?

She turned to me so our conversation wouldn't be amplified. "How does this work?"

"Sound is a wave, an invisible vibration that travels through a medium such as air, and because of the shape of the benches, the sound waves are concentrated and reflected." I tried to use the simplest words I could, but they clearly went over her head. I switched to Mandarin, but it wasn't just a language problem.

Even though she didn't understand, she nodded at me, one sharp movement. "I'm so glad you're here. You fit. You'll do well. I know you'll get into the best medical school and become the best doctor."

They were simultaneously the best and worst words. I tried to focus on the pride in her voice and eyes, but instead, my stomach shot into my intestines.

● ● ●

By the time we returned to Burton Conner, we didn't have to wait long for my father to pull up. From the SUV's trunk, my parents pulled out a giant cooler plus several plastic bags filled to the brim. And these weren't flimsy grocery store bags—they were behemoth ones bought for nickels in Taiwan and lugged back home across the Pacific.

"I did your laundry and brought you food for the week," my mom explained.

Gratitude welled into a lump that stuck in my throat like a Codd-neck Ramune bottle from my childhood. "Thank you so much, Mǎmá."

She waved a hand through the air. "It's so you can devote all your energy to studying."

My family did *not* mess around when it came to academics. My yéye had passed away during my father's studies in graduate school, and his family didn't tell him his own father had died until the semester ended. It was the reason I lived in perpetual fear that my parents were sick or dying and they wouldn't tell me until it was too late.

After the clothes were put away, we stood awkwardly, crammed into my tiny room with our arms folded over our chests. I shifted my weight from one foot to the other.

"Well, I guess we should let you study," my mother said.

I laughed. "You guys drove all the way here. Let's go get dinner together."

"Are you sure you don't have homework to do?" my father asked.

"I'm all caught up."

He nodded, and off we drove to Chow Chow, no discussion needed to decide our destination. I forced myself to ignore my craving for pizza.

When we parted later that night, a small piece of my heart broke off and went home with my mother. Would I ever see this version of her again? Somehow, as the physical distance between us increased, so did her hold on me.

VOICEMAIL FROM MY MOTHER

Mei! You're still pinching your nose, yes? It's already naturally big, so don't worry—you will make money in the future. But it doesn't look good. Pinch it twice a day, twenty minutes, so it's slimmer. More feminine. You know what? I'll bring you a clothespin. This is your mǔqīn.

CHAPTER 5

(Of course there is no chapter four. Mămá Lu would faint at having the number four—which in Mandarin sounds like the word for *death*, therefore making it unlucky—as a chapter number.)

Rash Decisions

There comes a time when every parent

must have the ever-important sex talk with their child. Unfortunately for me, my version consisted of the following: *Sex is a crime before marriage and an obligation for a wife*, and, *Do not get a Pap smear or use a tampon because you will deflower yourself prematurely. How will your future husband know your looseness is from that tool they use, not another penis?*

None of that was useful, well, ever. So when a burning itch hit me down below, I had no idea what the problem could be, and my only solution was to scratch it by squirming.

Around three in the morning, my chair was about to lose its

upholstering. The itch was so intense I'd even endure the cow's hoof to cure it. I had no choice but to—God forbid—look at it. I knew I had to get over my uneasiness with nether regions before becoming a doctor, but I thought I had more time. It wasn't that I was afraid of my body—more like I didn't know what to do with it.

I closed the bathroom door and dragged the trash can in front since there were no locks. Then I undressed and took a deep breath. With my right foot propped on the sink, my hands grasping the wall, and a flashlight between my teeth, I tried to get a look at my vagina in the mirror. Well, not my vagina exactly—more distal, in the crease and spilling over onto my inner thigh.

The door opened.

The germ-ridden trash can careened into me, and I lost my balance. The flashlight fell from my lips, my scream echoed down the hallway, and I crumpled into a heap on the floor. Shockingly, my first thought was not my nakedness; it was the dirty communal bathroom floor.

I glanced through my sprawled arms to see a stranger peering in concern. A boy. Of course. Now my nakedness took top billing.

"Get out!"

"Sorry! The doors—they don't lock!" His arm was draped over his eyes, but his tinted cheeks screamed, *Yes, I saw your lady parts!*

I picked myself up and slammed said door. "No shit, Sherlock! Why'd you kick it in?"

"I thought it was stuck!" Pause. "You, uh, might want to get that checked out. It's pretty red."

"Oh my God, stop talking!"

My cheeks flushed the same shade as my rash. I wanted to

chuck the flashlight at the mirror to shatter the maladjusted girl staring back at me.

With my pants only half zipped, I flung the door open, flew past the boy whose face would be forever burned into my memory, and made my way straight to the MIT medical clinic, or "MIT Medical," as we called it.

Two hours into my wait at Urgent Care, I had fully zipped my pants and ticked through a list of possible diseases crawling on my chair. I scooted my butt to the edge, which made the itching worse. When my squirming attracted the attention of my neighbor, I scanned the room, wondering how many of my fellow waiting room patrons knew what was going on in my head—or worse, down below. What did they think I was in for? Anxiety meds? Something to help me sleep because I was an overstrung Asian? I fumed at the stereotypical assumptions, then hated myself for being the one who'd come up with them.

I watched a bug-eyed boy scan the room with shifty glances as if he were guilty of something. My guess? Something totally awkward straight out of *American Pie*. His eyes caught mine once, then stayed away.

I watched two frat guys, not because they were attractive, but because it was impossible not to stare at a car wreck. Their voices projected the names of all the girls they'd "banged" this week, making it clear that their mothers were their only female visitors. My guess? They were waiting for a friend to recover from alcohol poisoning.

"Me-eye?" The nurse looked up from her clipboard. "Is that supposed to be Mia? Mia Lu?"

I raised my hand like a nerd, taking the name butchering in stride thanks to a lifetime of practice. At least Mia was a pretty name—poor Tze-Hsing Nguyen was always demoted to *Huh?*

I tried to settle onto the exam table, but the paper crinkled with every wriggle, demanding unwanted attention. My thighs locked together even though I knew I would have to flash my goods in a few minutes.

"What brings you here today, Mia?"

"I, uh, have a rash." I pointed to my vagina. "It itches. And it's red." Or so I was told.

The nurse asked the usual questions and left me to change into the dreaded hospital gown, which provided as much coverage as my discount mobile carrier.

Then the awaited knock at the door.

Please be a female. Please be a female. Please be a—

"I'm going to look at your rash," said the male Indian doctor with a heavy accent. Without meeting my eye, he unceremoniously pushed my gown aside and looked for a second. Just one.

"It's herpes," he said to the nurse, still avoiding eye contact.

A strange garbled noise escaped from my throat before I managed to rasp, "That's impossible."

He ignored me and threw several packs of surgical hand scrubs onto the table. "Use those. Then see a gynecologist."

"I can't have herpes. It's physically impossible. Unless I got them from a toilet seat, or the bathroom floor . . . or a pair of pants"—I glanced down at the brand-new jeans I had on—"but according to the latest studies, that's not possible."

The doctor gestured for the nurse to explain why I was wrong, then left the room.

"Don't worry. There's patient confidentiality," she said, monotone. "We won't tell your parents you're sexually active. Now, would you like a pregnancy test today?"

My voice rose. I wanted the itching to stop, but more so, the nonsense. "Wouldn't herpes hurt? This isn't painful, only itchy. And since when is herpes treated by scrubbing it? None of this makes sense!"

"You don't have to be embarrassed. There's no judgment here. Now, pregnancy test?"

I shoved the hand scrubs into my bag and hopped off the table. "No thanks. You'd probably tell me I'm pregnant."

"Then you need a test. If you're pregnant, we can help you. There are people you can talk to."

Grabbing my clothes in a huff, I stormed out in just my gown, my inner volcano—aka Lu-suvius—bubbling ominously.

Across the hall, I pushed the bathroom door open. And there, crouched over the toilet, her arm disappearing into the hole, was a slim Asian female in a white coat.

"What the hell?" I took a second to compose myself, then said, "May I ask why you're fishing for poo?" I desperately wished this wasn't something I'd have to do in the future as a doctor. Was this really the best way to retrieve bowel samples? Just the thought made me need to bend over the toilet myself.

"I dropped gauze in here," she said in a *you're-clueless* tone.

"Are you kidding me? Just flush it."

She regarded *me* as the weird one just as a nitrile-gloved hand emerged with the evil gauze. "I can't do that. It'll clog the toilet."

"How is that any different from toilet paper? And don't you regularly flush much larger things? If not, we really must write the author of *Everyone Poops*. They'll have to rename it *Everyone Poops . . . Except*"—I glanced at her name tag—"*Dr. Chang*."

She dumped her gloves in the biohazard bin. "Huh. You're right. I never thought about that. Maybe that's why the janitor stopped responding to my emails about retrieving stuff from the toilets. It's just that, my parents always told me anything foreign in the toilet would clog it, including tissues, cotton swabs, gauze. . . ." Her voice trailed off.

I waited for her to say something else, something that would clarify things a little more, but she just walked past me, completely silent, her head lowered and shoulders hunched. Since I knew that level of embarrassment intimately, I let her pass without meeting her eyes.

After changing and leaving the flimsy robe in a heap on the floor, I slunk home, a spitting image of the mysterious Dr. Chang.

VOICEMAIL FROM MY MOTHER

Mei! I heard from Mrs. Ahn who heard from Mrs. Lin that Ying-Na just got her third sexual disease. Glad you will never have to worry about this. Focus on studies, not boys. Because you have Eugene. Well, if you nab him soon. Call your mǔqīn so we can set that up. Remember, only cats, no pandas.

CHAPTER 6

Future Mei

Two flimsy robes in one week.

"Dr. C. will be right in to see you," the nurse said, flashing me a smile before she closed the door. Well, this appointment was already looking better. As was my rash, though it hadn't totally disappeared yet.

There was a timid knock at the door, so quiet I barely heard it.

My eyes widened when I saw the gynecologist, who pushed her glasses to the bridge of her nose, then stuck a limp hand out. I was still frozen as she said, "Chang. Dr. Chang. Tina Chang. No, just Dr. Chang. But, um, I guess you knew that."

Apparently her posture the other night hadn't been from

humiliation; even now, as the authority figure, she was the epitome of subservience, hunching so much she appeared to be trying to hide herself. Or maybe she was thinking about how I had caught her with her hand in the toilet.

She was all business, no conversation—surprise, surprise—and immediately following the introduction, she pushed my gown aside. My leg muscles tensed instinctively, but the damn stirrups kept them in place even after Dr. Chang wheeled over a giant magnifying glass.

Diagnosis: allergic reaction. Embarrassment level: as high as when my mother talks about her period in public.

But despite the mortification, I relaxed because the Mǎmá Lu in my head had finally stopped chattering. Up until now, it had been a nonstop stream of: *Eugene does not want a wife with herpes. How will I ever marry you off now? I told you not to sit on public toilet seats.*

As Dr. Chang rattled off a list of potential sources—new lotion, perfume, body wash—I shook my head repeatedly while trying to puzzle out the answer myself. After running through a mental list of yesterday's events, it hit me. "I never washed my new jeans before wearing them," I told her.

Dr. Chang delivered a monotone rundown of the treatment—apply over-the-counter hydrocortisone cream and wash the contaminated pants—followed by, "Questions?" in a tone that implied *no questions allowed.*

Ignoring her obvious desire to wrap up, I asked, "Do you like it? Being a doctor? I'm premed."

"Yes. Being a doctor is a great job. Respectable. Stable."

I examined her in a new light, the future version of myself. "But how do you *like* it?"

"It's great." Her tone remained flat, same as all her other sentences, making it impossible for me to interpret her true feelings. She could've been ecstatic or miserable or anywhere in between.

She stuck a palm out, signaling an end to the conversation.

Desperate for answers, I extended the handshake longer than allowed by societal norms. "Did your parents pressure you to be a doctor?" She tried to pull away, but I tightened my grip, crossing into freak territory. "Are you happy? Is there something else you wanted to do more? Please. Just those questions."

She sighed, giving in. "I liked math, but there are no job prospects with that." Mustering all her oomph, she yanked her hand free in one aggressive swoop, then left, again with no good-bye.

I sat for a minute staring at my sweaty palm, now empty. My body shuddered even though the room was perfectly warm. *I know you'll get into the best medical school and become the best doctor,* I heard my mother say in my head.

I dressed in a haze, and then, because I couldn't get her sad aura or hollow eyes out of my head, I tracked down Dr. Chang's office. One meek knock later, I was in her cramped, cluttered space.

She looked up from her paperwork briefly, then lowered her head again. No words. Not even an eyebrow raise or muscle twitch or frown.

I swallowed. "I was wondering if I could shadow you today for your last few patients."

She remained bent over her work, and I felt the need to fill the silence. "It's just . . . I'm desperate for some answers, and I thought you might understand." I took a breath. "I'm worried I don't have what it takes to be a doctor. I, um, don't really like germs."

Her eyes finally met mine through her thick glasses. "You're too young to be worrying so much. Just enjoy college, and by the time medical school comes around, you'll be ready. If I can do it, you can too."

"I want to know what I'm getting into," I said, when I really meant, *I'm terrified I won't be able to get over my squeamishness.* "Please. You won't even know I'm here."

With a sigh, she snapped her folder closed and walked out of the room—still no words. I followed behind, not sure if I was supposed to until we stopped at the front desk for me to sign a privacy agreement.

As I followed her to the next patient, I wondered if the lack of conversation would turn out to be a blessing or a curse. After the knock, I came face-to-face with Valerie, the junior from my floor who had laughed during my BB-8 fiasco.

"I'm Dr. Chang. Tina. Dr. Tina Chang. The nurse tells me you think you have a yeast infection, which you described as white and flaky, like cottage cheese?" She tapped the stirrups and rolled a massive light over.

If I hadn't been so disgusted, I might have reveled in witnessing my bully under such compromising circumstances.

Valerie pointed a rigid finger at me. "She goes."

I held my hands up in submission. "Fine with me."

After darting out of the room, I tried (and failed) to quell my turning stomach. *It'll get better with experience,* I lied to myself as the nausea turned into fear. *But what if it doesn't? What if I can never eat cheese again? I love cheese!* My stomach cartwheeled. *What if one day I vomit into my patient's vagina?*

Dr. Chang emerged, walked across the hall to the microscope, and placed a slide on the stage. She looked for a second, then waved me over.

Holding my breath—I did *not* want to taste *that* through my nose—I forced myself to peer into the lens. The stringy rods and circles were innocuous enough, but knowing where they came from made me dry heave. I nodded quickly to Dr. Chang, then retreated.

"*Candida albicans.* Yeast infection. We'll give her an antifungal for two weeks. The medicine can be oral or vaginal. We'll use vaginal in this case since it's not that severe and topical treatments have fewer side effects."

Not wanting to picture Valerie treating her yeast infection, I just nodded.

We made our way down the bleak, deserted hall to the next patient. As soon as we entered, the middle-aged woman said, "Hey, Doc, there are floating chunks in my pee. Is that bad?"

Dr. Chang picked the sample up with only a flimsy paper towel between her and the cup. "When was your last period?"

"Honey, I haven't had my period in years. I'm fifty-six!"

I held my fist over my mouth and suppressed a gag as Dr. Chang announced she would be running some tests to diagnose the swirling mystery flakes. For once I was thankful for my terrible eyesight, which prevented me from seeing the chunks. I inched over to the hand sanitizer in the corner while trying not to breathe too deeply—the sterility of the cleaning chemicals was worsening my headache. I barely heard the woman's answers to Dr. Chang's questions about diet, recent changes in behavior, and medical history.

I did manage to smile at the patient before leaving, but it promptly fell when she said, "I don't know how you guys do this. The smell that's been coming from down under—*whoo*! *P-U*!" She waved a hand in front of her face. As if I needed more clarification.

Outside the door, Dr. Chang fumbled in her pocket with her free hand. Unable to locate a pen, she jiggled the urine sample toward me, still only protected by a flimsy paper towel. "Can you hold this for a sec?"

With a few fingers, I grabbed the cup so gingerly I almost dropped it. Instinctively, my other hand whipped forward, and now I was grasping the specimen like a warm mug of tea. I adjusted my grip so only the pads of four fingers touched.

Dr. Chang arched an eyebrow. "It's pee, not a bomb."

"Contaminated pee with chunks in it. And it's slightly wet." I swallowed hard. "I don't think I can do this."

"I'll say. You know you're going to have to do much worse in med school, right? Dissect a cadaver, rectal exams, abscess drainage, central lines—" Her voice cut off when I leaned against the wall for leverage. She cleared her throat. "You'll get used to it. We all do." But her voice was reedy with doubt.

I know you'll get into the best medical school and become the best doctor. I saw the pride in her eyes, the pink MIT MOM shirt, and I bent over, supporting myself on my knees. I was going to be sick.

• • •

That night I shampooed three times and scrubbed my skin raw. As soon as I was clean on the outside, I fled to the Porter Room to cleanse the inside. *It's going to be okay,* I told myself. Dance would save me; I would detox at night, recovering from the day, and make it work.

The dimness of the room cloaked me, making me feel safe, hidden, and alone, free to express myself in the only way I knew how. It was just me, the linoleum floor, and emptiness for what felt like miles.

My heebie-jeebies from the day—and the chunky pee— manifested as full-body shudders and jerky limbs, hitting before the music even started.

The bass pulsed within me, and I nodded to the beat, eyes closed. Okay, this was it. This always drained me, helped me work through anything.

The air whistled through the vents, then brushed my cheeks. I embraced the frustration within and kicked, punched, and leaped, stretching every muscle until it could stretch no further, a rubber band about to snap. The fear traveled down my arms, the sinew serving as tracks, and exited through my extended fingertips.

But with each burst of energy, I didn't feel release. Something was different. My feet slipped on the tile that should have caressed my toes and allowed me to turn endlessly. My limbs didn't feel like extensions of my body—they were burdens, weighing me down and dragging me around. The wind through my hair wasn't refreshing—it made my head pound with bursts of pain.

Before, there had never been anything dance couldn't resolve. But I never did find my calm that night.

VOICEMAIL FROM MY MOTHER

Mei! This is important so listen carefully! I read that colleges are handing out birth control pills. Do not take them, you hear? They will mess up your eggs and you will have a hard time getting pregnant. Then Eugene will leave.

Call me back! This is your mǔqīn.

CHAPTER 7

Punting

I knocked on Dr. Chang's door with my free hand, a box of green tea in the other. I couldn't look at the partly smushed, twenty-five-cent bow slapped on top because it was too apt a metaphor for how I was feeling: I was grateful she had let me shadow, but it had done more harm than good.

My newfound knowledge that I was terrible at the one future my family wanted for me had made me squirrely this past weekend. At Chow Chow, my parents—scratch that, my mom—had asked me question after question about my study group, who was who, what we worked on, and how much I was loving biology.

One word: exhausting. I'd felt like she was circling all my

secrets, trying to sniff them out one by one. Maybe she had noticed my reluctance to meet her eye, or maybe she knew I had gone through two papaya smoothies because I was using a full mouth as a way to avoid questions. Maybe she had smelled the deceit in my sweat, my aura, my vague answers. Maybe I was losing my grip on reality.

Dr. Chang opened the door a crack, stared at the box for a moment, then let me in. She grabbed the tea and inhaled for a full minute. I squirmed, not sure what to do while she sniffed with her eyes closed. I almost felt like I was intruding.

"Thank you for letting me shadow," I said unnecessarily, just to fill the awkwardness.

She smiled—actually smiled!—and I had to keep myself from doing a double take.

She placed the tea on her desk beside a mountain of butter, the kind you get from restaurants with rolls. When she saw me staring at the pile, I expected her to either blush or give me a normal explanation, but she did neither.

"They're free with meals, so why not stock up? If I'm paying ten dollars for lunch, then I deserve all the butter I want."

I imagined her and my mother out to a meal, both sweeping things into their purses. It was like when two of your personal monsters teamed up, the Joker and the Riddler working together to make Batman feel as awkward as possible.

Dr. Chang pointed at my dangly earrings. "They're pierced. Your parents let you?"

"Yeah. My mom took me in fifth grade." I mimicked her lecture voice as I recited her favorite mantra. "There are no ugly women, just lazy women."

Dr. Chang referenced a superstition. "Isn't she worried all the money will leak out the holes in your ears?"

I tapped my big nose. "Well, I got this baby, so I'm financially set."

She nodded, completely serious, as if my answer were logical. I wouldn't have been surprised if the next words out of her mouth were, *But you still have to pinch it to make it slimmer. Have you tried a clothespin?*

A girl burst into Dr. Chang's office, startling us. The intruder yelled, "Your treatment didn't work, and I still have fucking chlamydia. It burns when I pee now, no thanks to you."

"Uh . . ." Dr. Chang's eyes darted over to me. Clearly I was violating doctor-patient confidentiality.

I started for the door, my clothes rustling, and the girl turned around.

Oh. My. God. It was Nicolette. Was there chlamydia all over our dorm room? I grabbed the desk to steady myself. So. Many. Things. To. Disinfect. If human combustion were possible . . . *poof.*

For the record, I didn't care about her sexual history—more power to her—but chlamydia = bacteria = OMG.

Something flashed across Nicolette's face, but it was so fast I wasn't sure if I was hallucinating. Next thing I knew, she was grabbing the arm of Dr. Chang's office chair and yanking it toward her in a flourish. "I'm not leaving until you fix this."

Dr. Chang cleared her throat, the softest *ahem* of all time.

"Wait—why don't we take this to an exam room? Or at least let me put some paper down."

Nicolette looked at her for a moment, piecing it together, then sat with gusto. "Are you serious right now? Do you think it can travel through my clothes or something? No wonder I'm still not cured; you don't know anything!" She wriggled her butt side to side. "By your logic, I just had an orgy on the subway. I'm probably crawling with herpes and syphilis now too. Forget the chlamydia."

Dr. Chang wrung her hands, her eyes straying to Nicolette's pelvis every few seconds . . . which she must've seen . . . magnified.

Nicolette peered at Dr. Chang the way kids used to inspect my dried squid snacks—with curiosity and confusion. "How can you be a doctor if you're like this?"

Dr. Chang and I exchanged a glance. Then she said, more to me than Nicolette, "You compartmentalize. It's doable. You'll learn, Mei."

Nicolette burst into laughter. "*You're* going to be a doctor, Mei? Your closet has more hand sanitizer than clothes. And what's up with the weird tissues everywhere?"

I don't like to touch your things, and apparently for good reason, I wanted to retort but held back.

Nicolette gestured to Dr. Chang from head to toe with the wave of a hand. "Is this what you want to become?" she asked me.

"Will you please go to the front desk and make an appointment?" Dr. Chang begged.

With one last wriggle, Nicolette uncrossed her long legs and strode to the door.

Dr. Chang rushed over with latex gloves and CaviCide spray,

which broke me out of my post-chlamydia-stress trance. As I watched her scrub, I saw it as a sign of hope.

If she could compartmentalize, maybe I could learn to do it too.

• • •

Being at MIT Medical post-rash-investigation was the one situation in which I didn't want to see the spiky outline I was constantly searching for . . . so of course there he was, in all his six-foot-something glory. And when I say glory, I mean yumminess.

I froze, not sure if it was worse to miss this opportunity or to have to explain why I was there.

He walked by without turning his head my way, obviously just passing through the building as a shortcut to the other side of campus. I breathed a sigh of relief. Then immediately yelled, "Darren!"

When he turned, I was still frozen in place, a little disoriented at how I hadn't been in total control just now. Maybe it was the rash.

His face lit up. I wish I could say mine did as well, but I was too busy fighting my urge to itch the still-lingering rash while simultaneously trying to come up with a lie as to why I was hanging out at the health center—free pamphlet? Free condoms? Free lollipops?

"Mei! What brings you here? Everything okay?" Darren called out as he made his way over to me.

Why do I do this to myself?

"I was just, um, passing through," I said. Then I realized I was pretty far into the actual building, in front of the gynecology reception desk. Of course. It couldn't have been anything less embarrassing. I started to ramble. "I mean, well, I bought this new pair of jeans, and then, well, there must've been something on them—and really, you should wash your new clothes before wearing them. . . ." I took a breath. "I was just passing through. Like you."

"Sounds complicated," he said, the amusement on his face matching his voice. "I'll keep your tip in mind. I've been grabbing all the free shirts around campus to avoid doing laundry." He pointed to the tee he was wearing, which said PUNT in bubbly, half-formed letters right-side up and TOOL upside down—MIT lingo for putting off work for fun (punt), or to toil away studying (tool). I silently thanked the campus life brochure for teaching me those. "I'm glad the 'tool' is upside down," he continued, "or else people would think I was calling myself a tool, which I would be if I were wearing a shirt that said 'tool.'"

"True, but you'd be even more of a tool in an 'I love beaver' shirt."

"I do love beaver though," Darren said with a straight face. (Yes, I blushed.) He dug around in his messenger bag before emerging with a stuffed TIM the Beaver. "He's too cute and cuddly not to love."

I laughed. Instead of revulsion, which my mother had led me to believe was the only possible response to my loud, openmouthed "man-laugh," Darren grinned at me—genuinely, I think, since it reached his eyes.

I could get used to that.

"Do you carry that around with you everywhere?" I asked. A microscopic part of me hoped it was true so that I would finally know something embarrassing about *him*.

He tossed TIM from one hand to the other. "I picked this up from the activities fair for my sister, Sally."

I mock wiped sweat from my brow. "Phew. Because between

the two of us, there can only be one stuffed animal hoarder." I laughed to myself about how Horny was still my little secret.

He smiled so wide I could see that his bottom teeth were slightly crooked. His gaze never left my face as he asked, "Are you free right now?"

"Right now?" I sputtered. "I mean, yeah, I'm free." And finally I removed my foot from my mouth. "No better time for some punting." I gestured for him to lead the way.

We walked to Building 6, then ducked down a small, abandoned hallway that was empty except for a rusty metal door.

"Are you ready?" he asked, the excitement dancing on his face.

"Um, depends what's on the other side. I might need a minute if this is a Narnia-type situation."

Darren chuckled. "In our dreams."

He reached an arm up to push the door open, and when the navy blue of his shirt neared his face, his eyes turned darker—more mysterious somehow. Anticipation thrummed through my veins, and for a second I let my imagination run wild with possibility.

The door opened to reveal a secret outdoor garden. The courtyard was filled with golden sunflowers crammed so tight they blended together.

He swept a hand in a princelike gesture, and I stepped over the threshold into another world.

"What is this place?" I asked, my lips turning up into the grin reserved for after-midnight spoonfuls of Nutella.

"Whatever we want it to be."

"A place to dream," I answered immediately. And for a moment I let my dance-studio pre-prima-ballerina dreams back in. Let myself enjoy that I was in this secret garden between lectures and that maybe, just maybe, it was okay to enjoy Darren's company for a few brief minutes. "Do you know what you want to major in?" I asked as I walked among the flowers, touching a petal here, a stem there.

"I'm thinking Course Seven," he said, using the MIT lingo for biology. Everything here was numbers—the buildings, the courses, the majors; we had our own language.

I pressed my lips together, holding back. If I told him I was also going to be Course Seven, he would expect us to gush about biology together, in which it would inevitably be revealed that I actually hated it. Then I would have to explain why I had to major in it when it put me to sleep, and that was a can of carnivorous worms I had to keep sealed or else the worms would eat my sanity.

Oblivious to my inner flailing, he continued. "I'm thinking about going into academia in the future, but I'm open to other options." I briefly wondered if my mother valued money or prestige more: Professors made less but were respected, especially in Chinese culture. "My parents will probably freak out that I could end up anywhere— they want me close to home—but oh well." He shrugged like it was no big deal. "We'll figure it out."

I refrained from asking more about his parents. I couldn't bear to hear how much easier things were for him. "What do you like about biology?"

"I've always been curious about how living things work, starting when I was a five-year-old kid with a My Body and Me kit. Man, I used to carry that thing around with me everywhere." The faraway look in his eyes made me want to see what he was seeing, maybe absorb some of that dreaminess for myself. "I also love that research is a puzzle, and finding the solution sometimes involves unconventional thinking and out-of-the-box experiments. Like, apoptosis was discovered while tracking *C. elegans* cells through development without knowing what kinds of interesting things they would find. Then they worked backward to figure out the genetics. I can't think of anything cooler than that."

I nodded, thinking about how inspiring it must've been to be at MIT when Bob Horvitz was recognized for his groundbreaking work. "And they won a million-dollar award for it. Not too shabby." Why did I have such a hard time with a subject that yes, was kind of amazing when described by Darren this way? Was it because I knew what was at the end of the tunnel, waiting for me, and I couldn't separate my doctor future from the rest of it? "Nobel Prize aside, you don't think it's frustrating that you can try for years to find the answer to one thing, only to get the answer to something else? It feels so"—I waved a hand in the air, trying to locate the right word—"unpredictable."

He shook his head. "It's exciting. An adventure. A quest to find the answers to life's mysteries." He gestured grandly with his arms, trying to illustrate the expansive unknown with wide circles.

Seeing his fervor, I blurted out, "I love your passion." As soon as the words were out, I regretted it (like usual).

But when I peeked over at him, he was smiling.

"Thanks," he said, then shifted his gaze upward. "And thanks for coming here with me," he said to the sky, slightly shy and completely adorable. "I just found it the other day and it was too cool to keep to myself."

Part of me hoped he had wanted to show one shy, non-blond girl in particular, while the other half dreaded it.

He dropped his gaze back to me. "Now that I've told you about *my* dreams—"

"Sorry, I've got to go," I blurted out, checking my wrist for the time even though there was no watch there.

I wasn't ready to tell him. Talking about my secret dreams brought them closer to reality, which could never be. And that included him. *No Japanese boys*, I heard in my head, my mother's words like nails on a chalkboard.

"Where're you headed? I'll walk with you," he offered.

"Sorry. I'm in a hurry." I was already one foot out the door.

"When will I see you again?"

"When there's another student in distress, needing saving," I joked, because it was easier.

"Then I'll be sure to start telling the MIT sex joke constantly. Maybe incite some fights over whether the Logs or the Chorallaries are better—or maybe just commit all-out blasphemy by saying a capella sucks."

I faux gasped, and we shared one of those conspiratorial looks that happens when you find that rare person who shares your sense of humor.

I punched him on the arm lightly (because I'm awkward) and left promptly (because I'm a coward). It was even harder for me to do than return to my chlamydia-infested room.

VOICEMAIL FROM MY AUNT YILONG

Mei Mei! Năinai and I are coming to visit, and I have a surprise
for you! Get us some egg tarts from Chinatown, okay? Twenty or
twenty-five of them. For Năinai. Not me, of course. I'm on a diet.
Tee-hee-hee-hee . . .

CHAPTER 8

Archduke Ferdinand

Even though exams were coming up and my parents believed schoolwork was of utmost importance, Năinai (my father's mother) was the exception. So when she and my aunt Yilong descended upon Massachusetts for a surprise visit, I was expected to drop everything—which is how I found myself at home dragged down by my textbooks and all my secrets. My family couldn't know about the Porter Room, or how I'd fallen asleep in several biology lectures, or that I had freaked out over pee and flaky cheese.

And . . . I hadn't backed out of teaching dance. In fact, I had already taught two Sundays' worth of classes, and I'd never felt so alive, so in the exact place I was supposed to be, wondering why I had missed out for so long. Which only made it worse.

I needed the dance classes more than I needed their approval and what they didn't know wouldn't hurt them, right? I could do this—keep it from them, keep everyone happy. There were good secrets and bad, and this was a good one, right? Those existed?

"Mei Mei!" Aunt Yilong called in her high-pitched voice, squeaking on the last syllable and clutching me to her chest. I coughed out her sickly sweet perfume and rubbed my tongue against my palate to get rid of the acrid taste.

She pushed me back for a closer inspection. "Look at you! I can't believe you're in college already! And at seventeen—*bùdéliǎo!*" I smiled, my lips lifting with my spirits.

But then she kept going. "Hmm, maybe some more exercise though? Getting chubby."

I clenched my teeth, unable to thank her with the obedient, *Yes, Aunt Yilong, xièxie.*

Instead, I turned my attention to Nǎinai, who was seated at the dining room table with her trademark walker beside her.

"Mei Mei, eat your vitamins," she said.

I bowed slightly. "Yes, Nǎinai, *xièxie.*"

Aunt Yilong pushed a grocery bag toward me, excitement raising her voice even higher. "I brought you a present."

"*Xièxie*, you shouldn't have." I reached into the bag and pulled out a dark red sweaterdress large enough for Yilong and plain as could be—rounded neckline, long sleeves, and a single seam at the waist. At my aunt's urging, I pulled it on over my clothes. The hem pooled on the floor and the chest area was at my waist.

To end this, I said, "*Bù hǎo yìsi*." The phrase is used as a formal version of "thank you," but literally translated means "I'm embarrassed." I chuckled at my own joke, then felt completely alone.

Aunt Yilong stowed the now-empty plastic bag so it could make the trip back to her hoarder's den. When we visit her home, we have to eat meals in fifteen-minute shifts because of the lack of space on the dining room table. I used to wonder how Nǎinai put up with the mess, but then I saw her Taiwan apartment, filled to the brim with trash and every insect imaginable.

"Let's go to Chow Chow. I'm so hungry I could die." Yilong gestured to me. "And what a perfect opportunity to wear your new dress."

I began protesting, but my father shut me down with a glare. *Dèng yi yǎn*, more powerful than words.

When we reached the restaurant, I decided to own it, just like in junior high when my wardrobe consisted of flowered leggings and neon hoodies. I held the dress up with two dainty fingers, a princess waltzing into a ball, not a stinky-tofu-scented hole-in-the-wall. Just like seventh grade, it didn't work. A few patrons pointed and giggled. Others stared. One older woman openly cackled, taking full advantage of her revered elderly status. Out of the corner of my eye, I saw my father duck his head in embarrassment. Satisfaction coursed through me even though I was the *pìgu* of the joke. That'll teach him to think before his next *dèng yi yǎn*.

Before we had even sat down, Mrs. Pan rushed over, flashing Hanwei's picture in my mother's face. Except this time, she was armed with an entire album. "See how precious he is? Look at him here, age six, playing the guitar for an entire audience. They all cheered so loud."

I remembered that sad performance my mother had dragged me to. The ten of us in the audience had clapped only because we could tell how much pressure poor Hanwei was under.

I thought my red dress might have been enough to turn Mrs. Pan away, but then I remembered she wanted me for her son because of MIT and my money nose, not my fashion sense.

She flipped through the pictures frantically, as if she knew her time was limited. "And look, so handsome at his college graduation. He finished with honors."

My mother pushed the album away. "I'm sorry, but Mei is spoken for. Mrs. Huang and I have been talking."

Mrs. Pan huffed. "The Huang boy? I heard he joined a fraternity and is on the fast track to becoming a drunk deadbeat. Is that what you want for Mei? Hanwei has never had a sip of alcohol in his life."

If I hadn't been the piece of meat the two dogs were fighting over, this might have been funny.

Mrs. Pan snapped the album shut and stalked off, her head in the air to hide her hurt pride.

Nǎinai nodded her approval at my mother. "Good. You taking care of Mei. That way she won't end up like Xing, turned by the devil."

I swear to God, my mother smiled.

And I sank lower into the pile of manure that was my future marriage.

We ordered so much another table had to be dragged over. Before I had even used hand sanitizer, my father attacked, slurping up beef noodle soup so violently broth spewed across the table. He didn't become *Lu Pàng* by caring what others thought.

After dishing food to Năinai, Yilong stacked her plate five layers high. A few *bāo*s and pork balls tumbled off and she hurried to scoop them back on top.

"You know, Mei," she said between bites, "you should think about going on a diet. Or you should start exercising, like Băbá. Did you know he could've been in the NBA? He turned it down for computer science."

I mashed my lips together to hold the laughter back. Once a week, my father huffed and puffed around the gym with other fifty-year-olds. There was more heavy breathing and yelling of Chinese obscenities than exercise.

"He's a regular old Jeremy Lin, all right," I said, expecting to end the conversation since no one would understand my reference.

"No one is as good as Jeremy Lin," my mother said.

"Lin-sanity," Năinai added.

I choked on my tea. "Do either of you know who Michael Jordan, Kobe Bryant, or LeBron James is?"

Năinai smiled. "Eat your vitamins."

I answered my own question. "They're basketball players."

"We don't know them because they're not as good as Jeremy Lin," my mother said with a shrug.

I had forgotten about what I like to call the Asian Club Phenomenon—that my family didn't know Brad Pitt or

J. K. Rowling, but they knew Lucy Liu and Amy Tan. Was it because so few Asians broke into pop culture that they felt a sense of shared pride, or was it because they felt a bond with every Asian, even the strangers we bumped into at Kmart and Costco?

"Too bad you didn't go for it, Bà," I said. "You could have been Lu-sanity. Well, that doesn't really work. Lu-nar eclipse. You know, because you would eclipse everybody."

Năinai nodded. "Lunar. We use lunar calendar."

I nodded at her, too distracted to care that she hadn't gotten my joke. A rare opportunity had presented itself, but it was so risky I was jiggling my leg the way my mother hated. "Do you guys think Jeremy Lin's mother was right to let him pursue his NBA dream?"

"Do you remember Peter Cheng?" my mother asked. "You got locked in the bathroom at his house when you were little. Well, he was roommates with Jeremy Lin. And Peter is now a lawyer, making tons of money. I heard he bought his fiancée a three-carat diamond. Huge! The size of my fist." She held up her tiny clenched hand to demonstrate. "So at least Jeremy Lin went to Harvard and has that degree as backup."

The weight on my chest lightened . . . until Yilong spoke a second later.

"Jeremy Lin probably went into basketball because he wasn't good at medicine or law. Don't worry, Mei. You will make the best doctor. Plenty of job offers, plenty of money."

Năinai nodded. "You won't end up like your māmá. Jobless. No offers."

My mother's shoulders slumped forward, her posture matching her position in the family—the lowest, almost invisible.

Yilong added, "Your năinai told her again and again to get a job, but nobody wants her."

And I lost it. "My mother dropped out of graduate school to take care of Xing and me," I fired back. My mother grabbed my arm, trying to shush me. I shook her off.

Yilong glanced at me with wide eyes, then rested her gaze on my mother. "If you'd taught her better, she'd be more obedient."

I balled the tablecloth in my hands, squeezing to try to calm the bubbling Lu-suvius. I couldn't win here. If I let any snark seep out, they would only attack my mother's parenting more, but saying nothing meant I agreed that obedience was a virtue. I tried to *tombé, pas de bourrée* in my head, but there was too much frustration coursing through my veins. My fists remained tight, and I hoped it was enough to show my dissent without feeding the fire.

In the ensuing silence, during which I could hear my own heartbeat, Năinai's eyes glazed over as they always did before a flare-up of her dementia. As the cloudiness grew, I knew she was being taken farther and farther back in time. Her episodes often involved Communist Revolution flashbacks, mistaking my father for her husband (and arguing with him), or reliving my brother's disownment. That last one was the most common. Her eyes would fill with tears as she cursed Xing's girlfriend, the one who'd gotten him disowned, and then she'd pound her fists on the table, her leg, the person next to her until the episode passed.

Năinai looked to my aunt as she yelled, "Yilong! Don't talk to *her!*"

She spat the last word at my mother, the way she normally spoke about Xing's girlfriend. "Not until she gives me a grandson!" She turned to my mother. "You can't sit with us until I have my *sūnzi.*"

This was a new one. My head swiveled from my mother to Yilong to Năinai, wanting to hear more yet dreading it. My voice cracked as I tried to clarify, "Năinai and Yilong didn't speak to Mămá until she gave birth to a son?" I didn't even know who I was asking.

"Enough," my father barked. "Mā, you have two grandchildren. One is sitting beside you. Remember? Remember Mei?"

Năinai looked at me and her eyes gradually focused on my face, which was a shrunken version of my father's. As she took in my familiar lucky Lu nose, she smiled. "Mei Mei," she cooed, as if I were still a child.

My father leaned over to me. "Năinai isn't doing well. You need to make more time for her. There's no one in the world she loves more than you."

Except Xing. Those unspoken words hung between us, just one of many hidden truths floating in the air. I could never compare with "most excellent," *zuì yōuxiù* Xing, who was the coveted eldest son of the eldest son.

Yilong poured the leftover oil from the shrimp onto her plate and dinner returned to normal. Well, normal for when Yilong and Năinai were here. Năinai stared at me with half-blank eyes while my aunt chattered about the article she'd just read that said if you swung your arms three thousand (yes, three *thousand*) times a day, you'd live a longer, healthier life.

I actually missed my mother's criticisms and fussing. I considered chewing with my mouth open just to get her to slap my hand and remind me to "be a lady." Or maybe I should prop my leg up on the chair—my favorite eating position always made her hiss, *You look like a villager!*

But I held back. I was afraid she wouldn't do anything—just like how she hadn't swatted my jiggling leg—and it would only remind me how she became a ghost in the presence of her in-laws.

So we ate in uncomfortable silence heavy with secrets and repressed anger—in other words, a normal family dinner. Unfortunately, this was just the calm before the shitstorm.

Since Yilong and my parents' backs were to the entrance and Năinai's eyesight was even worse than mine, they didn't see him come in. But I did. And *she* was with him.

Maybe it's not him, I told myself—I hadn't seen him in years. But I knew I was deluding myself. He was a younger, thinner Băbá, complete with white Reeboks and sideswept hair.

My brother and his petite Taiwanese girlfriend exchanged a loving glance. Her sleek, stylish bob framed her face perfectly, swishing gracefully with her neck movements. Then he slipped his arm around her tiny waist, routine, but her face lit up as if it were the first time.

My mind scrambled, trying to piece this image of her with the one my parents had forged in my mind. They had led me to believe she was the devil, breaking up our family for her own evil kicks. Not this seemingly sweet girl. An actual person.

Xing met my stare and froze.

My brain flooded with memories. Xing reenacting Sailor Moon episodes with me. Xing buying Horny for me because my parents had been too frugal. And worst of all, Xing, the last time I saw him, burying his face in his scarf, unable to tell me he wouldn't be seeing me for a long time. Four years, it turned out.

My pulse quickened. I was trapped.

I snatched my father's chopsticks out of his hand so he couldn't chuck them across the restaurant when the inevitable battle broke out. The pork ball they had been holding rolled down his shirt as one chopstick slipped through my fingers and clattered to the floor.

Oops.

He raised an eyebrow at me. As he turned to signal the waitress for a new pair, I realized I had just shot Archduke Ferdinand. If I hadn't done anything, maybe they wouldn't have noticed. Maybe Xing and his girlfriend would have left.

My father's hand fell to the side when he spotted them. I braced myself for his Lu-suvius eruption, but it came from my mother. She charged over and grabbed the girl's left hand.

"You proposed?" My mother spoke only to Xing, as if his fiancée weren't human. "Even though you know we disapprove? How could you disgrace us like this?"

"It's nice to finally meet you," Xing's fiancée said, clearly lying. "I'm Esther."

Her response shocked me like a pulse of electricity. Even after all that had transpired, she had taken the high road.

I ran over on the heels of my father, hoping to be able to do something, even if it was merely being a buffer.

My mother's eyes scanned over Esther, the scowl on her face deepening when her pupils passed over the brown highlights in Esther's hair. I could hear her in my head, clear as if she had spoken the familiar words aloud. *Only criminals dye their hair.* I found myself hoping that Esther didn't have any other strikes, like a tattoo or multiple piercings.

My father was surprisingly calm, which was scarier than Lusuvius. "Xing, your mother and I are so disappointed in you. If you marry her, that will be it. No chance of reconciliation. Forget our address, our faces, our names. You're dead to us." He gave me the eyeball. "*All* of us."

I hunched, wanting to disappear.

By now Năinai had grabbed her walker and made her way over. She waved a shaky, accusatory finger at Esther. "She-devil!"

I waited for Yilong to rein her in, but she stepped forward and put her hands on her hips, joined forces.

I should've known better. Yet after seeing Esther in her perfectly smooth, human flesh, everything was jumbled.

Năinai was more lucid than I'd seen in a long time. Unlike my mother, she spoke directly to Esther, in Mandarin. "If you love him, you would offer your fertile sister to him in your place. But since you are selfish and refuse, now I have to resort to praying for your death."

Holy shit, did we just time travel a hundred years back?

The strained smile vanished from Esther's face, and she bit her lip. I couldn't tell if it was to keep from crying or to keep from yelling obscenities. Hell, *I* was about to start yelling.

I wanted to reach out to Esther, maybe stand in front of her as a human shield, but my traitorous feet were rooted to the ground.

Xing's eyes were dark and cold as he pulled his fiancée out of the line of fire. "Do not *ever* speak to her like that again," he said directly to Năinai. I instinctively tensed as if I were the one being scolded.

Năinai stumbled, throwing herself onto the walker, which creaked under her full weight. When Yilong's arms reached out to support her, Năinai let go and slumped to the floor.

Yilong screeched, high and piercing, not caring that we were in public. "Look what you've done to her!"

Both my parents rushed over, the excess of arms entangling such that Năinai remained on the floor as everyone fought over who would help.

Xing used the mess to escape with Esther. He gave me one last look, and there was so much that transpired between us in that second, but I didn't know how to interpret it. I opened my mouth to say something, but . . . there was nothing. Not that it mattered. He was gone before anything could have come out.

I'm sorry, I eventually mouthed to no one. But sorry for what, I couldn't put my finger on. I wasn't on my parents' side, right? I mean, what had come out of Năinai's mouth was so fucked up there were no words for it . . . yet by remaining behind, I had chosen a side.

Once Năinai was back in her seat, my mother hissed, "This is what happens when you disrespect us, Mei."

I knew all too well. All Xing had done was fall in love with a reproductively challenged woman.

• • •

The ride home was silent except for the 1950s Chinese music blasting from the speakers—the same songs that had played in my tone-deaf father's car for the last ten years. The lyrics I normally found humorous now seemed to be mocking me. *Zhè bǎ nítǔ* no longer just meant *this handful of dirt*—it meant *you're trapped; you aren't a part of this culture; you aren't a part of anything.* Then they morphed into accusations that I was betraying myself, my true self. *Jiǎrú wǒ shì yígè yuèliàng* was not just *if I were a moon*—it taunted me, saying, *You're a coward; You can't be anything you want, only what others want.*

At home everyone made a beeline for the makeshift altar, which comprised a folding table covered in gold cloth. A photo of Yéye sat in the middle, unsmiling—the same portrait that usually hung at the head of our dining room table, eerie and omnipotent. Around his picture sat bananas, peanuts, and Kit Kat bars—his favorite foods. As a child I'd had a hard time imagining this austere stranger loving Kit Kats—better known to my family as *Yéye táng*, or *grandfather candy*.

We always honored him around this time of year, the anniversary of his death. Năinai paid her respects first, as always, and completed her version of worship while seated, refusing to give her late husband more. I suspected Năinai kowtowed only to stay in the ancestors' good graces.

After Năinai, my parents took their places a few feet apart, facing the portrait. They stared at Yéye as they clasped their hands together and raised and lowered them once. Then they kneeled and kowtowed three times, craning their necks to look at the photo between each bow. One final clasped arm raise on their knees finished the ritual.

Worshipping was serious business. No smiling, no laughing, no talking—which of course meant it had taken all my strength to suppress my giggles as a kid.

After Yilong took her turn, I stepped forward. When I was little, this ritual had been a necessity to honor my ancestors (and on Chinese New Year, to get my *hóngbāo* with a crisp twenty-dollar bill inside). Now it had morphed into just what you do, like how you brush your teeth twice a day or eat dinner at night. Just going through the motions, not really feeling or thinking.

As I robotically raised my clasped hands for what felt like the thousandth time, I couldn't stop picturing the last worship with the entire family, BD. Before Disownment. My parents had just finagled a copy of Xing's senior-year transcript, which had taken many phone calls, too many threats, and probably some misdemeanors since Xing had made sure the transcript was never to be sent home. He was already accepted into medical school, his future secured, but my father had spent our rare family time screaming at him for getting a C. Xing had stormed out without worshipping Yéye. Did he know then that he would never be back in this house, be a part of this tradition again? And I couldn't help wondering . . . was I following in his footsteps?

I couldn't let it happen. Because unlike Xing, I couldn't handle being on my own. He had always been rebellious, often choosing the wrong path on purpose just to piss our parents off. The opposite of my instincts.

As soon as I finished the last arm raise, my father cleared his throat. "Seeing Xing should have jolted you, Mei. Study hard. Bring honor to our family. Do not disappoint us. You know the stakes."

Xing and I are different, I told myself over and over as I tried (and failed) to fall asleep.

• • •

At four in the morning, extra pressure on my bed stirred me from my hard-earned sleep. Without opening my eyes, I knew the unwelcome visitor was Năinai—the only person with the ~~gall~~ elderly status to regularly intrude on her sleeping hosts in the hopes of waking someone to keep her company.

She spoke in Mandarin. "Mei Mei, you need to learn obedience. Just look at your father, the epitome of *xiàoshùn*—always putting me first, never asking questions. He was obedient to Yéye until the end—no, past the end. After Yéye's death, your father paid the proper respect, refraining from cutting the hair on his head and face for a hundred days."

That wasn't noble. Just sad. The only way my father knew how to express himself to Yéye was through an archaic tradition done after death.

"But don't worry, your father wasn't always that way. It can be learned." She guffawed suddenly, loud and throaty, startling me.

"He was so naughty as a child. How he loved to eat. Whenever I gave him money for a haircut, he would spend the dollar on beef noodle soup and just accept the beating that followed. So naughty, just like Xing."

My heart ached for my father, who grew up in a different time and had it so much worse. Had he been scared? Confused? Resentful? The few times he had talked about Yéye, he'd spoken with such reverence.

Nǎinai inched closer and leaned over my still torso. "One time, Yéye caught him smoking and used the cigarette to burn his arm. Your father never smoked again."

I pictured the three welts of scar tissue on my dad's arm. Whenever I asked where those came from, he just grunted. Nǎinai obviously didn't know he continued to smoke for years, a pack a day, in the basement. The only way Yéye helped him quit was by dying of emphysema. So many secrets. So much left unsaid. I was guilty of the same, like father like daughter, carved from the same *mùzi*.

She patted my leg. "Try harder. I know you can do it. You're at MIT because you're a hard worker, like me. Did you know I joined the army to escape the Communist War? Then, in Taiwan, I argued my way into the police academy."

For the first time since the onset of her dementia, I felt that thread that connected us. I used to look up to her for her independence, the fight she had inside. My chest used to puff when my father told me I reminded him of her, the highest compliment he could give.

But then she pressed a finger to the off-center mole on my

forehead, which was visible now that I was lying down and my bangs had fallen to one side. "We should remove this. I could cut it off for you, to help you catch a man."

And with that, our moment was over. She shuffled out, muttering about finding a knife for the goddamn mole that had plagued me my whole life.

After wedging a chair beneath the door handle to keep Nǎinai and her knife out, I tossed and turned for hours, haunted by my father's past, Xing's past, and my future.

MY MOTHER YELLING THROUGH THE DOOR TO WAKE ME UP

Mei! Put on sunblock. You look like charcoal. Your mǔqīn knows best.

CHAPTER 9

(Not a) Candy Bar Wrapper

When my father dropped me off at Burton Conner, my mother darted out of the car after me, claiming I needed her help because my room was *luànqībāzāo*. Even though she did proceed to tornado through, sucking up dirty clothes, gum wrappers, and hair ties while clucking her tongue at me, I knew she was here because she couldn't stomach any moře Nainai or Yilong. In another hour, max, they would be on a plane out of here, but I guess even that was too much. Understandable.

I had anticipated this, hiding my dance shoes (which were calling to me like they knew I needed them) in a pile of Nicolette's (hopefully chlamydia-free?) clothes. The polka-dot socks on top marked the pile as hers, which my mother would know since she bought most of my clothes and *why you need colorful socks? The plain ones are cheaper.*

But still, every time my mother breezed close to the buried treasure, I stopped breathing. Luckily, she was too appalled by the mess to pay much attention to me.

"If you don't learn to clean up, maybe Eugene won't want you."

"I'm sure tiger Mrs. Huang will be wiping his butt until she dies," I muttered from my desk. I was trying to drown out the tongue clucks with a p-set (MIT lingo for homework).

"Mrs. Huang is not a tiger; she's a horse. And you're right, she will probably live with you once you're married. Except *you* will need to clean up after *her*. The only reason Năinai doesn't live with us is because Yilong never married. Poor Năinai, having to deal with that. If you don't marry, I would be so ashamed I'd never show my face."

I scooted my chair closer to the desk and hunched over my paper. *Drop-copy-decrease-chain*, I chanted in my head as I differentiated, trying to tune her out—the only defense in this situation. I wish she had taken up my offer to walk around MIT again. I'd been hoping to re-create that day from a few weeks ago, but she had said no—reluctantly at least—citing that she didn't want my father to have to wait on her if we took too long (heaven forbid).

Suddenly, my mother screamed. An I'm-getting-murdered, make-your-eardrums-bleed kind of scream. I covered my ears so fast I stabbed my temple with the pencil in my hand. Fortunately, it was the eraser side.

My head whipped toward her. She was perfectly fine, standing there in one piece, holding a candy wrapper. "Jesus, Mǎmá. So I ate a candy bar. Calm down. That scream should be reserved for 'I'm dying.'"

"How could you? This is Ying-Na level stuff!" My mother stomped up to me and shoved the wrapper in my face. "Mei, you should know this already: Sex is a crime before marriage. Ying-Na did the sex, and it ruined her life."

When my eyes focused enough to make out that my mother was actually holding a *condom* wrapper, it was my turn to scream. I backed away from the giant bacterium. "That's not mine!"

She took another step. The wrapper was inches from my nose now. "That's what you would say if it *was* yours!"

"Maybe so, but it's definitely not mine—it's my roommate's!" I fought the urge to hyperventilate—could chlamydia be breathed in through my mouth?

To my relief, she threw the wrapper to Nicolette's side of the room. She looked from the lacy underwear strewn across the chair to the bottles of makeup on the desk. "We'll need to see if we can get you a new roommate," she grumbled. "Don't confront her though. Amberly Ahn confronted her roommate. Then her homework was changed in her sleep! Can you believe that? She had a semester full of Bs—the horror!"

I suspected Amberly merely used her roommate as an excuse for her grades (and I tucked that idea away for future use), but I wasn't going to get in the way of my mother working her magic to get me a new, possibly chlamydia-free roommate.

My mother went back to cleaning, but before she could touch any of my stuff, I snatched the hand sanitizer off my desk and squeezed a gigantic glob across her knuckles. She narrowed her eyes at me, and I knew she was saying, *I hope this doesn't interfere with your future.* My struggle with germs was an unspoken tension, and I often had to hide it from my parents to avoid fighting. I was used to sneaking sanitizer on beneath the table, in my pocket, behind my back.

To change the subject and avoid the land mine, I said, "I saw on Facebook that Jade moved in with her boyfriend."

My strategy worked. "*Aiyah!* Really? How could her mother let that happen?"

I ignored the implication that I would never be able to move in with a future boyfriend, which I already knew anyway.

"*Bú xiàng huà!* I bet you they're having the sex," my mother said, nodding her head. "No one can live together and not have the sex." She returned to cleaning up. "Good for you, Mei, avoiding these temptations. I taught you well." I patted myself on the back for earning free brownie points. My abstinence wasn't exactly by choice, but I might as well collect the perk associated with it. "Like I said before, this is why it's important to have the right boy. One who won't pressure you. Eugene."

I cringed into my p-set.

"Eugene will never take you if you're dirty, sullied by another person," she continued, oblivious to my nausea. "Don't let your roommate infect you with her bad behavior. Peer pressure happens when the other person is jealous. So if she tries to make you feel bad, remember it's because you're better than her."

She stopped folding clothes, and my radar *ping*ed. I wasn't sure what serious (and possibly embarrassing) conversation was coming, but I knew enough to get out of there. Unfortunately, I wasn't fast enough.

"Mei, we need to talk about what happened last night at Chow Chow."

I held my breath. I actually *wanted* to talk about Xing. More than anything. Not because I was confused (which I was), but because I hadn't heard my mother talk about him in years. And after yesterday, if we didn't even mention him now, it would mean he was really gone. The bar was so low—even if she brought Xing and Esther up just to curse at them, I'd have some hope. Because then they would at least exist, be important enough to still get under her skin.

She sighed. "It was nice of you to stand up for me, but you need to learn that's not how it goes."

I exhaled quickly like I had been punched. I wasn't surprised that she hadn't brought him up, but I wasn't okay with it either.

She didn't even notice my reaction and continued. "In the future, your mother-in-law, Mrs. Huang, will be number one in the family. And right now, in our family, Nǎinai is number one. You can't disrespect her or talk back. I'm scared you're too headstrong, and it will be a problem when you get married."

Only if I marry a Chinese person with traditional, unrelenting parents . . . like you and Bǎbá.

"But that's why I think Eugene will be a good match," my mother went on. "I think his parents will be better. I'm trying to set you up with a good boy with a good upbringing from a family I know. I'm trying to save you the heartache I suffer. . . ." Her voice trailed off, and she left her sentence vague, no details.

"Mămá, if you don't want me to go through what you went through, wouldn't it be better if I married someone *not* Chinese? Or at least someone with parents less overbearing than Mrs. Huang?"

My mother paused for a moment, but only one. "Marrying another Chinese person who understands your upbringing and values—that's what creates a solid foundation for a strong marriage. Remember Kimberly Chen? Her mother didn't object when Kimberly married that Spanish boy. Now they're divorced."

"I doubt they divorced because of their different backgrounds. Many people get divorced."

"None of my friends are divorced."

"None of them are happy, either," I muttered.

Seeming not to hear me, she barreled on. "I'm sure Mrs. Chen regrets it now. Kimberly is left with two kids, and no one else will marry her. Can you believe she let that happen to her own daughter?"

Umm, yes? Because she's not an oppressive dictator?

My mother gasped, and I instinctively scooted my chair away, anticipating another non–candy bar wrapper. But when I turned around, she was holding up the calculus test I had "accidentally" left out. The *100* at the top was so big and red I could see it from across the room.

She smiled at me, a hint of pride in the curve of her lips, exactly as I had hoped for. "I can tell how hard you've been working, Mei. My good girl, spending all her time studying."

I tried to bask in her pride, to feel the glow from inside that came only every few months such that I had to store it away and ration it out . . . but all I could hear was my heart pounding in my ears, *trait-or, trait-or, trait-or. Quit teaching dance* had been on my calendar every day the past few weeks, but so far I'd been oh for twenty. But it wasn't getting in the way of my studies, right? Except for the sixty on my biology p-set, which was burning a hole at the bottom of my drawer.

"Mămá? Why is it so important to you that I become a doctor?"

She busied her hands with folding as if the topic made her nervous. "You can't end up like me, Mei. You heard them last night. No respect for me. As a doctor, your husband and in-laws will be better to you. They have to," she said, more to convince herself than me, it seemed. "You need power in your relation-ship. If you earn your own money, your husband can never use it against you."

"Can't I do something else? A different job, also respectable?"

"Doctor is the most respectable, and you have the smarts to do it, Mei. Don't worry. You won't end up like me. I've been planning for you since the beginning. Since you came out a girl. And I'm still planning. Always planning. I do your laundry and bring you food so you can devote all your time to studying. So get good grades, okay? Don't let me work myself to the bone for nothing."

I've always been jealous of my friends whose parents kissed their cheeks, read them bedtime stories, bought them whatever toys they wanted. But my parents showed love in different ways: shopping exclusively at garage sales, reusing napkins and Ziplocs, never treating themselves to the furniture or vacations they coveted. It was so I could go to the best school and end up with a stable career where I would never have to sacrifice like they did. To them, a secure future was the ultimate gift a parent could give. How could I refuse them when this was their motivation?

Except Esther wasn't what they said she was, a tiny voice whispered in my head.

"What is it?" my mother asked, breaking into my thoughts.

"What do you mean?"

"I can tell—something's bothering you."

"Really? You can tell?"

"Of course. I'm your *mǔqīn*."

My chest twinged. "Nothing's bothering me. I'm just . . . thankful that you want the best for me and that you've sacrificed so much to get me here. Thanks, Māmá. You gave up your own education and career for me."

My mother balled socks angrily. "I could've been successful, too. I went to Tái Dà, National Taiwan University—the Harvard of Taiwan! I did better than Bàbá, and certainly better than Yilong. Yet I don't have anything to show for it."

Each ball she threw into the pile further pounded into my head that my mother's demands, her criticisms—they were because she wanted better for me. I tried not to think about the fact that she was so unhappy.

Or that Xing and Esther had looked so in love.

Or that the pressure was boxing me in, restricting my airflow, with no end in sight.

VOICEMAIL FROM MY MOTHER

Mei! Good, you didn't pick up. You are supposed to be in
<pause> five . . . one . . . one . . . one . . . right now. Why so
many numbers? Call me at two fifty-five when lecture ends.
It's your mǔqīn.

CHAPTER 10

Queens

Nicolette groaned in her sleep. I froze, hoping to stave off what usually came next. The hoarse, *Must you be so frickin' loud?*

I jumped when she spoke.

"Why do you see your parents so often? It's, like, every week. You know that's not normal, right?"

Nothing about me was normal. Maybe if she were around more, she'd have figured that out already. I wasn't even seeing my parents today, but she didn't get to know that.

I didn't say anything. Wasn't that what she liked about me anyway?

She yawned. "Tell them to get a life and stop inserting themselves into yours."

I burst out laughing. I couldn't help it. Nicolette opened one eye and squinted at me. "You're an odd egg. What's so funny?"

"You wouldn't understand."

"Try me."

"They're just . . ." My mind blanked. Fuzzy screen, jumbled words, emotional soup. "Traditional," I finished lamely. "Not that that's a bad thing," I added quickly.

"If I had to see my parents every weekend, I'd fake my own death."

"That's pretty extreme, don't you think?"

"So is seeing your parents every weekend in college."

My anger bubbled to the surface. She didn't know anything about them, my situation, how hard it was to straddle two cultures. What gave her the right to Judge Judy my life?

Before I could come up with a conversation-ending retort, Nicolette rolled her back to me. "Just sayin' . . . Maybe stop hanging out with them and go out a bit more."

Easy for her to say.

I slammed the door on my way out, hoping it jolted her from her half slumber. That was for insulting my parents. And for the condom wrapper.

• • •

As the Dartmouth Coach chugged along the road, Helen Mirren's *The Queen* played sans sound on all thirty or so TV monitors overhead. I couldn't help but feel proud of my independence even though it was sad that this was such a big step for me and a regular day for everyone else on the bus.

This was the first time I'd ventured out on my own (not count-ing that time I had snuck to Walgreens to buy tampons despite my mother's directive to "not deflower myself prematurely"). Thanks to the internet, I had figured out the subway, found the bus that ran from South Station to Hanover, New Hampshire, then crossed state lines—all without my parents. And once I'd done it, I wondered why I had never thought to do it before. Following directions? Super easy. Going unknown places by yourself? A little scary, but also kind of exhilarating. Reason for leaving? After the crap-storm that was this weekend, my past, present, and future were broken and jumbled, pieces floating around and crashing into one another. So I was running away to Helen, the only high school classmate who'd been mother-approved (aka Taiwanese) and thus my only friend.

The mix of pride, excitement, and anxiety churned my stomach. Or maybe I was just carsick. I hadn't thought far enough ahead to bring a vomit bag. Hopefully on this day of firsts, it wouldn't be my first time throwing up on a stranger, too.

At least we were getting close. According to the online sched-ule and my phone's GPS, we were fifteen minutes away.

The bus bucked over a pothole, and I grabbed the seat in front of me as my stomach flipped. A tiny moan escaped from my lips (so embarrassing), and I desperately hoped my seatmate didn't hear.

"Are you okay?" she asked, her voice sympathetic.

"Sorry. Yeah. I'm fine." I took a second to calm my insides, then leaned back in the seat and closed my eyes. "I get motion sickness. I probably shouldn't have been watching the movie. It wasn't even any good—I was just bored." *And trying to distract myself from the thought-tornado inside my head.*

"I know, right?" She gestured to the screen. "It's just Helen Mirren, in makeup, talking. I mean, yeah she earned an Academy Award for it, but it's not like we get to experience any of that with the sound off." She chuckled. "And you know what? They play that movie every trip. It's my seventieth bus ride, I've changed majors three times, and yet that goddamn movie is still the same."

"Wow, *seventy* bus rides?"

"My girlfriend goes to Dartmouth and I'm at MIT."

"I'm at MIT too!" I felt an automatic bond form between us. Was this what my mother felt with other Asians?

"I'm Jenn," she said. Luckily, she didn't hold her hand out.

"Nice to meet you! I'm Mei." I barreled on to fill the silence, just in case a handshake was still on the horizon. "So, seventy trips, that's gotta add up."

Her features darkened for a moment, and I could tell she was contemplating whether or not to show me a window into something important but private. I knew that look all too well—I struggled with it every day growing up, when I didn't know how to explain my parents to my classmates. By junior high, I'd stopped trying. It only led to more questions and a bigger target on my back for being different.

She took a breath. "The price of bus tickets is worth the small sacrifices of drinking less coffee and using the library's textbooks instead of buying my own." Her eyes lowered to her lap. "Sarah's my family. My parents didn't handle my coming out well. They made me choose between them and being who I was, so . . ." She looked right at me, and I felt like she somehow knew about me, Xing, and the similarities between our parents. "It was an easy decision, yet it wasn't, you know?"

I sighed, heavy enough that I was pretty sure Jenn knew I had some experience with this, at least remotely. "I'm sorry you had to go through that. I hope they come around. And if not, they don't deserve to have you in their life."

Jenn smiled, more open, and she relaxed her shoulders. "Thanks. I'm lucky to have met supportive people like you since the falling-out, which helped a little. I lost so many people over this—not just my parents, but other family who tried to convince me that my mom and dad were doing this because they loved me, and I should try harder to work it out with them."

"That's bullshit," I said, the words flying out before I could think. My hand flew to my mouth, partly because I had said the word "shit" out loud but more because I hadn't realized I felt this way. I was brought up to believe questioning your parents was immoral, but on the outside looking in, I sided wholeheartedly with Jenn. My parents had never talked to me about homosexuality—maybe because they avoided all politically charged topics, or maybe because we never talked at all. Whatever the reason, I had formed my own opinion over the years, hadn't flinched when Jenn first mentioned her girlfriend, and now was appalled by her parents' actions. Of course they were wrong.

And then it hit me.

Why hadn't I thought more about Xing's situation when it happened? In the years to follow? I only knew the curses my parents threw. Only their side. I hadn't questioned their actions because there wasn't a choice to be made—I simply *had* to choose them since I lived under their roof.

I never thought my parents could be wrong about anything, but the seed of doubt that had been planted this weekend was sprouting.

I opened my mouth to ask Jenn more, but because we were pulling up to our destination, she said, "My last name's Green," implying I should look her up. "Don't hesitate to reach out if you ever need anything!"

"I'm happy you found Sarah. I wish you two the best, and I really hope your parents come around."

Jenn pulled me into a hug, and, uncharacteristically, I embraced her back.

Helen was waiting for me, perky as ever in a green and white Dartmouth tee that had been cropped into a cute tank with scissors (and not very sharp ones from the look of it). She waved frantically, and I wondered how she managed to look so cute doing something that would've made me look desperate.

She wrapped me in a hug the second my foot touched asphalt. Two hugs in two minutes—that was a record for me.

"Lunch first?" she asked in her singsongy voice, and after nodding, I let her loop her arm through mine. Helen's touchy-feely-ness had been so off-putting to me at first—ten-year-old me had been so startled the first time she hugged me that I had accidentally smeared ice cream in her hair—but over time I had grown to expect it (and maybe even crave it, though I would never tell her that). She had been the most normal part of my high school experience, and there was something so calming about being back with her.

Helen introduced me to 90 percent of the people who walked by, each with a name and a description—Charlie, the best Christopher Walken impersonator you'll ever meet; Jake, the best beer pong player. . . . Basically, everyone was the best at something useless. I wondered what I would be, but she just introduced me as *Mei, my friend from high school.*

She seemed to be the queen of campus. Another Queen Helen. The difference between us couldn't be more pronounced, like molten lava cake and red bean dessert soup. And it only became starker as we made our way, arm in arm, into the Dirt Cowboy Café, which I originally read (with a zap of panic) as Dirty Cowboy Café. But there weren't any men in cowboy hats and assless chaps dancing on the bar. Just rows of coffee beans on one side and a display of pastries on the other.

I was initially frazzled by the plethora of options written on the wall, but then I remembered how far I had come to get here today. With confidence, I ordered a turkey sandwich (safe) and a parsley-carrot juice (yee-haw!).

I sat beside Helen, whose head was swiveling to and fro, clearly searching for someone.

"I just heard that the guy I'm crushing on checked in here," she whispered so softly I barely heard. It took me a moment to fill in the blanks, half the words having disappeared into her pale-pink lipstick.

"Checked in on Facebook?"

"Shhhh!" She waved her hands at me, drawing way more attention than my four words had. "Duh, on Facebook." With one more scan of the perimeter, she settled into her chair. "He's not here yet. So, how's MIT?"

"Good," I said instinctively, in the same way you answer *I'm fine* regardless of how you're actually feeling. "I mean, I like it," I said sincerely. "I fit in there better than I did in high school." I ignored Helen's snort, which she didn't try to cover up. "But there's still a bit of a disconnect."

"Do you think it's because you're younger?"

I shrugged. "I mean, no one knows I'm younger. It hasn't come up."

"Yeah, but you *are*. You're supposed to still be in high school, worrying about parents and grades and the mean popular kids."

"Um, I still do that."

She laughed. "You should've come here with me, Mei. I could've helped you shed your stiff exterior." Then she said what I was thinking but wouldn't have voiced aloud. "But I guess that wasn't really an option with your parents."

I stiffened.

Helen looked at me warily. "Ease up, soldier. I know better than to say anything negative at this point."

I laughed, short and forced. Ms. I-Hold-Nothing-Back used

to rail on my parents, calling them dictators, tiger parents, *qíguài*. And each time, despite the fact that I had been complaining just moments before, I'd defend them, inciting a fight. Eventually, we learned to steer clear, but it didn't make me any less tense when we circled it.

"You know, I didn't even have to apply to MIT. Remember?"

Of course I remembered. I felt like she was just rubbing it in at this point.

Before even visiting, Helen had told her parents she didn't want to go to MIT because she didn't want *that kind of college experience*, whatever that meant. You know what her parents said? *Sure, Wei Wei, whatever you want.* Her parents called her *Wei Wei*. Taught her Mandarin. Yet she didn't have to go to Chinese school because she didn't like it, and she didn't have to strive for MIT/Harvard and accept Dartmouth as a shameful consolation. Her parents had thrown a party when she was accepted early decision, while mine hid Xing's Dartmouth attendance away in shame.

I realized that I had come here partly because I wanted to know why our experiences had been so different. Her parents were from Taiwan, just like mine. They had immigrated here for graduate school, just like mine. Yet Helen had boyfriends, spoke her mind, and her only house rule growing up was *Don't let the dog poop on the bed*. I bet Helen never suffered from Lu guilt—you know, that special brand of disgrace, responsibility, and shame bred by an environment where most things you did weren't good enough and unconditional obedience was expected.

Other childhood acquaintances popped into my head like

whack-a-moles. Kimberly Chen, who married a non-Chinese guy and then got divorced . . . Jade, who moved in with her boyfriend without a ring on her finger . . . even Hanwei, whose mother hadn't cut him off when he'd decided to pursue music.

Suddenly I saw the spectrum they represented. It had been right before my eyes, but I hadn't seen—or more accurately, had *refused* to see. Before, I had blamed my culture, but that wasn't the problem. It was so much more complicated than that. It was a clashing of personalities and *interpretations* of cultures. How would my parents and I ever find a solution to this impossible mix of opposing ideals and desires? No right answers. Only a long list of wrong ones.

"Helllooooo." Helen waved a hand in front of my face. "Did you fall asleep over there because of the all-nighters you've pulled doing homework?"

"When people ask you what you are, what do you say?"

She quirked a brow. "Are you okay?"

I nodded, then waved my hand to draw the answer out.

"Chinese, I guess. Why?"

"Do you feel Chinese?"

Her eyes narrowed in confusion. "Of course. I speak the language, my parents are from Taiwan, and I mean, c'mon, look at me! Supercute Asian girl!"

She felt Chinese but didn't feel constrained by it like I did. Maybe I was the problem. Maybe I could learn from Helen. But we were so different I couldn't isolate her views of the culture from the effervescent bubble that made up the rest of her. And mixing red bean soup with lava cake was disgusting.

I barely tasted my turkey sandwich as Helen chatted to me about her crush, Nate, and his blond curls and tanned skin. I grew so accustomed to her voice that it blended with the background din and I didn't notice when her mouth clamped shut. She whacked my arm—not very subtly—and I finally caught on when I saw curly blond hair out of the corner of my eye.

Maybe Helen and I weren't so different after all. Even Queen Helen turned awkward in front of her crush.

"Go talk to him!" I said, nudging her foot with mine under the table.

She shook her head frantically, packed up her sandwich and mine, then dragged me out with a viselike grip.

"Why didn't you talk to him?" I asked.

"Are you kidding me? He's a junior! And didn't you see him? He's gorgeous! *So* out of my league. I might have a shot when I get into Tri Delt though. I think I've got that in the bag now."

Lava cake and red beans.

The next few hours felt like a blur. I met student after student, all perfectly pleasant, but soon they jumbled into person-soup and I couldn't remember one name from the next. Maybe it was because our conversations were short, meaningless, and rehearsed, or maybe it was because I couldn't focus with everything going on in my head.

On the return bus, I slumped in my seat and stared at the nondescript trees flying by. Somehow, even though I was seeing clearer than before, I felt more trapped.

VOICEMAIL FROM MY MOTHER

I heard from Mrs. Tian who heard from Mrs. Lin that Ying-Na
tried to make it in LA as an actress but couldn't. They even
stopped paying her to take off her clothes. You're studying hard,
right? Make me and Bǎbá proud. This is your mǔqīn.

CHAPTER 11

In Stereo

As I strolled past the Johnson Ice Rink, my name rippled in the distance. I glanced around. Maybe a stranger had said the word "may," not my name, but then I made out a familiar jagged outline of hair.

I strolled, trying to suppress my eagerness, which resulted in an embarrassing quick-slow-quick-slow trot—like I *had* the trots. Darren and three of his friends had skates slung over their shoulders. He introduced me to a lean Latino male, Billy; a cute brunette named Penny; and a short Indian freshman, Amav, who was also Penny's boyfriend. I recognized Billy and Amav from Chow Chow.

I smiled ear to ear as I shook hands with each of them. New friends. Who seemed genuinely happy to meet me.

"Free skate is going on for another hour. Want to join us?" Darren asked.

My pulse quickened. I hadn't been able to Rollerblade in junior high PE—what horrors awaited me on ice? And I knew from my online stalking that Darren was on the MIT hockey team.

No, I definitely couldn't join them. "Sorry. I have to—"

Darren's face drooped, his eyebrows angling down and his smile dropping into a frown. His disappointment was so endearing that imaginary Mămá Lu disappeared along with my fear of embarrassment.

"Well," I amended, "I guess I can get to my p-set later."

When he pumped his fist in the air, I blushed. Penny shot me an encouraging smile, which I returned.

I requested size eight skates from the sweaty dude behind the counter, reminding myself I was hanging out with all of them, not just Darren. Totally chill.

I took a seat beside Penny to emphasize that point.

"Are you an avid skater, Mei?"

"Uh, no. I've never tried it. But I dance, so maybe some of my balancing skills will transfer over?"

Darren scooted down the bench until he was directly behind me. "I didn't know you danced." His eyes twinkled as he said, "I know a thing or two about *pas de bourrées* and *piques*."

My mouth went slack, and I stared until my tongue dried out. "You speak dance."

"My sister is really into jazz, and I've listened to her talk about it my whole life."

I was glad my mouth was already open. I snapped it shut, scratched my head, wiped my nose with my finger—anything to cover up the longing I was feeling toward him. Even if he stood up and did a *pique* on the spot, it didn't change his background or mine.

"Such a show-off," Billy said, breaking my bubble when he reached over me to smack Darren's knee. "Don't be fooled, Mei— he can't dance worth a damn. It's all talk."

Darren chuckled. "How would you know? Last I checked, you haven't given me the opportunity to waltz you around the floor. I accept your challenge."

Billy rolled his eyes at me. "See what I mean? All talk."

"But he offered to prove it," I said. It felt so good to be included, to be seen.

"Uh, *no*," Billy said with emphasis. "He just knew I'd refuse to dance with him because *I'm* a rotten dancer."

Darren held his hands up in submission. "I never said I was a *good* dancer. But I dance." He splayed his long, wiggling fingers into jazz hands. "For fun. No idea how I look doing it and never intend to find out."

I couldn't help imagining Darren flailing his gangly limbs around. A-dorable.

Annnd cue the guilt sweats. Imaginary Mămá Lu couldn't even give me one freaking second.

"It's all good, Mr. Tall, Dark, and Handsome," Penny said to

Darren. "You don't have to be great at everything."

Amav pouted. Before he could speak, Penny leaned down, kissed him, and said, "Don't worry, darlin'. I personally like 'em short, cute, and spunky."

Amav picked her up, making her squeal, and they left to skate in their private, romantic bubble.

My eyes followed them around the rink, wondering if I'd ever be able to have that with someone. It seemed so difficult to find to begin with, let alone among the few fertile Taiwanese doctors my parents approved of. And it didn't help that I seemed to be attracted only to spiky-haired forbidden fruit.

Once my skates were fastened, I clutched the seat and raised my butt a millimeter at a time, eventually standing successfully. So far so good. I held on to the side of the rink as I stepped onto the ice, but the second I let go, my torso flew forward.

Darren skated a graceful arc around me, his arm encircling my waist. "I've got you. Try to bend your knees a little, and keep your feet shoulder width apart." He exaggerated his stance to demonstrate.

I couldn't focus on anything with his hand burning a hole in my side. I had dreamed of affection like this for so long, but I never thought it would come with so many complicated strings.

I must have tensed because Darren let go. And, of course, I went flying forward again. He tried to grab me, but my flailing arm socked him in the stomach, and we crumpled into a heap on the cold ice.

Oh God.

"I'm so sorry," I said from beneath Darren's left arm and leg. "I should just crawl out of here on my hands and knees. That'd be less embarrassing."

Darren laughed, loud and genuine, which put me more at ease as we untangled.

I stood slowly, trying to locate my center and use my dance training to keep myself upright. I tried a few short, choppy steps, but at this rate it would be graduation day by the time I finished one lap.

"Um, could you maybe help me out a bit?" I rationalized it was for my safety (and his). Perfectly innocent.

His arms were as cozy as a Snuggie. I took a deep breath to relax my muscles, and I finally allowed myself to sink into him.

To my dismay, I started to get the hang of it after a few snail-paced loops. But, fortunately, Darren's arm remained snug around my waist. As our feet glided in almost-sync, I forgot about the other crap in my life and lost myself in his body heat, the crackling energy of the other skaters, the sound of blades scraping.

Billy skated over, jumping to a stop and spraying ice bits over our feet (and our moment). "Guys! I just heard from someone that LSC starts tonight! We have to go! If we catch Saferide, we can get there before previews start. C'mon!"

He was already speeding toward the bleachers before we could respond.

Darren turned to me. "Want to go watch a movie in a lecture hall?"

"But it's Tuesday."

"Exactly." He grinned, crooked and boyish with just the right amount of mischief. It sent a thrill through me.

The MIT Saferide was packed, forcing us to cram in the aisles, grabbing on to whatever we could to stay upright. I tried not to think about the bacteria crawling on the shuttle and now my hands.

"This is the most spontaneous thing I've ever done," I called out to Darren.

His gaze met mine over the other passengers' heads. "Then I'm really glad we're doing it. Among other reasons."

Unsure how to respond, I fumbled in my bag for something—anything.

The shuttle lurched to one side, throwing me against a stranger. The guy glared at me despite my apology, and Darren squeezed closer, using his body as a barrier between me and the disgruntled student.

I secretly hoped for another lurch, but none came.

We followed posters for "The Lecture Series Committee" to 26-100, the largest lecture hall on campus. As we took our seats, Billy acted as if we were attending opening night of a Broadway show. I squirmed to make sure I was still in the wooden lecture seats, not cushy velvet.

Ouch.

Billy patted Penny's knee like an excited child. "I've been hearing about all this MIT stuff for forever from my bro, and I can't believe I get to do it all myself now." Penny rolled her eyes playfully, like she'd already heard him say this a thousand times. He rubbed his palms together. "I'm ready to yell. I hope the picture cuts out or something."

There were a few hundred people spread across the stadium seating. The lights dimmed and the front brightened as the projector flipped on. A few patrons whooped.

Giant letters appeared on the screen, and a male voice announced over the speakers, "Coming soon . . ."

The entire audience (except me) yelled, "IN STEREO!"

I looked around, wondering momentarily if they had all been possessed. The audience chuckled together.

As a trailer for next week's screening came on—an action flick—the sound cut out. Explosions continued to fill the screen but in silence.

Someone from the far right of the room yelled, "L-S-C!"

"SUCKS!" yelled three hundred people.

"L-S-C!"

"SUCKS!"

The chanting continued among other chatter. "It's the first showing of the season, damn it. We're only one trailer in!" "C'mon, projector guy! Get your shit together!"

I pictured the projectionist flailing around his tiny space, driven more frantic by the taunts.

"Give him a break! He's doing his best!" I yelled. I had tried to project, but my voice only reached a couple rows around me.

"It's a tradition here," Darren explained, his eyes slightly wide with . . . surprise? Amusement? "LSC has been around since the forties, when technology still kinda sucked. Whenever the film used to have problems, everyone would shout so that the projection guy would see and fix it. I think now they make mistakes on purpose just so we can yell—or at least that's what Billy's brother says. It's lighthearted."

"Sounds mean-spirited to me."

He smiled, his eyes still dancing in a way that made me feel warm. "Just be glad no one's hacking into the system to change the movie to porn or something."

I tried to cover my flushed cheeks with some forced laughter. "And the 'in stereo'?"

"It's a holdover from the fifties. The previews used to start by saying 'Coming next week, in stereo,' and even though that's long gone, we still yell it out."

"That's . . . interesting." I didn't really get it. But I guess any inside joke is fun when you're inside it. Too bad I was still feeling my way around in the dark, trying to find the door that would let me in.

I sank into my seat, trying to feel like I was a part of the crowd. Like I belonged. Maybe if I faked it, it would eventually come true.

Darren slid his arm across the back of my seat. Without thinking, I curled into him, feeling snug and warm, like when we were skating.

But only for a second.

Now that I didn't have an excuse—like how our canoodling was for my safety or his—the Mǎmá Lu in my head roared. I couldn't deny it—between the movie setting and the dimmed lighting, I was full-on disobeying them.

Xing and Esther and the explosion at Chow Chow popped

into my head. I couldn't go down this road. Worse, I couldn't take Darren down this road.

So when he started to lean closer, I ran. Just shot up out of my seat, mumbled that I left the stove on (I mean, *what?*), then started excusing my way past the other patrons.

The tangle of legs crowding the row and the reluctance of the students were quicksand, slowing me such that Darren and his long legs easily caught up.

Outside in the hallway, he asked, "Was it because I put my arm around you, or because I mentioned porn?" He paused. "I'm willing to take back one of those . . . the arm."

I chuckled, which he took as an invitation, inching closer.

The laughter drained out as I took a step back. "I can't. We can't. But not because I don't want to. It's . . . complicated."

He sighed. "Because your mother disapproves of me?"

Of course he had noticed at the restaurant—Mămá Lu wasn't exactly known for her subtlety. I looked away, not wanting to know what he was thinking.

His voice was barely above a whisper when he asked, "Is it because I'm not Chinese? Or because I'm Japanese?"

Both. "It doesn't matter."

"Well, what do *you* want?"

No one had ever asked me that before, including myself. It almost felt forbidden. Partly because it *was*, by my parents. But mostly because it made things harder. Which meant . . . I already knew what I thought.

I think I had stopped asking myself what I wanted after the

pre-prima-ballerina dream turned nightmare. Dreams could hurt you if they didn't come true, but if they never existed in the first place . . .

"That doesn't matter either."

His eyebrows angled up in surprise. "How can you say that? Of course it matters. It should be the *only* thing that matters."

I shook my head. "You don't get it. You must not know the kind of pressure I'm under, the type of guilt I feel."

He folded his arms over his chest—tired, not confrontational. "I have a lot of pressure from my parents too. I don't come from very much, and there's a lot riding on me and my ability to provide for them in the future."

Strike two, I couldn't help thinking. My mother once broke up with a boyfriend because he was the eldest of six and would have to provide for the rest of his family, meaning it wouldn't leave much for her and her not-yet-born kids.

"And," Darren continued, "my parents didn't want me to go to MIT. They wanted me to stay near home, go to a local school, and not *abandon them*." He made air quotes. "But I got a free ride here, and when I visited, I knew I had found my home. I didn't let them get in the way of what I knew was best for me, and I don't regret it at all."

"I'm sorry," I said sincerely. "I didn't mean to imply anything about your situation, and I'm sorry about the pressure you have and what you had to go through to get here. . . ." I trailed off, unable to say what I was thinking, that it was different for him. Because what did I know? Just like how he didn't know anything about my circumstances. "Look, what I feel—the sense of duty—it's debilitating, makes me feel so ashamed that I don't even care what I want."

"It's okay not to agree with them," he said gently, as if I were an animal he was trying not to spook.

"Not to them. They believe having different opinions makes me a bad person. In Taiwan during my parents' childhood, filial piety was as much a part of life as breathing—ingrained from birth, expected from everyone. Confucius's Twenty-Four Filial Exemplars—one of the first lessons in school—spoke of warming an icy lake with your naked body to catch fish for your mother, tasting your father's feces to diagnose his medical condition, and feeding yourself to the mosquitoes to spare your parents' blood."

Too far! Too weird! the alarm rang in my head. I snapped my mouth shut.

Darren's eyes had first widened during the Filial Exemplars and seemed to still be going.

After a beat, he said, "That's absurd."

His words cut into me, each syllable a pinprick. He didn't understand. But maybe it was better if he never did. Because no matter what, this would end in flames, and it was cleaner to extinguish it now, small and contained, than later, when, say, a certain tongue clucker could be involved.

Even though I tried, I couldn't keep my voice even as I said, "Not as absurd as going after a girl who can't be with you. Can't you take a hint?" I hated myself. And I hated myself more when pain flashed across his face. *It's for the best,* I told myself even though I couldn't tell anymore whether it was me or Mămá Lu talking.

The pain morphed into sadness, such a contrast to his usual brightness. "Maybe I saw something in you that isn't there. I didn't realize you were so brainwashed that you couldn't think for yourself."

I turned and ran. And I didn't stop, not even when he yelled after me.

• • •

No one understood me or how hard this was. How I felt like I had to split myself in two, neither of them truly Mei, just to make everyone *else* happy. The one person who I had thought would get it was too busy impressing sororities, and the one person I had wanted to get it had said, *That's absurd.* The words made me cringe, made me want to disappear. Made me crave the one person who *would* understand.

I took out my phone and dialed. I didn't have much hope—he had stopped taking my calls years ago—but I had to try.

"Mei?" Xing sounded like he had just seen a ghost.

"Hey, Xing Xing," I said, calling him by his childhood nickname.

"Is everything okay? Are you okay?"

My eyes filled with tears. "I miss you." I took a breath before I could say the words—the traitorous, condemning words. "Congratulations on your engagement."

"Thanks. That means a lot."

I took another breath. "Can we see each other soon?"

A pregnant pause. Then a protective timbre surfaced in his voice. "I don't want you to get in trouble with them. If they find out, they might cut you off. No tuition, no roof over your head . . ."

This was the brother I remembered—the one who always tried to keep me safe. Who would play Chubby Bunny with me to make me forget the bullies at school, then call the principal to send them to detention.

I mustered my waning courage. "They won't know."

Xing was quiet for a moment. "Of course. Let's meet for dim sum in Chinatown at noon tomorrow."

I wiped my tears away roughly.

VOICEMAIL FROM MY MOTHER

Mei! Yilong sent me the article and maybe you should try swinging your arms three thousand times a day. It's supposed to help circulation.

Oh, and speaking of circulation, I read about these spoons that fight fat. I ordered them, of course. You press and push, push the fat away. Poof! Your belly needs it! Luckily your forearms and calves look good. Those are my genes. These spoons will make you měi, Mei.

I know you get out of class in ten minutes! I expect a call then! It's your mǔqīn.

CHAPTER 12

Mei-Ball

At the dim sum restaurant, I saw Xing
first and needed a moment before I could alert him to my presence.

He was so familiar (always on his phone, not paying attention
to his surroundings), yet I didn't know this person in front of me
with lines on his face and wearing a button-down instead of a
hoodie. Part of me wanted to reach out and touch him, to make
sure he was really there. My parents had scrubbed him from our
lives so thoroughly I used to pull out his Dartmouth sweatshirt
just to make sure he hadn't been a product of my imagination.
That ratty sweatshirt was all I had left of him since my parents
had thrown his stuff on the lawn, then changed the locks. I hated

my shiny new brass key, which had replaced the worn silver one. I refused to carry it with me and was locked out of the house more than once, but somehow it felt better to sit and wait on the porch than to carry physical proof of my brother's nonexistence.

"Xing?" I finally said.

When he saw me, his face completely brightened, the way it used to when we made blanket forts. But then the hesitation crept in. We approached each other slowly, not sure what to do. A handshake was completely weird, but so was a hug since we never did that even before our four years apart. We ended up with an awkward turtle dance, where he stuck his arms out reluctantly, I sort of bobbed and weaved a bit, there were plenty of jagged starts and stops, and finally we managed a one-second hug where he patted me on the back and I didn't fully enclose my arms around him.

Um, success? I guess that was the most affection any Lu ever exhibited.

Our table was tucked in a remote corner, accompanied by wobbly chairs and a stained tablecloth. A Chinese woman, a stranger, stared at us from across the restaurant. Was she judging my chunky figure or American clothes? Probably a mix of both.

Most of the waitstaff spoke Cantonese, not Mandarin, so we ordered by pointing to dishes on passing carts. As usual, many servers ignored us, some were rude, and others tried to push the less popular items like chicken feet. The best carts never made it past the central tables, so Xing took a cue from our father and chased down the shrimp dumplings, stuffed eggplant, and turnip cake.

Only, he managed to do it without creating a *Lu Pàng*–size scene.

The smell of the food stirred up memories of lazy Sunday afternoons with my family, stuffing ourselves so full of shrimp we could barely move. Even my mother's clucking tongue had been silenced by thousand-year-old egg congee.

And now we were divided. Those memories were fading.

Xing and I clicked our chopsticks together—a toast he had created to distract my younger self from our parents fighting about the thermostat, my mother's cooking, the amount of tofu in the house. Well, more accurately, it was my father yelling as my mother cowered.

My shoulders relaxed, falling away from my ears. Okay, we could do this. *Yíbù, yíbù*, until we took enough steps to wade through the crap.

But then it was like my brain couldn't take it anymore—the chopstick toast, the dim sum smell, the fact that Xing felt both like my blood and a stranger. . . .

I hated myself at the moment, for lots of opposing reasons. I hated that I had let this go on for so long, let others decide for me that my only sibling was going to disappear from my life. I hated that I was disobeying my parents right now, choosing the person who had so easily abandoned me and ignored my subsequent phone calls.

And I hated myself for adding yet another secret to my already overloaded plate. It was like trying to contain three spoonfuls of stuffing in a dumpling—it was so overfilled the skin barely met on any side. All the secrets threatened to spill at any moment. If I ever tried to finish the dumpling, it would explode when I squeezed—meat and veggies everywhere.

This had happened to me, literally, when I was little and learning how to make dumplings. It seems like it should've been a small issue—maybe even something many parents would have laughed at and given the child a pat on the head for being cute—but to my parents who grew up with nothing and scrimped and saved every grain of rice, wasting food was punishable. That was when I learned life was unfair.

I knew the danger of what I was doing, yet I had done it anyway. There was no one to blame here but me. I had called Xing first.

Shit. Maybe I should run for it now while I still could. We hadn't actually spoken yet—it was salvageable.

But then he smiled at me, and I remembered. How he knew my—correction, *our*—parents, and I didn't have to explain myself. He knew the culture, not just as a whole, but through our little window.

We didn't speak as we loaded our plates, and it shouldn't have surprised me—we had four years of ground to cover—but it still made me anxious. What if too much had been lost to time and we could never get it back? What if it would never be the same again and he would forever be a stranger?

"How could you just disappear like that?" I blurted out, my voice shaky. "I tried to call you so many times."

Xing's mouth was open, a piece of eggplant a few inches away, but it slipped from his chopsticks and clunked onto his plate, spraying sauce. He was frozen for a second before closing his lips. . . . But he left the sauce where it was, which reminded me that he was still the same person I remembered, never cleaning up after himself.

I could see him turning the words over in his head and it sent a zap of frustration through me. "Stop filtering everything, Xing. Just tell me what you're thinking, the truth. Not some pretty answer you think will resolve everything."

He spoke immediately, the words falling out fast and a bit jumbled. "I didn't want to make you choose. I bowed out so you could keep your relationship with them. You need them more than you need me."

"How could you decide all that without asking me?"

There was a long pause. "You're right. I shouldn't have. But you were so young. I thought I was doing what was best for you."

"Best for me? You shoveled a bunch of crap on me when you left. I had to fix everyone whenever your name came up, and worse, I had to become the perfect Taiwanese poster child to make up for all the shame you caused. I was never let out. I missed prom. I became this sheltered, awkward turtle destined to be an outcast no matter where I went. You weren't there to tell me about the world, and because of you, Mom and Dad made sure I never saw it. Now I'm a seventeen-year-old college student who's never been kissed and who'll end up with the guy who peed on my foot because you couldn't try to make it work with our parents."

Okay, that may have gotten away from me a bit. But when I raised my gaze to meet his, I saw in his eyes that he understood and he was sorry. We shared a sad, knowing smile.

Then a shadow crossed his face (and I couldn't help but think how much he looked like my father in that moment). There was an edge to his voice as he said, "Mom and Dad and especially Năinai are so backward in some of their thinking." *Offer up your fertile sister* rang in my head. "There's no working anything out with people like that. So you're right. I didn't try that hard, at least not after that night. . . ."

That night. That night had haunted me for so long. I had watched from the stairs, too young to fully understand but old enough to know something was different about this fight.

Xing had pleaded, begged on his knees, for our parents to give Esther a chance. But when they yelled at him to *gŭn* and roll out the door, his face had changed. It was like I could see the ties breaking, see everything drain from him to the point where he no longer cared what they thought.

"How could they throw away their son over a girl they hadn't even met yet?" Xing's voice was rising. "One strike and . . ." He slashed his finger across his throat.

Esther's reproductive challenges had been the sole reason for Xing's disownment. Her congenital endometriosis was caught late, and doctors informed her she may have trouble conceiving. Otherwise she was perfect, even by my parents' standards: intelligent, Taiwanese, beautiful . . . or so Xing had said. My parents had refused to meet her. Not bearing grandchildren, especially if you were the firstborn son, was the worst kind of disobedience possible. And not only was Xing the firstborn son of a firstborn son, but he and my father were the *only* sons in their family. Double, triple, quadruple whammy. I never understood what was so bad about having fewer Lus in the world, but to my parents it was a crime.

"I'm sorry they were so hard on you," I said, placing a palm on Xing's.

He patted our pile of hands with his free one. "Thanks, Mei-ball—it means a lot."

That nickname hadn't touched my ears in so, so long, and hearing it now, my heart was bouncing in my rib cage. I felt us taking one step forward, together.

I wanted to tell him how much he meant to me and how much I had missed him, but I didn't know how to say it. So I said the next nicest thing I could think of. "You and Esther looked happy."

"Thank you. You're so kind." He smiled, intentionally revealing the chives stuck in his teeth.

I laughed, my insides warming at the game we used to play. With my tongue, I pushed shrimp bits onto my incisors. "You're so welcome, good sir."

"Tell me, what's new with you?" he asked, his voice serious but his mouth full of turnip. It helped decrease the awkwardness of how he was asking me to sum up the past four years.

"I'm at MIT. I like it."

"Premed?" he asked, but it sounded more like a statement, like he knew I didn't have a choice. Which, well, he *did* know.

I gave an imperceptible nod. "Do you like it? I mean, I assume you're a doctor now?"

He nodded. "It pays the bills. I'm in my first year of an internal medicine residency, still at Tufts. I'm thinking about doing gastro-enterology, you know, endoscopies and colonoscopies."

I couldn't help cringing. "Was it hard to get used to doing those?"

Xing sipped his tea, oblivious to my nausea. "Yeah, it took some time. I used to laugh whenever I thought about the colonoscopy recovery room, where the patients can't help farting up a storm. The attending threw me out my first day. Now look at me! I just told you about the room without even cracking a smile."

I laughed, deep and throaty. Xing joined in, and the hearty sound filled me with memories. Xing reading me comics—Chinese or English, depending on our mood. Xing joking, asking me whether I thought Wang Leehom's parents were prouder of their Taiwanese pop star son or the son who went to MIT. (We both agreed: the MIT son.)

"That is *not* what I meant," I said between laughs. "I was asking if you were ever grossed out."

"Sure, but I have a higher tolerance than most. You have to find what you're okay with, you know? The nice part about medicine is that there are a lot of options. And most important, I feel secure in my future. I know Mom and Dad have their faults, but this was something they were right about—picking the right major and career is so important. I have friends who are barely scraping by with no end in sight. At least I know that in a few years I'll be pulling a decent salary. Which is more important now than ever . . ." He trailed off, and his words hung in the air for a moment.

I felt like I was missing something but wasn't comfortable enough to ask. "So you never wish you did something else?"

"That's an entirely different question. I'm just saying that, practically, it's important to find a career that can put a roof over your head and offer enough stability that you can sleep at night."

I wasn't sure if I was talking to my brother or my parents. How could this person be the same one who had done the ultimate rebellion and walked down the disownment path, eyes open? "Medicine's not the only stable career," I countered.

"True, but there will always be a need for doctors, and there aren't many of us making a measly pay. There's just less variance than other fields. And it's respectable, right? You're helping people, making a difference."

My stomach flip-flopped, and for once, the smell of shrimp balls was making it buck even more. He was supposed to relate to me, make me feel better, but now I felt like the only person left on my own strange Mei-planet. Instead of telling him about my fears, my struggles, my secrets, I shoved them deeper, making the goddamn dumpling even fatter and more unmanageable.

"Don't worry, Mei-ball. You'll love it when you get there. I promise."

I stuffed my face with shumai and mumbled, "Chubby bunny."

Xing laughed, but I couldn't smile, and it wasn't because my mouth was full.

VOICEMAIL FROM MY MOTHER

Mei! I read today that using a tea bag more than twice will give you cancer. You're not doing that, are you? But you shouldn't use it just once either—waste of money. Use it exactly twice, okay? Call me back immediately! This is urgent! Oh, and it's your mǔqīn.

CHAPTER 14

(Since I'm Chinese-*American*, we also do not have a chapter thirteen. Equal superstitions.)

MIThenge

Hearing Xing talk about medicine in the same tone as my parents had made me wonder . . . was I also brainwashed? Immediately after Darren's accusation two days ago, I had resented him for what he had said, but now I was scared it was true.

So I hunted Darren down, orchestrating our bumping into each other because, I don't know . . . I wanted to see if he would take it back?

Except it didn't go quite as smoothly as I had pictured in my head.

Since I knew he was taking 7.012 (like me), I decided to go to my first biology lecture in weeks. As the professor droned on and on about G proteins, my head lolled back and forth in half sleep—fishing, my mother called it. What a far cry from multivariable calc, which kept me awake and attentive, grand jeté–ing across the floor in my head while taking copious notes. Math was a language I spoke, one that was the same in every culture.

But clearly I did not speak biology. By the end of class, my head was on my little foldout desk, and I didn't wake until the after-lecture rustles started. And by then I had lost the spiky-haired outline previously sitting four rows in front of me.

The paper from my notebook stuck to my cheek, ripping when I sat up. Because, of course. I scooped my things up, then charged into the herd of students in the hallway. Thank God for his height. I chased after him, squeezing through chattering groups and almost tripping over a few legs. When I finally got close to him, I suddenly didn't know what to do. In my head I pictured tapping him on the shoulder with a coy, *Fancy seeing you here.* In reality, I shoved his shoulder with a little too much force, then opened my mouth like a fish, nothing coming out.

When he saw me, the corner of his right eye crinkled the way it did before he teased me. "How'd you catch up to me so fast?" Oh God. Of course he had seen. "Not a fan of G proteins, I take it?"

"Didn't get enough sleep last night," I lied, not wanting to fight about the titillatingness of G proteins. There was defi-nitely a joke in there somewhere, which would've come to me if I weren't so overwhelmed at the moment.

At the east end of the Infinite Corridor, Darren sidestepped to lean against the wall, out of the stream of traffic.

I joined him, keeping a space between us—I wasn't sure what the social norms were post-fighting-about-Filial-Exemplars. I opened my mouth again, an apology loaded on my tongue, but nothing came out. Maybe because I still stood by my reasoning for saying what I did. Maybe because Mămá Lu was holding the words back.

Darren cleared his throat. "I'm glad you caught up," he said, and I relaxed a little. "I wasn't sure if you wanted to talk to me." I held my breath, willing him to say it. "I'm sorry about what I said—I didn't mean it. I was just overwhelmed with the mosquitoes and the feces and . . . You can understand that, right?" And finally I exhaled.

But even though I was breathing again, I still felt tense. And that was when I realized, it didn't matter what he thought. It was exactly as he had said—it was what *I* thought that mattered. And right now I had no idea where I ended and my parents began.

Darren stuck his neck out slightly, peering at me curiously until I realized I hadn't responded to his apology.

"Oh! Uh, don't worry about it. I'm used to it . . . people not understanding. My parents sent me to school without knowing English and with pork floss sandwiches for lunch. My classmates thought they looked like pubes!" I forced a sad little *ha-ha*.

"That's terrible. That must've been so hard for you." I was so used to being the *pìgu* of the joke that I just stared at him, unsure what to do with his sympathy. After a beat he said, "I know it doesn't make it better, but when I said all that stuff last time, I was trying to help. Because I care."

I raised an eyebrow. "Weird way of showing you care."

"Sorry, I just spoke my mind without thinking. You wouldn't know what that's like." The teasing crinkle reappeared.

"And I'm sorry I butted into someone else's business. You wouldn't know what *that's* like."

Our concordant man-laughs filled the space around us, and for a moment I couldn't help wondering what could have been.

"Thanks for apologizing," I said sincerely, even though it didn't have the cure-all effect I had been foolishly hoping for. "I'm sorry, too, for the record, for what I said." I punched him lightly on the arm. "I'll see you around, Takahashi." I used his last name in the hopes that it would create some distance and emphasize the friend border.

"Wait." He held a hand out briefly before running it through his already-disheveled hair. A nervous tic, perhaps? "I want to make sure you understand why that whole thing with your parents was so important to me. MIT was the best decision I ever made, and I didn't want to see you go down the wrong path for the wrong reason. I know it's not easy to go against your parents—and clearly I don't fully get what it's like for you—but I also know it can be worth the fight sometimes. And I'm not talking about me or us or, you know, anything specific. . . ." His cheeks colored slightly. "I mean in general. Because I'm guessing there's a lot there to unpack."

It was such an understatement I almost laughed, but the weight of what he had said kept it at bay.

I understood where he was coming from, but that didn't make

the situation any easier. I had to force my next words out. "Thanks for trying so hard, but I have to go."

I turned to leave but froze when I saw the students gathered in two single-file lines on either side of the hallway. It looked like the end of *Grease*'s "We Go Together," except Rizzo and Kenickie weren't dancing down the middle. Instead, the center was purposefully empty. Eerie.

Before I could ask what was going on, it happened. The hubbub silenced, and all eyes, including mine, homed in on the window at the other end of the corridor. The setting sun glided into view and rays lit up the west end of the Infinite. Within minutes, the disc filled the window, emblazing the entire 251 meters in a honey-golden glow.

The other students trickled out, having seen and taken a selfie, but I continued staring. That is, until Darren's tall frame blocked the view, casting his shadow over me.

His voice was warm honey, just like the sunset. "MIThenge is like the Lost Ark; you can't stare at it too long. Except in this case, you'd just damage your corneas."

My gaze fell to him, but he was a mere outline, my eyes having been overwhelmed by the light. *Just like how we would never see eye-to-eye*, I couldn't help but think.

"I wish things were different," I said, the sentence coming out easier with him blurry. But as my vision returned, the rest of the words died away, disappearing into the folds of my tongue.

Cautiously, he said, "Just because your mother is, um, extreme, doesn't mean we can't be friends." I said nothing. "What if we

don't talk about our parents? What if we just work on p-sets?"
When I still didn't respond, he said, "What if we just dance?"

And he broke into a jig, stomping around and flailing his arms.
It was so sudden and out of place that all I could do was stare, just
like everyone around us was doing. But he didn't care. His eyes
were on me and just me.

He finished with a heel click and swung his arms out, wiggling
his jazz-hand fingers. With a hopeful smile on his face, he held the
pose, waiting expectantly.

I shook my head at him. "I can't believe you just did that. I broke
out into a dance at school once and the other kids called me a nut."

"Well, if being a nut means being fun and yourself, then you
should be proud. I can only hope I'm a nut too. We can be nuts
together, Nut One and Two, tag-team duo, out to save the world
one almond and crappy tap dance at a time." He cleared his
throat. "Since we're going to be fighting crime together, maybe we
should exchange numbers, for the sake of the world, of course."

Why the hell not? He could've looked me up in the MIT
directory, but this felt respectful and gentlemanly—asking my
permission.

I wrote my number on his hand, old-fashioned. The pen
glided over his skin, and it made me want to touch him to see
if it felt as smooth as it appeared. Impulsively, my left palm met
his, and I pretended like I was merely steadying it, as I would
any ho-hum piece of paper. My fingers met rough calluses, and
for some reason I found that more intriguing. Rugged, like he
wasn't afraid of getting down and dirty. Or maybe I would've

found it hot no matter what, just because it was part of him.

As I wrote extra slow, I asked, "Does MIThenge happen every day?"

"Twice a year." His eyes never left my pen on his hand.

"And we bumped into each other right before it? What's the probability of that?"

"Well, given that there's always stuff going on at MIT, the probability we'd bump into each other before *something* is pretty high. But as for bumping into each other before MIThenge, specifically, we would have to take into consideration how often we bump into each other normally, the fact that our class together got out right before it started . . ." He tilted his head to the side, thinking. "The chances are roughly one in a hundred fifty," he finally answered.

"Really?"

Darren shrugged. "Your guess is as good as mine. But I impressed you for a second, didn't I?"

"Would've been more impressive if you'd been right." I playfully poked his biceps with the pen before putting it away. Yes, I looked at his arm as I did it, and yes, I liked what I saw. Was there such a thing as hockey arms, you know, like swimmers' shoulders?

"I'll keep that in mind for next time," he said, emphasizing the last two words ever so slightly. "Good day, Lady Peanut." When he tipped his imaginary hat to me in farewell, I saw him in a different light. Unfortunately.

It would've been easier to stay mad.

VOICEMAIL FROM MY MOTHER

Mei, call me, your mǔqīn. You're supposed to be free right now!
Where are you? Are you sick? Have you been swinging your
arms? Do you need me to come over with the cow's hoof?

CHAPTER 15

Ruth

I hunched over my desk, burying my nose in a textbook and pressing my hands between my thighs to hide the guilt sweats. I was so scared my mother would just look at me and know I had seen Xing. And know that I was seeing him again later today, not actually hitting the books with my ever-expanding fake study group like I'd told her.

It was starting to get too tangled. Earlier I'd had a brain fart and referenced Penny's physicist dad, only to remember that it was fake Billy's dad that was the physicist. Then I had to fumble and tell her *both* their fathers were physicists, to which my mother had said, "I thought Penny's father was a doctor." I had to summon every ounce of acting ability to convince her she was mistaken.

"What's this?" My mother snatched up my biology exam from the drawer she'd been snooping in. I'd been so distracted I'd forgotten about the secret hidden at the bottom. She waved it in my face. "A seventy-two, Mei? That's an F in our book. What happened to the other twenty-eight points?"

My mother would never understand the concept of grading on a curve and that the 72 was really a B+. But still, a B+ wasn't good enough, even with MIT's pass/fail grading for first-semester freshmen.

At age six, when I had presented my spelling test to her with a smiley face inked next to the 98, she had asked, "Where did the other two points go?" I used to tell myself this kind of tough love was what got me into MIT, but at that moment I wanted to rip that biology test into a million satisfying pieces.

I had worked my *pìgu* off for that 72 in a subject I hated as much as the cow's hoof. So many hours in the library, forcing myself to learn about—*yawn*—signaling pathways and bland-as-rice enzymes, all for them. All for a tongue cluck and a stern look.

"Do we need to get you a tutor?" my father asked.

"Mei, you should be doing the tutoring, not getting tutored." My mother threw the test onto my desk. "If you're not careful, you may not get into medical school."

That would be a relief, I thought before I could stop myself.

• • •

I lied to Xing for the first time. I told him I was dying to get a taste of medical school, and when he had grabbed the bait and ran, talking about how medicine was so exciting and I was going to love the adrenaline of it, the science, the satisfaction of helping people, I hadn't said a word. So not a blatant lie, but a lie by omission. Yes, another one. Was this my alter ego now? Or worse, just me?

I was determined not to let Xing find out that today was not an exciting glimpse into my future, but rather a test to see if I could make it work. To see if I could handle things better than the last time. If anyone could help me see the fun in medicine (or in anything, really), it was Xing.

"You're going to have *such* a blast today, Mei-ball. Gross anatomy was my favorite med school class. You'll never experience anything like this again, that first sense of wonderment and wanting to know more—how we all tick, how to find the problem, how to fix it. This is the kind of stuff that gets me through the harder parts."

He had this faraway look in his eyes, and for a moment I thought he might even tousle my hair or something, but then I remembered we were Lus: no unnecessary physical contact. But his talk worked—I could hear my heart beating in my ears.

Or maybe that wasn't excitement. Maybe it was anxiety.

Xing introduced me to my tour guide for the day—a short East Asian girl dressed in wrinkled, cerulean scrubs and beat-up sneakers. I followed Anna down multiple flights of stairs. Now that I was separated from my optimism—aka Xing—my stomach was in knots, ironically caused by the prospect of seeing other peoples' stomachs . . . and intestines . . . and livers. The space between me and the innards was growing too small too fast.

As soon as we reached the basement, the smell hit. It was vaguely familiar—corn chips, I realized, but mixed with a suffocating chemical odor. Yet another thing permanently off my grocery list (in addition to cottage cheese, of course).

I dug in my pocket for the Tiger Balm (the Asian cure-all) that Xing had told me I would need to put in my nose for the smell.

Anna grabbed my elbow. "Hey, you okay? Give it a minute—your nose just needs to adjust." She glanced at the beads of sweat on my face. "This is exciting. Fun. Don't be scared or nervous or whatever it is you're feeling. It'll be better once we're actually in front of the cadavers, when you can see everything, just like Dr. Lu said."

I ignored my bossy companion and took a moment to collect myself, needing a few extra seconds after hearing the words "Dr. Lu."

Then I ripped the Band-Aid off, passing through the double doors quickly while holding my breath. It escaped in a whoosh when I spotted the rows and rows of body bags, most of which were open. The cadavers were yellow-gray, slightly deteriorated, even more dead than I expected. In various parts—the leg, arm, and neck—the skin was cut away, the fat cleaned out, with only muscles, tendons, and nerves visible. The whole image was so unnatural, so disturbing, like a horror movie come to life.

The ease with which the medical students milled about felt so out of place I stopped to stare. One student leaned against his cadaver's leg as if it were an extension of the exam table. Another excised neck fat in the same manner one would hack apart a fatty rib-eye. The bodies were no longer human. No one looked at them, and the ones who did saw *past* them.

I felt someone grab my arm, and I numbly followed Anna's tugs to a group at the back of the room.

The balding professor—Dr. Wilson, according to his hospital badge—patted the cadaver's ankle with a gloved hand. "How's Ruthie today?"

The students chuckled, and with a satisfied smirk, Dr. Wilson walked to Ruth's partially dissected neck. "Who can locate the cervical sympathetic ganglion?"

All six students raised their hands. Several held strong and still in a salute while others waved. Both obnoxious, but in different ways.

Dr. Wilson pointed to Anna. After parting Ruth's carefully incised neck tissue, Anna thrust her gloved hand in and emerged with the gray, knotted nerve. She tugged the chain so it extended past the plane of Ruth's neck like an overstretched rubber band. The smug look on her face was more nauseating than the smell.

"Excellent work." Dr. Wilson chuckled. "It's like a treasure hunt."

A sadistic, twisted treasure hunt for serial killers, maybe.

The gray elastic between Anna's fingers snapped back, and she jumped in surprise, moving away from Ruth.

"Don't worry. She can't hurt you," Dr. Wilson said, his voice dead serious, as if he were imparting new wisdom. "Consequently, what a perfect opportunity for more learning. If Anna had indeed injured Ms. Ruth's cervical sympathetic trunk, what would the medical ramifications be?"

He absentmindedly picked a hand from the four in the air, this time a squat boy with a stubbly chin. The student's voice was monotonous, as if he were reading from a textbook. "Horner's syndrome, whose symptoms include miosis, ptosis, enophthalmos, and anhidrosis."

Could I ever be happy memorizing textbooks and spewing them back to professors? I asked myself even though I already knew the answer.

"Correct," Dr. Wilson said, then shifted over to Ruth's head. "Okay, enough review. We're going to get into the brain today." He picked up the electric saw. Its half-moon blade was lined with jagged teeth and the bloated, boxy handle looked impossible to hold, let alone control. "Which one of you wants to do the honors with the Stryker?"

Six hands shot in the air so fast I wondered if I had misheard. Did he just ask, *Who's scared to use the tool specifically designed to cut through bone?* Shouldn't everyone's instinct have been to run the other way, not fight for a chance to use it?

Anna's outstretched arm was the straightest and most desperate, but Dr. Wilson pointed to the burly boy with gargantuan hands. Everyone crowded around Ruth's skull, and I fought the tide to plant myself by Ruth's lower half.

The saw came to life with a high-pitched whir. If my eyes had been closed, I might have thought an airplane was somehow landing in the basement. But I didn't dare close them for a second, not with an active bone saw in the hands of an inexperienced operator.

There was a gleam in the boy's eyes as the blade arced through the air, meeting Ruth's cranium with an intensified screech. Flecks of skin and bone splattered onto the surrounding students, but they didn't notice—all except one boy, who flinched and rubbed his mask with his double-gloved hand. Unbeknownst to him, the movement smeared the debris instead of removing it.

I was pulled to him like *Lu Pàng* to a scallion pancake. Clearly, he was the only other sane person here. Sidling up to him, I yelled over the noise, "How long did it take you to get used to this?"

His head whipped toward me as if he were surprised by my sudden appearance. "Maybe two sessions? I shower afterward and have the hospital clean my scrubs." He pushed me closer to Ruth. "Once you get in there, you'll feel better. Why don't you pick up the forceps and take a look through the leg muscles?"

"No fucking way!" I yelled just as the saw fell silent. Crap. I could practically feel the veins in my cheeks dilating. *Vasodilation, presenting as flushed cheeks, or blushing*, I heard the squat boy say in my head.

Dr. Wilson glared at me, then returned to his cool-professor persona with a fake smile. "Everything okay?" he asked a little too sweetly.

"Yes. I apologize. I'm, uh, a visitor, and I was just . . . a little thrown off by how calm everyone is around the cadavers. It's still pretty new to me."

Dr. Wilson chuckled even though my lie was as exposed as Ruth's neck. "This is nothing. In my day, when I was a student, we didn't even use gloves. We ate lunch, hung out here, but now the rules are stricter. Who knows how much formaldehyde I accidentally consumed, and I'm still here."

I retreated to a corner far from this potential psychopath.

By the end of the day, I was bathing in my own sweat. I didn't know how I was going to do this—get through medical school, make this my life. A few hours and I was ready to immerse my entire body in a hand-sanitizer bath.

"Well?" Xing asked me, a hopeful smile on his face as he drove me home.

"I'm never eating corn chips again."

"Oh yeah, the smell. Like I said before, it takes some getting used to." He paused. "Wait, was it really that bad?"

"What do you mean?"

"I know you. You use humor as a defense mechanism." I gazed out the window, unable to look at him. "Talk to me, Mei-ball. What happened?"

At the sound of my nickname, I gave in. Fell apart. Became me. "I can't do this. I just . . . I can't."

"Well, what did you enjoy about today? Let's start there."

A tear escaped from its pool at the corner of my eye. "Nothing. I enjoyed nothing." My voice was a whisper, as if my words scared me. And they did. Because I knew the weight of what they meant. If I deviated from this path, it would be another behemoth secret from my parents, and it would be like shoving another *biānpào* into my overstuffed, overheating brain, and it was just a matter of time before one firecracker fuse ignited, leading to an epic explosion of domino proportions. Dance had been my gateway lie, an easy one that didn't feel completely wrong since my parents had bought me my first pair of ballet shoes. But then it all just kept building and building, one secret at a time so it seemed doable, until now there was no more room.

Xing was glancing at me every few seconds, clearly unsure what to do. "What was so bad about it?"

"Do you ever struggle with thinking things are dirty? Worrying where they've been, what germs are on there?"

His eyebrows shot up. "Do you?"

Duh, I wanted to yell, but I stayed silent instead. How come we knew certain pieces of each other inside and out but then were oblivious to others?

Xing thought for a moment, then said, "Honestly? That stuff isn't really an issue for me. I guess one time I carelessly shook hands with a scabies patient and it was a little gross thinking I might have gotten mites again"—Again?!—"so . . . yeah. That bothered me."

I would have never made the mistake of touching that patient, I thought. *And if I had, I would have immediately doused myself in mite poison or whatever. Burned my clothes, took a scalding shower, cut my hair, et cetera, et cetera.*

"We're different," I said, the blue ribbon of understatements.

And I knew then what I had subconsciously known all along. I couldn't be a doctor.

I hugged my knees to my chest, my arms wrapped tightly around them. Xing's eyes raked over me, shifting from the tears running frightened down my cheeks, to my arms, to the fact that I made sure not to touch my shoes to any part of my body because, obviously, germs.

And I saw when he got it. Well, as much as someone like him could. His face completely sagged, those premature lines becoming so pronounced I could have stuck a penny between the folds.

"What now?" he asked me.

"You were supposed to be the one to answer that."

I didn't bother with the Porter Room that night. I knew it was futile.

Incoming text from Darren

Do you have trouble ordering coffee? Because of your unique name?

Me

No, they just write May.

after a minute

Duh. I should have realized that. I was trying to be smooth and segue into asking you to coffee. I was going to dare you to tell them Lady Peanut when they asked for your name.

☺

Is that a yes? Because I like you a latte (as friends, of course, as previously stipulated).

I like how much you espresso yourself.

I'll chai not to be late.

😮

after an hour

I like you too, for the record. As friends, of course.

CHAPTER 16

Hot Chocolate

Outside Darren's chemistry lecture, I leaned against the wall, one ankle over the other, trying to look nonchalant. Like what I imagined a friend waiting for another friend would look like.

His texts had arrived during my regular dance therapy session, but I was barely moving—just a sad middle-school dance, stepping side to side with limp arms flanking my hunched, hopeless body. It was as much as I could bear to move.

I liked to personify the Porter Room because he had become such an integral part of my life, and when I danced, it was like I was conversing with Mr. Porter about my thoughts and emotions.

When I stomped my anger into his tiles, he supported me, vibrated with me, and told me, *I got you.* When I dragged my feet, sweeping them across the floor to paint my sadness into the linoleum, he absorbed my pain and told me it would be okay. But even Mr. Porter hadn't known what to do with my side to sides.

I spotted Darren first, naturally, since his hair was spiked above the plane of heads. Another reason my mother would disapprove. She hated "the spike," as she called it. *Why they have to do that? Looks so angry.*

Darren greeted me with an uptick of his chin (perhaps a we're-just-friends gesture?). "Hey, Princess Pecan."

"Hey," I answered softly. I wanted to joke back, but the words caught in my throat. I was so scared to cross the friend border that I kept myself as far from it as possible—in Awkward Territory, next to the Babbling Brook of Insecurity.

We fell into step, and even though he tried to hide it, I could tell he was walking a little slower so that I could keep up with his long strides.

In Killian Court, a middle-aged East Asian man with thick glasses broke from a pack of tourists to approach Darren and me. He pointed to each of us, then asked in a heavy accent, "Stu-dents?"

I nodded.

"Picture?" he asked, a hopeful smile on his face.

I reached for the high-tech camera cradled in his arms. "Sure. Do you want the dome in the background?"

He pulled away sharply as if I were trying to steal his firstborn son. He shook his head, then pointed the camera at us. It seemed he wanted a photo of Darren and me, but that made as much sense as *Lu Pàng* playing in the NBA.

The tourist waved a hand, motioning for Darren and me to move closer into the frame of the photo. Darren obliged, even playfully pointing to the MIT logo on my shirt. The camera clicked, capturing my face twisted with bewilderment, and the man was gone before I could puzzle out what had happened.

When Darren spotted my arched eyebrows and wide eyes, he mirrored my confusion. "That's never happened to you before?"

"I don't walk through Killian that often."

"Well, get ready. Because the tourists always want pictures of MIT students, and if they want a picture of me, then they'll definitely want a picture of the cute . . . I mean . . ." He looked away, embarrassed, as his voice trailed off.

I couldn't help a small smile no matter how large my mother loomed in my head. "Thanks, but I doubt they came here because of the student body's good looks," I joked. If the tourists were anything like my maternal grandmother—whose English vocabulary consisted of "hello" and "MIT"—then they were here because to them, the campus was a must-see, the golden goose. "For the record, I'd rather they want a picture of me because of my brain, not my looks."

Darren nodded his approval. "Good priorities." He leaned a tiny bit closer—almost imperceptibly so, but I was hyperaware of him. "And for the record, I agree—nothing more attractive than a big, beautiful brain. Just, you know, in general. I'm definitely not talking about anyone in particular."

Um, this friends thing might be even harder than I originally thought.

At the Student Center, Darren strolled up to the window. "How do you like your coffee?"

"Oh, no, I—I'll get it myself," I stammered, still intent on getting hot chocolate even though I knew how juvenile it would look.

He paused, perhaps debating whether or not he should put up a fight, then stepped aside, probably because of the friend stipulation. "Ladies first."

I stepped up to the counter. "Hot chocolate with whipped cream, please." My shoulders hunched, Dr. Chang style, but then I heard my mother's voice in my head: *Stand up straight so you look confident. And so your breasts look bigger.*

"Actually, that sounds good," Darren said to my surprise. "I'll have that too."

We paid separately and, with drink in hand, I made a beeline for my favorite couch—the overstuffed, least-pilly love seat. But Darren motioned outside. "How about sitting by the river?"

"The river?" I parroted, hoping he would remember it was freezing today.

"We don't have to, but it snowed! And this is my first snow in ten years! C'mon!" He waved his arm once, and with it my no swung to a yes.

While I bundled up, he held the door open, waiting patiently until I walked beneath his outstretched arm. As soon as I stepped outside and the wintry chill hit, I regretted my decision.

We made our way to the benches lining the Charles. I grasped my cup the entire way, desperate for some warmth to seep through the gloves onto my frozen hands.

After sweeping snow off the seat, Darren motioned for me to sit. While I balanced precariously on the edge, not wanting to bathe in a pool of melted snow (and worrying what germs were on there), he sat like a normal person, favoring a comfortable butt to a clean one.

"You seem pretty comfy for a Southern Californian."

"I'm frozen on the inside. But it's worth it. This is one of my favorite places."

I followed his gaze to the frozen river dusted with snow. I hardly ever looked at it despite having a view from my dorm. How had I missed its beauty for so long?

"Chow Chow used to be one of my favorite places," I said, "but recently it's been more stinky tofu than home. It's been exhausting seeing my parents every weekend." *Especially with all the secrets.* Last visit, I had been so stressed answering my mother's questions I accidentally ate a clove of garlic, mistaking it for a clump of onion. I couldn't exhale out of my mouth for two days after without gagging at the smell. "I thought I'd be more independent in college."

"Yeah, I picked up on their protectiveness," he said with a light-hearted chuckle.

"They're just so traditional." I peered at him over my cup. "Do you struggle with that?"

"Sorry, I can't relate. My family has been in America for three generations. I don't identify as Japanese. I mean, I *am* . . . but I'm also American. My parents' pressure to keep me close to home isn't related to the culture, at least not that I know of. I think they were just scared that once I left I'd never come back, and since I'm the first to leave the nest, they had an especially tough time."

"Was that really hard for you?"

He chewed his lip for a second. "Yes, but not any more than expected. It made it easier that I was going away to MIT, which they're proud of, and because of the financial aid. And they sort of knew all along that they weren't going to sway me, no matter what. It wasn't as difficult as it seems for you. At least, from what I've heard."

I leaned forward, my elbows resting on my knees and my cup dangling between my legs. "I have such a . . . complicated . . . relationship with them." I took a breath, then said words I had never admitted out loud before. Words I'd barely admitted to myself. "I don't agree with them sometimes . . . a lot of times."

The Pavlovian guilt started to wash over me. I waited, half-expecting the ancestors to send me a warning sign, maybe in the shape of a blizzard, but the only movement was Darren tilting his head to urge me to continue.

"They think that just because they're older, they know what's best for me and my future." I paused to glance at him, then clarified. "Specifically, my career. But they don't know me well enough to know what I want." Hell, *I* barely know me well enough.

"What do your parents want you to do?"

I hesitated. For a second I was transported back to the courtyard, when he had first asked about my dreams. I still felt the urge to run, but then his warm, caring gaze met mine, and I caved. "They want me to be a doctor."

His eyes widened. "Uh-oh."

It was only two sounds, not even a real word, but it sent all the walls up. I waited, my muscles frozen in anxious anticipation.

He faux coughed, fidgeted, then finally said, "You, uh, use your hand sanitizer a lot. And when we were on the Saferide, you touched the handle with as little surface area as possible, which wasn't all that safe, by the way. And . . ." He (finally) trailed off, probably because my cheeks were flushed—their contrast to the cold air was jarring.

His voice softened. "I mean, hey, I get it—all the studies show how effective hand sanitizer is. I should really carry some with me too. But, uh"—he nudged me—"you seem to have a thing about germs?"

I surprised myself by laughing. "Okay, you made your point."

The teasing crinkle appeared. "Nothing to be embarrassed about. You're perpetually clean and you always smell like pomegranate. Seems like there's only upside."

"That's because you haven't fully seen in here," I joked, tapping on my temple. I was so used to hiding this part of me that it was instinct to deflect. Though really, all I wanted was to tell him more, just to hear him say over and over in different ways how all of this was okay.

"*Yet*," he said. "I haven't fully seen in there *yet*."

I tried to will my heart to stop beating so damn fast. "You know, it's ironic—I think it's my mom's fault I'm this way. She used to bring our own utensils to Chinatown, saying that their silverware was too dirty."

"Yet somehow she trusted the food they made?"

"Just one prime example of Mămá Lu's airtight logic."

He chuckled, then said, "Well, if doctor isn't your dream job, what is?" The warmth in his voice alleviated the heaviness of what he was asking.

"I would love to open a dance studio. I think."

He beamed. "I was going to guess something with dance. The way your face lit up when I mentioned *piques* . . ." He placed a hand over his heart. "It made me want to learn."

My leg jiggled. "I actually dreamed of opening a studio when I was younger, when I was too naive to know my parents had already planned out my life."

Darren scooted to the edge of the bench to face me. He placed a hand on my knee, and I froze like the surrounding ice. "I think it's selfless how much you care about your parents, but I think you deserve better than sacrificing who you are for their sake."

"It's not selfless when I do it out of fear. Or guilt."

He leaned back, sending snow flurries in the air. My leg felt hot where his hand had been. "I don't think it's that black-and-white," he said.

"It's not a panda?"

His lip quirked up on one side (the right, never the left). "No, not a panda."

"Well, whatever it is, make it disappear. Then this would be easy."

He waved his arms like a conductor. *"Kiemasu!"*

I shifted away, startled.

He laughed. "It means 'vanish.' There was this Japanese magician my sister and I loved as kids. We used to practice terrible magic tricks and yell *'kiemasu'* at each other."

I committed the new word to my vernacular. "Can you show me a trick?"

He swept his hand over his hot chocolate, yelled *"kiemasu,"* then shook the cup, the absence of sloshing proving his trick successful.

I laughed, deep and unladylike.

He grinned at me, so huge I could see most of his teeth, and my eyes immediately homed in on his slightly tilted lower canine, the one that became visible only with his biggest smiles. "I think *'kiemasu'* sounds better than *'abracadabra,'* don't you?" he asked.

"Definitely. And it's better than *'bújiànle,'* too, for the record."

"Do you speak Chinese fluently?"

I nodded. "And I had to go to Chinese school every Sunday from ages two to fifteen to learn how to read and write."

"I've always wondered, do you translate everything in your head first?"

I paused for a second. *Wǒ xǐhuān shuǐjiǎo. I like dumplings.* "No. I guess you could say I think in Chinese and English. Meaning, I don't stop and translate, like I did in high school Spanish."

"Wow. That's amazing. Sometimes I wish I had grown up speaking Japanese . . . though I'm glad my parents didn't send me to school without knowing English."

"It doesn't have to be so black-and-white," I said, nudging him lightly. "And you already know '*kiemasu*.'"

"Yup, that and '*arigato*.' Just a couple more lessons and I'll be hosting my own Japanese magic show. Together we can be the Nutty Magic Duo—I'd let you saw me in half. And"—his right eye crinkled—"I'm sure your mom would totally approve of you being a magician."

We laughed together—loud, long, resounding belly laughs—before falling into a comfortable silence.

The wind swirled snow flurries around the icy lake and in my heart. I could feel some of the resistance planted by my parents melting away, and it was terrifying.

VOICEMAIL FROM NĂINAI

Mei Mei? Study hard and go to acupuncture, okay? I hear about your bad grade. Remember, seven eggs a day will improve your memory. And eat your vitamins.

CHAPTER 17

Ancestor Lu

As Xing and I waited in line for our museum tickets, he thanked me for accompanying him to the limited-time *Terracotta Army* exhibit. "I've been dying to see these my whole life. Remember when Mom used to tell us about them?"

"Of course." I could picture us clearly, sprawled across Xing's childhood bed, looking at pictures of clay soldiers and listening to Mămá tell us about Emperor Qin Shi Huang and his desire to protect himself in the afterlife. "I've always wanted to see them too."

The memory helped ease some of the guilt, but there was still a whole buttload left. I had thought maybe it would get better the more I saw Xing, but obviously that made zero sense. The fewer times we met, the easier it would be to explain away if my parents ever found out, so each additional visit was diving further "into the fire pit," as my mother always said (and yes, she had used that in reference to Xing choosing Esther).

Esther was busy with work (as a dentist, I'd learned recently), and while I wanted to meet her for Xing's sake, I was relieved. I wasn't ready to put a personality (especially a good one) to her face. I was weighed down by enough guilt for just seeing Xing. If meeting Esther had been added to my sins, I would have—*poof!*—combusted on the spot, destroyed by my own *biānpào* secrets. Every Chow Chow visit, I felt like a spy—a terrible one who sweated through all her clothes. But every time my thumb hovered over the delete contact button or I considered turning down an invitation to meet up, I heard Xing's laugh, our chopsticks clicking together, and I couldn't bring myself to go through with it.

At least we're doing something Chinese today. Learning about our culture, I tried to convince myself.

After Xing waved my Hello Kitty wallet away and paid for both of us, we strolled through the introductory hallway in silence, reading about the discovery of Qin Shi Huang's tomb. Was Xing also hearing our mother's voice, imagining her reading to us from the *Xiǎo Kēxuéjiā* (*Little Scientist*) books of our childhood?

In 1974, a farmer dug a well and found the collapsed tomb and broken terracotta warriors, I heard her say as I looked at black-and-white photos of the excavation site. *The paint from the soldiers flaked off when exposed to air,* she said as I looked at a replica of what the soldiers would have looked like in their original colorful glory. *Since the technology is not there to preserve these relics, most of the tomb has not been excavated yet,* she reminded me as I stared at an aerial photo of the mausoleum, the giant unearthed mound screaming, *Think of all the treasures in there!*

I desperately clung to these memories, to this version of my mother, the one who just wanted to spend quality time with me. No clucking tongue. I wish I knew how to bring her forth.

When we stepped into the room with the life-size terracotta warriors, Xing and I both froze, taking it all in. The sculptures had clearly been broken into many pieces and put back together, the break lines still prominent despite the rehab. Their dusty, pewter-colored faces were more lifelike than I would have predicted, with wrinkles and expressions sculpted in.

Xing pointed to the warrior in the display case to our right, the one wearing sleeveless armor and long trousers. "Doesn't that one look like us? Maybe we're related to him."

Every face was different, unique, based on a real-life soldier. I took in this warrior's slightly bulbous nose and pronounced cheeks. He was so familiar, what I would picture my ancestor to look like. I felt tied to these artifacts, as if a piece of me were in them as well. Perhaps that really was the case with this soldier here. Possibly a Lu. I knew he was inanimate, just a lump of molded clay, but when I stared into his blank, pupilless eyes, the shadows from the dim lighting made it appear as if he were staring into my soul, judging me and all my secrets.

I spoke to the glass. "Sometimes I'm so proud to be Chinese, and other times I resent it so much. The obligations. Duty to family. *Xiàoshùn.*" Each word felt like charcoal in my mouth—bitter and out of place.

"I know what you mean," Xing said. "Sometimes I wonder if Mom and Dad are particularly tough because they immigrated here. Maybe they feel like they have to hold on to traditions tighter to make up for leaving."

I nodded as he spoke. "And since they're not there," I realized, "they can't evolve with the times—they're still holding on to traditions they grew up with from an entirely different generation."

I turned away from my possible ancestor to face Xing. He had traces of resentment around his eyes, the same shadows that had first appeared the night of the disownment and never left, only took root.

"I think I understand your position more now. Because of, you know." I couldn't even say it out loud, how I wasn't going to be a doctor. There were a *million* different possible careers out there. All I had done was decide one wasn't for me, and yet it felt like a crime. Because it was. To them. "I was always more hesitant than you to question Mom and Dad or disobey them. But I guess sometimes you're put in a position where you have no choice."

He sighed. "I wish you never had to learn that. I wish you were still young and naive and had goggles on to shield you from everything."

"Me too," I whispered.

● ● ●

"Mei," my mother said over the clean clothes she was putting into my drawers. (Sigh, she does so much for me.) "I just heard from

Mrs. Ahn who heard from Mrs. Lin that Qin Shi Huang's terra-cotta warriors are here! I forget which museum they're at, but your bǎbá knows. Do you want to go?"

I swear I almost peed my pants. Maybe I did, a little.

I lived in constant fear of messing up one of my lies, and now, *ta-da!* Here was a mammoth, slap-me-in-the-face opportunity to take a scissor to my finely woven web, which was barely holding up as it was. And if that sounded dramatic, then *good.* Because this was the worst.

So I definitely couldn't go because I *definitely* would let something incriminating slip, but that meant I would need more lies to stack on top of the other lies to explain why I couldn't go.

Shit. I was a lousy Jenga player.

"That sounds so fun, Mǎmá, but I have exams coming up and I think I should really be studying." I couldn't say any more because my heart was threatening to rip in two. Was I giving up a chance to see the version of my mother I craved so badly?

"Of course. Good girl. Are you going to study more with Billy, A-mah, Penny, Kim, Khloe, Kour-ney, and Kendall?" Man, that had really gotten away from me. "Tell me again where Kendall is from?"

"California."

"Right, right. And Billy?"

Crap. I had no idea what I had said last time. It was easier remembering the Kardashian facts than the random answers I had made up. Why hadn't I written all this down somewhere? It was like my fifth class, 5.317: How to Lie to Your Parents. (See what

I did there? What 5.317 spells upside down? TIM the Beaver would be proud.)

I deflected. "Did I tell you that Billy had to go home for a while because his grandmother got sick with pancreatic cancer? I hope everything's okay." And as soon as I said it, I kicked myself because I didn't know anything about pancreatic cancer, and now I was going to have to do some in-depth research.

"They shouldn't have told him. Especially with exams coming up." As she shut the drawer, I heard something fall off the dresser. "Mei, what's this?"

Since my back was to her, I didn't know what she was talking about, and there were a hundred things she could be holding that would be a firehose to my web. Maybe I peed a little again.

I turned slowly in an attempt to be nonchalant and ended up moving at way-below-normal speed. So I quickened slightly to make up for it and ended up all jerky and awkward turtle. She was holding my mascara and eyeliner, which I had taken out to make sure I still knew how to do stage makeup.

I didn't know how MIT's Association of Taiwanese Students (ATS) had found out about my Chinese dance background, but when they had asked me to be the entertainment for their night market event next week, I had agreed immediately. I felt such a pull to ATS, to Chinese dance, almost as if I was desperate to hang on to the bits of culture I still loved.

But even though no one appreciated a good night market more than my mother, she couldn't know about this, especially since she was still reeling from my 72. (I had caught her snooping in that drawer again.)

Then I realized why her eyes were so wide. She was jumping to conclusions, that I had a secret boyfriend. Which . . . well . . . crap. I had to steer her away from that, too. I wasn't doing anything wrong—well, not *really*—but if she started asking me questions about whether or not I had talked to *the Japanese boy*, it would get ugly, fast.

"It's Nicolette's," I said as calmly as I could. "You can throw it to her side. She uses up all the space in here." I hoped it wouldn't land in a chlamydia hot spot.

As my mother muttered about bribing the dean to swap my roommate, I had to calm my nausea by telling myself everything was fine; the lies weren't crumbling around me.

Which was, you know, just another lie to add to the bunch.

VOICEMAIL FROM MY MOTHER

Mei! I spoke with Mrs. Huang yesterday. She said Eugene is excited to meet you. He actually thinks you're pretty! You need to snatch him up before it's too late. Before your eggs get cold. You'll be thirty before you know it!

Call your poor mǔqīn back. Why you never pick up? I know you're not in class! Are you hiding something??

CHAPTER 18

Night Market

As Xing and I waited in the mall arcade for our turn at Dance Dance Revolution, I marveled at how people (me included) were willing to pay to jump around in a predetermined order.

The dim room reeked of pubescent teenagers. As I inhaled the pomegranate scent of my hand sanitizer, I was weighed down by the stack of quarters in my pocket and the baggage on my proverbial shoulders.

The teenage boy on the machine was sailing through level maniac, his legs flailing to the beat. The noise gave me the courage to ask Xing, "How did you know Esther was worth fighting for?"

He sighed—loud, long, and heavy. "I used to think of relationships the way Mom and Dad do—as a business transaction. They see it analytically, whether people match on paper, with the only goal being to raise a healthy family. Mom's own parents used a matchmaker. More practical than emotional . . ." He trailed off.

"But then you fell in love with Esther," I stated even though it should've been obvious. But I said it anyway, just in case, because in the back of my head, there it was, still niggling—had Xing chosen Esther just to piss my parents off, the way he had told them he was going to try to be the next Wang Leehom even though he couldn't sing?

Xing nodded sadly, as though falling in love with her was weary, not a blessing.

I asked the question that had never stopped bothering me. "Why did you tell Mom and Dad about her trouble conceiving before they'd even met?"

"For the same reason I used to sneak out in the middle of the night, refuse to worship Yéye, and skip my SAT tutoring classes: I hated the responsibilities as the eldest son. I had no idea it would go this far—really, I was just pissed that I never got to be Dad's *bǎobèi*."

For the first eight years of my life, I was not Mei, only *bǎobèi* to my father, his treasure. And for those same years, he was my *bábǐ*, the Chinglish word I made up for "daddy." When I was little, as soon as he walked in the door, I would latch on to his leg. He called me his *xiǎo zhāngyú*, which only made me act more like my *bábǐ*'s little octopus. I'd squeeze his leg with all my might and squeal when he took troll-like steps, swinging me through the air. Even though sons were sought after, my father had a side reserved for me and only me.

Xing never saw *Bábǐ*, only Bǎbá. A firm hand, all the time. I eventually saw that too, but when I was a child, it was only Chinese checkers, tickle fights, and octopus swings.

We may have grown up in the same house, but Xing was right—our experiences were different because of our gender and the order in which we were born.

"I'm sorry. That must've been hard for you," I said. "I'm also sorry that everything blew up the way it did."

He gave me a wistful smile. "You can't pick who you fall for."

You-know-who popped into my head—infectious laugh, crooked smile, and all.

"I used to think Mom was more open-minded," Xing continued. "She didn't seem to want us when we were little, and I thought maybe since she'd struggled with the culture, she'd be able to . . . I don't know. Understand? Change? I guess either Dad or her upbringing has too strong a hold on her."

The more he spoke, the further I was pulled down. Even though I had started it, I tried to end the conversation by nodding toward the now-empty machine.

As I stepped onto the familiar DDR platform, Xing waved a dismissive hand at me. "Don't fret, Mei-ball. You're too young to be worrying about all that. And who knows? Maybe the person you end up falling for will be someone they approve of, so no use

175

wasting energy on it now. Use your energy for DDR—you haven't beaten me yet!"

My feet danced around to match the arrows coming up on the screen—second nature for me at this point—just like how I was robotically floating through life, adapting to each scenario, never truly being myself.

• • •

Even though I thought Taiwan was dirty when I was little, even though strangers on the street would come up to me and tell me I was fat, my nose was huge, my clothes were weird—it was my Elysium. The only place my parents didn't fight, laughed with us, and opened their wallets. We would actually *do* things together—go to museums, visit the aboriginal villages, learn about Taiwanese history. And every night we would go to the night market. My dad would break off to stuff himself with stinky tofu, and my mother would treat me to all the clothes and trinkets I wanted.

The Association of Taiwanese Students had turned the Student Center's Lobdell Dining Hall into an educational version of a Taiwan night market complete with dumpling vendors, Chinese yo-yo instructors, calligraphy stations, and a stage for entertainment. Me.

My crimson costume dripped with gold embellishments that caught the light, especially when I turned. The silk hugged my body and made me feel like the Dunhuang God I was supposed to be. I picked up my prefolded "flowers" (my props) by the "stem" (the wooden stick I used to control them) and took my starting position.

The *gǔzhēng* notes sang from the speakers, and the familiar trills of the Chinese zither transported me to another place. My dance world. Nothing existed but me, the real me. I wasn't Chinese or American—just a twirling, leaping force.

I started slow, my tiny steps matching the beat and my flowers twirling above my head. Cloud hands, they were called. I felt like an ancient Tang palace lady padding around the courtyard with my tiny bound feet, telling my story with my wrists.

The music sped up. So did I. With the crescendo, I threw myself in the air. As my legs separated into a perfect midair split, I swung my arms forward and the ribbons broke free from the flowers I had folded them into. Twelve feet of silk exploded from each of my hands. The audience gasped. I spun. My arms zigged and zagged, up and down, to form waves with the ribbons. They encircled me as if I were spinning in the middle of rippling water. I had chosen blue silk just for this moment.

The wind swirled around me. The ribbons were extensions of me, moving like an arm or a leg, completely in my control. Hours had been spent snapping them left, right, up, down so that each swing now looked effortless despite the energy involved.

I faced stage right and swung my arms backward, forming two parallel circles on either side of my body. My signature move. The loops were supposed to be perfectly round, but once I learned the backstroke, they developed a bump, an extra flick of the wrist. My old flamingo teacher always yelled at me, but I kept the rebellious curl. She had wanted us to look exactly the same. Programmed robots. But I didn't want to become invisible by conforming. That added ripple, though tiny, set me apart. Made me Mei.

The dance was over too soon, and I reluctantly returned to reality. I smiled at the audience as I took a bow, the adrenaline coursing through my veins—I could feel it in my fingertips, my toes, my brain.

As I exited the stage, my beloved ribbons bunched in my arms, I was swarmed. By *guys*. Their deep voices blended together, and my head swiveled left and right, trying to match words to faces.

"Where'd you learn to do that?"

"Those stick-streamer thingamabobs are so cool!"

"Do you think you could teach me?"

"Smooth moves!"

If it weren't for what they were saying, I might've thought they had mistaken me for someone else, but I was the only one with "stick-streamer thingamabobs" around here. Floundering, I started to respond to one person only to stop short and turn to the next. I sounded like a robot with a dying battery. Charming.

I flailed until I saw him, hanging back behind the group of guys, waiting. God, it had taken so much hemming and hawing for me to text him about tonight, and now, looking at him, I couldn't remember why it had been so hard.

Even though the other guys were perfectly good-looking and seemed nice, I wasn't interested. They weren't Darren. Besides, they were mesmerized by my thingamabobs, not me.

As I worked my way toward Darren, I politely waved the other guys off with my sticks.

When just the two of us remained, he pointed to my ribbons. "Fighting them off with a stick, huh? Literally."

I laughed, relaxing. "After I change, want to look around the night market together?"

"A chance to accompany the star of the hour? What do *you* think?" He winked.

I was in trouble. That one wink was enough to pierce me, melt me, and make me forget my parents.

In the public bathroom, I put on comfy jeans and a sweater, then dabbed hastily at my stage makeup. I managed to remove most of the bright colors, then peeled off the false eyelashes.

When I returned to Lobdell, I found Darren in the corner, a heaping bowl of Taiwanese shaved ice in front of him. It had been hard to spot him, but his long arms waving at me slightly awkwardly and completely adorably had helped me home in on the private spot. The pseudo-second level overhead gave the illusion of privacy but allowed just enough light in so that I could see the *bàobīng* in all its mouthwatering glory. The condensed milk dripped from one layer of fluffy snow to the next, flowing between strawberries, mango chunks, grass jelly, and gummy candy.

I scooted next to him—so we could share, of course. Perfectly innocent. "How'd you know this was my favorite?"

"I didn't, but I figured I couldn't go wrong with deliciousness on top of deliciousness. Besides, it's Taiwanese, like you, and I felt a little pull toward it." He coughed into his hand, as if he hadn't meant to go so far and was regretting it.

"Well, hopefully you'll still like it even though it won't talk to you about dog poo or Filial Exemplars."

He laughed—loud, infectious, and from his belly—and my God, it made me fluttery in a way I didn't know was possible from just a sound. All I wanted was to find a way to make it happen again.

His eyes were still alight with mirth when he pushed the starting-to-melt *bàobīng* toward me. "The star of the night market gets to go first."

I dove in, taking a bite so huge it left crumbs on my upper lip. The snowflake softness didn't melt on contact like in Taiwan, but the milky sweetness enveloping my tongue tasted the same.

"Holy crap, it's amazing." The words rushed out of my still-full mouth, too urgent to wait. I tried to be extra dainty with my napkin dab to make up for it.

Within five minutes, only a few errant ice chips remained—both in the bowl and around our mouths. I hadn't even cared that we were sharing, our spit mixing. In fact, I kind of liked it.

I picked up the bowl and shook it, the ice chips rattling around. "*Kiemasu.*"

"You learn fast." His smile was so broad a tiny dimple appeared on his right cheek.

I wanted to touch it. Kiss it. Memorize it.

I tried to turn away but couldn't. He was looking at me as if he truly saw me, past the outside and into my inner *měi*. I wanted to ask him to draw me a map so I could find it myself.

"Darren," I started but then trailed off, not knowing where I wanted to go. He tilted his head to one side, questioning, waiting patiently. Just like he had been waiting for me all along. "I can't just be friends with you," I finally said.

He stared at me for a moment like he wasn't sure if he had heard me correctly. Or maybe he was trying to decide whether or not to be the bad guy, the one to make me defy my parents. But I was already way past that. He was just one more spoonful of dumpling meat, one more *biānpào. He could also be the last straw*, a voice said in my head, but I shushed it.

Finally, after the longest thirty seconds ever, he raised a mischievous eyebrow. "That can be arranged."

"Does it bother you that my parents don't approve?"

"I only care what you think."

I grinned (a little goofily) at him, the only one who *saw* me. Liked me because of the same qualities that normally made me an outcast.

For the first time, I was thankful for those traits. Happy to be me. If only for a moment.

● ● ●

I was freaking out. Full-on about-to-pee-myself freaking out. Each one of my breaths was labor-intensive—a forced, shuddery inhale followed by a choppy exhale. I had to pull it together. My mother was going to know, figure it out.

But in my head I couldn't stop replaying the walk home with Darren. We hadn't kissed—which had left me both relieved and disappointed for so many reasons—but we had held hands the entire way. And he had hugged me before we parted. And told me he'd see me soon.

I was sure my face was part dreamy, part guilty. Guilt. Ga-ill-t. I'd thought, felt, and internalized that word so much it no longer held meaning for me.

My parents had surprise stopped by a mere twenty minutes after I returned to my room. I'd barely had enough time to put all my dance gear away.

And now I was standing in the chilly Burton Conner entryway, grabbing the bags of green tea they had brought, since by my mother's count, I had run out this morning (scarily, 100 percent correct), and she was worried I would need it tomorrow.

"Should I come up?" my mother asked. "Maybe I can pick up more laundry?"

Had I fully hidden my ribbons? What if the tail end was sticking out of my drawer? What if my mother opened the closet door and saw the costume I'd snuck from home? I stamped my feet to hide my shaky leg, hoping I just appeared cold.

"Thank you so, so much, Mămá, but I don't want to give you any more work."

"I'm going to do your laundry anyway—might as well do it now." The car door clicked open, the soundtrack to the devolving of my lies.

"No, please. I'm sorry—I was in the middle of a problem set and it's just still on my mind. I want to go write everything down before I forget, but I don't want to be rude because I so appreciate you coming all the way here."

The door closed again. "It was nothing, Mei. Of course we came. We're your parents."

"I love you." I barely got the words out I was so choked up.

They nodded at me and drove away without saying it back. I wasn't surprised, but I had never needed to hear those words more.

I retreated to my hideaway for the saddest, slowest dance session Mr. Porter had ever seen.

Incoming text from Darren

Konichiwa

Me

Ni hao

Someone told me today that at MIT the odds are good but the goods are odd. Do you think that refers to guys or girls?

after an hour of hemming and hawing

There's only one odd good I'm interested in . . .

immediately

I'd say your odds are good there.

CHAPTER 19

Clash of Cultures

An envelope jutted out of my dusty mailbox—a red flag. I never got mail.

My Chinese and English names were scrawled in calligraphy on the front, revealing what was inside without my opening it.

I slipped my finger beneath the flap and tore it open quickly before I could convince myself otherwise. The paper sliced through my flesh, and a drop of blood soaked into the ebony cotton. *It's a cautionary sign from the ancestors*, Năinai warned in my head. Previously, I would have laughed, but in this moment, her words sent a tremor through me.

The wedding invitation was red and gold (the Chinese celebratory colors) with half the text in English, half in Mandarin. I ran my fingertips over the embossed characters. My parents' names were glaringly absent.

How far we had come from my childhood days, when my father would run around the house with me on his back as the *xiǎo jī*, Xing and my mother chasing behind as the *lǎoyīng*, the eagles trying to catch the little chicken. I would squeeze my father close, especially when he rounded the corners at full speed. Xing would squeal as he ran, one of the few times he didn't have to be the responsible eldest son.

My chest ached with a mix of nostalgia, longing, and pain, and I had to remind myself to breathe.

• • •

For the first time at Chow Chow, I didn't notice the stinky tofu smell. I was too focused on the sweat pooling in my pits and hands. There was too much weighing me down. Death by secrets or death by my parents.

A vaguely familiar middle-aged Chinese woman approached our table. My mother took over pleasantries, bowing and gushing over the friend's haircut and outfit. "Goodness, we haven't seen you in ages. When did you move back to town? Mei, you remember Joyce *Āyí*, of course."

Joyce smiled at me. "Hello, Mei. It was a pleasure to see you that day at dim sum."

With the words "dim sum," I realized she had been the

"stranger" staring at me from across the restaurant. Before I could protest, she continued, "I waved to you and Xing, but you must not have seen me."

My father's rice bowl, which had been against his lips moments before, fell to the table. If he were a cartoon, steam would have been coming out of his ears.

Joyce backed away slowly, then scampered back to her table.

My parents began yelling at the same time, their words mixing into chaos. I opened and closed my mouth a few times but couldn't come up with a single thing to say.

Their voices crescendoed, each one trying to be heard over the other. I grasped my head with my hands, partly to cover my ears and partly because I felt like it was going to explode.

My father threw his chopsticks to the ground, and an eerie silence followed.

"I'm sorry," I said sincerely. But sorry about what, I didn't know. There was too much. Sorry we're so different. Sorry you don't understand. Sorry I hurt you when I didn't mean to.

"Did Xing pressure you to see him?" my mother asked, her face so creased with distress I wanted to do whatever it took to fix it. "Did you need help with something and didn't feel comfortable coming to us? Did you bump into him?"

I could lie. Say our meeting was an accident. Say he came looking for me.

I could agree to stop seeing Xing and Darren, try harder in biology, stop teaching dance. . . . Except I couldn't. I had already tried. And failed. If I lied, the real me would disappear.

I'd become that hollow shell, nothing but the emptiness I saw in Dr. Chang.

I couldn't keep the secrets anymore. They were already exploding around me. And now that one was out, it felt like the rest of the *biānpào* were set to blow regardless of what I wanted, regardless of what I did.

I gripped my glass so hard my knuckles turned white. "I saw Xing. On purpose. I reached out first."

My father shook his head. "That can't be."

My mother's voice was frantic. "Did you need to ask him about medical schools? Did you want advice on how to improve your application? Did you want to visit him at work so you could get excited about your future?" She was so desperate to find an excuse for me that I almost let her.

Almost.

She looked at me, and even though I was using all my energy to keep my face neutral, I knew she could sense my inner turmoil. "What is it, Mei? Just tell us."

I opened my mouth and my tongue touched the tip of my teeth, my palate, my lip, but no words came out.

"You can tell us," she repeated, softly this time.

I took a breath. "I reached out to Xing because I miss him. He's *my brother.* I just wanted to see how he was doing, make sure he was okay. It had nothing to do with your conflict or taking sides or disrespecting you." I paused. "I *did* also visit him at work, but . . . it was really hard. I wanted it to make me excited about my future. . . . I wanted that so much, but it did the opposite. I'm sure you've noticed how I have trouble with germs and—"

My father slapped the table. "Mei, this isn't up for discussion."

"Bǎbá's right. We laid out your future because we only want the best for you. You haven't even given it a try. A few hours doesn't count."

I shook my head. "But I *have* tried, and I know I can't do it."

My father straightened his spine. His voice was gravelly as he said, "Can't? That's not the daughter we raised. You can do anything. Where's that passion you once had? You used to be just like Nǎinai. A hard worker. What happened? Mǎmá and I didn't come to this country and work like dogs, giving up everything we wanted, just so you could throw it all away."

The wave of guilt hit me full-on, wrapping around and restricting like a straitjacket. I had to muster all my strength to continue down this traitorous path. "I know you sacrificed so much, and I appreciate it. I'm not throwing anything away. I'm still going to have an MIT degree, just like you wanted. I'll be able to get a good job. Please, just listen to me. I'm trying to tell you how I feel."

"Stop talking." His grating tone made me flinch.

But I ignored his command. "I just want to talk, like adults."

"You're a child."

I squeezed my eyes shut so I wouldn't have to see his sneer as I spoke. "I'm in college. I may be young, but it's only because you pushed me and pushed me, making me skip a grade without asking what I wanted. I'm seventeen only when it suits you."

"Have you no respect?" my mother whispered, aghast. "Haven't we taught you better than this? You're Chinese. Act like it."

"I'm Chinese-*American*. America has culture too. Why can't I identify with that also? What if I identify with it more?"

My mother's usually poised face turned down, revealing the wrinkles she normally worked so hard to hide from the world.

Look, I told myself. *Look at Mămá's sad, pained eyes, the utter disappointment in the frown on her face.* You *caused that.*

But why did I have to bear this burden? Why was I destined to be unhappy?

Life wasn't fair.

My mother shook her head, eyes closed. "Mei, people need to know where they come from. They can't know who they are without that. And traditions must be kept alive. Otherwise they die."

"It makes sense that you and Băbá care about keeping traditions alive since you were born in Taiwan. But it's different for me, for my generation. We were born here, live here. It's Chinese culture at home, American culture everywhere else. Do you know how hard that is? Can't we keep the traditions we like and alter the ones we don't agree with? Don't we get to choose who we are?"

Instead of answering my questions, my mother said, "First the boy and the"—she peered at my father—"candy bar wrapper, and, Mei, I found your ballet shoes and ribbons in your dorm room! And now this? Seeing your brother? Talking back to us? What's gotten into you? You used to *tīnghuà.*"

I closed my eyes briefly to collect myself. "I can't ignore what I want anymore. I can't do whatever job you pick, marry whoever you choose, or cut my own brother out because of an outdated tradition I don't agree with. That's not who I am."

The silence that followed was the heaviest and most painful of my life.

My father cleared his throat. His tone was even and practiced as he said, "Mei, you are not the daughter we raised you to be. I no longer claim you as my child. We will no longer be paying your tuition unless you come to your senses."

I grabbed the edge of the table as a wave of vertigo hit. My vision obscured and I swayed side to side. My breath hitched, and my reply tumbled out, unguarded. "Please don't do this. I'm trying. I'm doing the best I can. Can't you see what this is doing to me? Please!"

My father stood. "You, you? What about the damage your words have done to *us*? When you stop thinking about only yourself, we'll be here."

I wanted to shove all the secrets back in. Back where they couldn't hurt anyone except me. But the dumpling had exploded— meat, veggies, and secrets everywhere, unable to be gathered up and shoved back into hiding. And a tiny part of me was glad. I hated that piece of me. It was selfish, just like my father had said. It wanted the secrets out because I couldn't handle it anymore.

My mother's sobs shook her entire body, but her face was to the wall so our gazes wouldn't meet. My father looked past me. To him, I didn't exist anymore. As they left—my father confidently and my mother reluctantly—I prayed they would stop. Turn around. Tell me they love me, were willing to compromise, and that I wasn't alone.

But, of course, they didn't.

I was going to be sick. I fled from the restaurant, rounded the corner into the alley, and slumped against the brick wall, completely spent from the exchange. As my body curled into a ball, my mind removed me from reality to make it bearable.

I didn't comprehend the magnitude of my actions until the SUV's tires screeched down the street. How could they leave me here? Memories of Xing packing his suitcase at various ages surfaced. That's right, my parents were experts at abandoning their children.

The ache of loneliness ballooned outward, engulfing every thought, a black hole. Eventually, the smell of the Dumpster and the creaking of the chain-link fence snapped me out of my haze, hitting me with another wave of dizziness as I transitioned back to the real world too quickly. I had forgotten my location (an abandoned alley) and my immediate surroundings (graffitied walls, decrepit furniture, and piles of rotting trash). But now aware of my horror-movie scenario, I hurried to the busy street. A screech of tires sparked a flicker of delusional hope, but it was merely a Porsche showing off, not my parents returning.

I jammed my palms into my eyes and told myself to get it together. I had to find a way home. Public transportation didn't extend this far, and I didn't have enough money for the long cab ride back.

Aren't you an adult? I could hear my father sneer.

I called Xing.

He answered with a worried, "Is everything okay?"

I took a shaky breath. "No, I, uh, had a fight with . . . them . . . and now I'm, uh . . ."

"Where are you? I'll come get you."

I didn't need to ask how he knew what had happened. And it made the tears stream down again.

After what felt like hours, Xing pulled up in his navy Corolla—the one my parents had bought for him. Had they asked for their money back? Did I have to start cataloging all the tuition and fees they'd shake me down for even though they knew I had nothing?

I looked from the sympathetic smile on Xing's face to the stuffed Doraemon doll in the passenger seat for me to hug. When I slid in and pulled the periwinkle cartoon cat into my lap, I traveled back in time to green-tea parties and make-believe—when I was young, naive, and happy. The weight on my chest lightened and I breathed easier.

"They're supposed to love me," I whispered.

"They do," Xing said, his eyes not leaving the road.

When I didn't respond, he sighed, then said gently, "I don't want to push you. It's been years for me, and I still don't really want to hear it most of the time. You get to be sad because this sucks. It hurts like hell, and there really isn't anything I can say to make it better."

I faced him. "Do you ever wish we had parents like the ones in sitcoms? The ones who manage the perfect balance between discipline, trusting their child, and defending them? Ones who apologize?"

He let out a mix between a laugh and a grunt. "They don't exist. It'll be easier once you accept that."

"Do you miss them?" My voice was as small as I felt.

"Every day."

"Does it get easier?"

"Every day."

The rest of the car ride was silent as I pressed my forehead to the window. The chill of the glass was refreshing, a contrast to the hot tears coursing down my cheeks.

• • •

That night, Nicolette's ringing phone jolted me from sleep. As soon as I woke, the disownment was on my mind, having never left.

In the light of day (well, technically it was still night, but I had been asleep the past seven hours), I realized the disownment was just the tip of the Culture Gap Iceberg. That fight may have been small in the grand scheme of things, but it represented a whole lot more. There would always be another decision, bigger than the last, to fight about. And there was no compromising. I couldn't become a semi-doctor or marry half of Eugene Huang or have part of a kid to please them.

There was no right or wrong here. No morality. Just two roads, leading in different directions but both ending in heartbreak. Life was, as I was finding out, Choose Your Own Adventure with most of the fun stripped away.

I didn't move as Nicolette shut her phone off. I didn't want to talk to anyone, especially her.

But she chose this moment to speak to me for the first time in who knows how long. "Hey, roomie." I was going to feign sleep, maybe even fake snore, but then she said, "Stop pretending already. I know you're up. You're not doing that weird half-snore, half-gasp thing you do."

I turned to glare at her and was met with a yelp.

"Holy shit, girl, what happened to you?"

I used my phone as a mirror. Tangled hair, puffy eyes, tear-stained cheeks—my appearance reflected the mess I was inside. I threw a slipper at her, then immediately regretted it, not because it pathetically settled halfway between our beds, but because my slippers were so freaking dirty. As I broke out the sanitizer (yes, I keep some nearby at *all* times), I retorted, "At least I'm not a poster for the walk of shame." Her smeared eyeliner and clumpy mascara were way worse than the bags under my eyes.

To my shock, Nicolette laughed—deep and jolly, not at all what I expected.

She sat up in bed. "Hello Kitty has claws!" Rude. Even if I did own maybe too much Hello Kitty apparel. "So? What happened? Gave it up for some guy only to have him dump you?"

I rolled over, facing the wall. "Not even close."

"Oh, come on, it can't be worse than chlamydia." Her voice wavered on the last word, and I wondered if her overconfident aura was just an act.

"Are you okay?" I asked, still staring at the wall. I didn't want to embarrass her any further.

"Yes." A pause. "I don't know what you think of me, but it's probably wrong, just so you know."

"I don't think anything about you, good or bad."

"Flatter me more, please. I just mean . . ." Her breathing deepened and she tossed in her sheets. "I was kind of a nerd in high school . . . and . . . no one ever looked at me. Then I got here, and I was cool somehow. Guys wanted to talk to and hang out with *me*. So I did, with most of them because I thought, *Hey, I'm young, may as well get to know everyone before committing*. But then, before I knew it, I had a bit of a reputation. So I played the part. I don't really know why."

I rolled back, and we faced each other across the room from our recumbent positions in bed. If the Goddess of Confidence had insecurities, then, jeez . . . maybe I wasn't as much of an outsider as I originally thought. "It makes sense. If you own it, then you're less of a target. Except people will still find a way to make fun of you."

She pulled her covers up to her chin. "You had a hard time in high school, too, huh?"

"Not just high school. Always. I wore neon leggings and sweatshirts with misspelled English for the first ten years of my life. Bums Bunny and Butman made me a target no matter what I did."

Nicolette laughed so hard our neighbor banged on the wall.

I glowered at her. "Thanks. I see you would've been one of my bullies."

"Sorry, but come on, Butman? That's hilarious!" She continued laughing, and I eventually joined in, but only for a second.

She flapped her comforter open, revealing a flash of navy-blue pajamas. "So I showed you mine; now show me yours. What happened last night?"

I hugged a pillow to my chest. "My parents disowned me."

"What does that mean? Aren't you eighteen?"

"Well, no, but that's not what I'm talking about. I told them I don't want to be a doctor—"

"Thank God!" she yelled at the ceiling. "That would've been like a dog trying to be a cat."

"And . . . some other stuff, and they cut me off. Physically, emotionally, financially. But it's more than just that. They think I'm a terrible person. Immoral. They're ashamed of me." I wanted to crawl under the covers and hide.

"If they're getting their G-string in a twist over something that trivial, then I say fuck them! Who cares what they think? You're the one who has to live your life, not them. And you're at MIT, for Christ's sake! How is that not enough? Now that I'm here, I could murder someone and my parents would still be proud of me."

Her words pierced through my brainwashing and I felt a little better. I considered saying, *Yeah, fuck them*, but couldn't bring myself to. I didn't actually believe the ancestors would strike me down, but I don't know, why risk it?

"I don't understand why making your own life decisions makes you immoral," Nicolette said.

When I didn't respond (I couldn't), she flung her covers off and jumped out of bed. "Come on, we're gonna take your mind off this shit. Get dressed."

Both our heads turned as something banged against our door. Not a knock, just one single *thud*. I pointed to Nicolette to ask, *Expecting anyone?* to which she shook her head. Since I was closer, I dragged myself over.

My foot landed on an ice puck and slid out from under me, sending me headfirst into the wall.

Nicolette flung the door open. After a beat, she yelled, "What the fuck, Arthur! You made my roommate hit her head. You're such an asshole!"

I peeked around Nicolette to see a torn Dixie Cup on the floor next to a red-haired boy wearing a Nu Delta sweatshirt.

"You're the asshole!" he yelled, flinging the cup at Nicolette. "You gave me chlamydia!"

After flipping her off, he bolted, moving with intoxicated swerves and dulled reflexes.

Nicolette slammed the door. "What a loser. I can't believe I ever thought he was cute."

I picked the thin circle of ice up off the floor and tilted it this way and that. It caught the light overhead, reflecting a yellow tint. It also smelled. Like Chinatown. Holy Mother of . . . Did this kid freeze his pee and slide it under our door so it would melt into our carpet?

Screaming, I chucked the frozen puck as hard as I could toward Nicolette's side. It shot under the bed, disappearing in a tangle of blankets. She scrambled over, grabbed the revenge pee, and hurled it out the door. It ricocheted down the hall, smacking against the wall periodically. *Whack. Whack. Whack.* Gross. There was a trail of chlamydia down the hallway now.

"Why have I held pee twice this year?" I screamed as I ran to the bathroom.

"Twice?" Nicolette's voice called after me.

I washed my hands ten times, scrubbing for a minute each with the damn surgical scrubs I'd received from Urgent Care. If they believed it could cure herpes, maybe it could kill the chlamydia crawling up and down my fingers. For the first time in my life, I worried I might faint. My mother would be so proud, except for the fact that it confirmed once and for all I could never be a doctor.

• • •

"Are you ready?" Nicolette asked, her hands on the back of the chair I was in. We were in MIT's secret tunnels—really, just underground corridors, but "secret tunnels" sounded infinitely cooler.

I was hanging over the precipice of a downslope, just one rolly wheel contacting the floor.

"Wait," I said just as she let go.

My scream filled the passageway, reverberating back to me and making me whoop even louder. As I picked up speed, I clutched the seat to keep from flying off. My loose hair tangled in front of my eyes, but I didn't dare let go to move it aside.

"Push yourself off the wall!" Nicolette screamed at me.

I flung my head to clear the hair from my vision and stuck my foot out just in time, pushing off and sending myself down the next hallway. My chair spun in a circle, making me giggle with dizziness. I felt so free. Free of secrets, if just for a moment.

As the incline decreased and the chair slowed, I finally let go and threw my hands in the air. I shrieked, feeling the anger, frustration, and disappointment escape my body through my lungs. The chair hit a bump. I tried to right myself, but it was too late. I went flying . . .

Straight into Darren.

He managed to wrap his arms around me as my momentum knocked him into the wall. The chair crashed and a wheel popped off. His messenger bag dug into my ribs, and I prayed that he didn't have a laptop in there. He was probably on his way back from the library and using the tunnels to stay warm.

I was still catching my breath when Darren said, "Chair surfing?"

"How does everyone know about this but me?" I was still pressed against him, our faces inches apart, and he was the only thing I saw. Meaning, I didn't see Nicolette approach. I had completely forgotten about her.

Her magenta lips turned up in a sly smile. "Well, well, what've we got here?"

I reluctantly stepped out of his arms and made introductions.

"We're helping Mei forget about her overbearing parents," Nicolette told him. "They disowned her earlier."

I was partly relieved that Darren knew and I didn't have to be the one to say it, but I was also peeved that Nicolette was speaking as if she were reciting the symptoms of a damaged sympathetic cervical trunk.

I gazed up at him. "*Kiemasu*, right?"

He smiled sadly, then nodded. "*Kiemasu*."

Nicolette clapped him on the back. "Want a turn?"

"I think I'll go flying immediately on account of these." He waggled a long leg. "That's a nice chair. Where'd you get it?"

She grinned proudly. "Did you see that Tech article about how three chairs went missing from the Reading Room?"

"That was you?"

"No, but it sounded like a good idea, so I went in and stole two more."

Darren raised his eyebrows at me. "I need to be more careful around you. You're running with the rough crowd."

Nicolette laughed. "Yeah, that hack we pulled last week during the football game? Where we tricked those Crimson preppies into spelling out 'Harvard Sucks' in the stands? That was all me."

"Hack" was MIT's term for sneaky pranks, and it spawned the word computer geeks use today. We liked to play jokes on other schools and put weird things, like cop cars, onto MIT's iconic Great Dome.

"Hey, is that where you are most nights?" I asked Nicolette. "Hacking?"

She nodded. "Yeah. What'd you think I was doing?"

"No idea," I lied, then flashed an innocent smile. She chuckled. My first guess couldn't be that far off; she hadn't gotten chlamydia crawling in tunnels and climbing on pipes.

"Come on, big guy, Hello Kitty," she said, nodding at each of us. (I rolled my eyes.) "You guys are in for a treat—just follow this hacker."

• • •

After weaving through the tunnels, a basement, and too many stairs to count, we made it to the door. Which door, I had no idea. I lost track of our whereabouts hundreds of steps ago.

"Keep an eye out for cops," Nicolette said as she turned the lock pick with expertise. "I just need another . . ."

Click.

"Ha!" she exclaimed as the door swung open. "Welcome to MIT's famous domes."

I followed Darren onto the roof of Building 7. From this height, the Boston skyline was visible both in the distance and reflected on the Charles River. Despite the lights on the horizon, the stars scattered across the dark sky shone brightly.

"Orion," I whispered, pointing at the constellation's three-pronged belt. My mother used to take me stargazing. The thought of her made my heart lurch.

Darren took my hand and we strolled toward the little dome. He ascended the neck-high platform first (chest level for him) and extended a palm down. I grabbed hold, thankful that it had warmed slightly the past few days and I was wearing my thin, flexible down coat (curated by scared-of-the-cold Mămá Lu, of course). With Darren's help, I heaved myself onto the limestone.

I turned to assist Nicolette, but she was nowhere in sight. That sneaky wonderful girl. No wonder she had spouted off so much information on our journey over here—she hadn't planned to come onto the roof with us.

Following Nicolette's advice, we scooted up the dome on our butts. The height didn't bother me, but I wondered what kinds of germs I was rubbing into my pants to bring home later. Bird poop? STDs from MIT students who'd once had sex here? There was definitely a picture making the rounds on Facebook of a couple doing it on the little dome. Maybe it was Nicolette, I realized. Maybe she *did* get chlamydia from hacking!

When we reached the local maximum (not the global one—that was the Great Dome), I snuggled against Darren for warmth. Just me and him, on top of the world, where nothing else could reach us.

"Saved anyone else recently?" he asked, staring at the stars overhead.

"Nope. The campus has been safe—no distress calls." I pictured someone beaming a dumpling into the sky to ask for my help and had to stifle a laugh.

The teasing crinkle appeared, along with a new, unreadable tilt to his lips. "So you haven't had to tell your Horny story again? How is Horny, by the way?"

My mouth slacked open. "You heard that?"

"Every word."

We burst into laughter at the same time.

"Well, that's mortifying," I said when, really, it wasn't. Back at Chow Chow all those weeks ago, I had thought Darren knowing about Horny would have been The Worst Thing, but now it was just funny.

When the laughs subsided, he said in his warm honey voice, "Actually, it made me notice you more."

Seriously? He hadn't looked my way once that day. The blonde popped into my head, and I shoved her out with a kick to her perfectly plump behind.

"Made you notice my weirdness maybe," I said as lighthearted-edly as I could.

"I prefer to call it 'uniqueness.'"

He leaned in to me, our knees interlacing and his sandalwood scent enveloping me. I wondered if he could smell my soap too.

He placed a hand over mine, and my palm immediately turned sticky, but propriety be damned—who said sweaty girls couldn't get the guy? Confidently, I weaved my fingers through his.

We looked into each other's eyes, no longer in the awkward way of stolen first glances, but in the I-truly-see-you kind of way. The chemistry between us was so strong I could practically see the forces—ionic, covalent, even van der Waals.

Our gazes wandered to other features, our path dictated by the moon's illumination. I followed the light to his cheekbones to his nose to the mole beside his lip, a pinpoint speck. Had I been sitting farther, I might have mistaken it for a crumb. Somehow I felt like I knew him better now that I had noticed it. A landmark for me to anchor on to.

When his gaze passed over my features, I didn't feel self-conscious. Just beautiful. The way Darren saw me. The way I now saw myself. It had come at a price, a steep one I still wasn't fully sure I wanted to pay, but . . . I felt *beautiful*, completely *měi*, even down to the off-center mole on my forehead, which for the first time, I didn't feel the need to hide.

He traced his index finger over the pale-pink scar on my chin.

"I tripped when I was little and there was broken glass on the ground," I explained.

He leaned down and kissed the scar gently, his breath trailing across my cheek. It was so tender. So compassionate. I turned my head, and our mouths met in an explosion of heat.

I had spent countless hours worrying about how to act in a

boy's presence, reading illicit romance books to try to learn what my parents wouldn't teach me . . . but now that it was happening, it felt so natural. I didn't need to think.

I gave in to my impulses, resting my hands on either side of him and pressing my torso to his. I felt his chest heave against mine, and then he wrapped his arms around me and pulled me to him as if he needed me closer than physically possible. I curled into his lap seamlessly, our limbs entangling.

He ran a hand up my back and into my hair, cradling my head. My skin tingled everywhere he touched, little jolts of pleasure that danced through my synapses. And his lips. God, his lips. They were so soft, caressing mine like silk. The tip of my tongue glided gently along them, feeling, tasting.

I wanted more.

Our tongues met, electricity pulsing through me and sending the butterflies in my stomach into a flurry. Our heads, lips, bodies moved in sync, almost as if we were choreographed.

When he pulled away, my breath came out in heavy gasps, forming puffs of fog in the cold air. He brushed my hair back with one hand and trailed soft kisses along my forehead, ear, and cheek.

A siren on the street below startled us, jolting Darren's jaw into my nose as we turned in different directions. I yelped in pain, then rubbed the sore spot with my fingers. Luckily, his arms had tightened at the noise and I hadn't rolled off the dome. In that moment, I realized just how precariously balanced we were.

"I'm so sorry!" he exclaimed. His cheeks were flushed—from

embarrassment or passion, I wasn't sure. He brushed a kiss along the bridge of my nose. "Are you okay?"

"Everything's perfect," I said, and meant it.

"Maybe we should get out of here before the sirens find us," he said reluctantly. "And before we freeze." He rubbed his hands over my arms.

As we slid down the dome on our *pigu*s, I said, "So . . . there's this wedding next Saturday. . . ."

He perked up at the word "wedding" and stopped scooting. "I like weddings. Dinner, cake, dancing—what's not to like?" He struck a pose with his hands, and I smiled, remembering his adorable, flailing jig from MIThenge.

"Would you want to be my plus one?"

"I'd be honored," he said, the excitement on his face matching the energy in his voice. "Whose is it?"

"My brother's."

His face fell, the brightness disappearing like a candle being blown out. "Will that be awkward given everything with, you know, them?"

"My parents won't be there," I answered as I returned to scooting, needing the distraction. "They disowned Xing years ago because they don't approve of his fiancée. That was actually a large part of my disagreement with them, in addition to the career stuff."

As soon as we were back on solid ground, he took my hands with both of his, squeezing once. The warmth traveled from my palms to my heart. "I'm so sorry about your parents, Mei."

Surprisingly, it was all I needed. I had thought my situation would require dissecting each piece, brainstorming my next step, maybe even creating a ten-step plan, but those simple words and a kind gesture were enough for now.

Maybe there was something magical about the dome. MIT. Darren.

He held on to my hand until we reached Burton Conner. As we walked, I ran my tongue along my swollen lips, feeling the tenderness to remind me of our kisses, that it wasn't a dream.

We paused at the dorm's entrance, where the front light illuminated everything. I snuck a glance at the dark, walled-off garden to the right, the complete opposite of the bright, public spot we stood in now. It felt too creepy to pull him in there, yet I didn't want to sneak another kiss in the open.

His hands pressed the small of my back, pulling my lips to his. The electricity sparked again, and I sank into him. I no longer cared who could see us. I wouldn't stop even if my mother were here, hands on hips, that cold stare boring into us.

Darren pulled away first, much too soon. "Chin up, Lady Almond. It'll get better."

"*Kiemasu*," I whispered, then vanished into the dorm like a magic act.

VOICEMAIL FROM NĂINAI AND YILONG

Năinai: Mei Mei, I'm disappointed in you. You a good girl deep down. Stop being foolish and fix this.

Yilong: Don't throw away everything we've given you. Don't be like Xing. Otherwise, you are no niece of mine.

Năinai: <resigned whisper> Eat your vitamins. . . .

CHAPTER 20

Dr. and Dr.

Midstudying, I scrounged through my desk, searching for a fix of dried squid, my favorite brain food. But I came up empty. Of course.

When I failed to convince myself that the knot in my stomach was because I was hungry and nothing else, I slammed the drawer in frustration, sending a photo loose from the stack of papers on my desk.

My favorite baby picture, tucked into my college-bound boxes in a last-minute sentimental rush. It fluttered to the ground, catching the light streaming in from the window.

Two-year-old me, dressed in a red, embroidered, cotton-padded *mián'ǎo* and navy-blue sweatpants that said PUMP instead of PUMA. My father was holding me—no, he was clutching me to him, his arms awkward and cramped from squeezing so hard. His cheek was pressed against mine, an uncharacteristic curve to his lips. And his eyes—they radiated love.

I was his *bǎobèi*.

And this *bǎobèi* was about to *lose it*. I snatched up my phone and ballet shoes, then retreated to Mr. Porter's open arms.

Everything felt tight. Too tight, like a coffin. My muscles screamed at me as I dissolved into movement without any warm-up. And as stiff as I was on the outside, the inside was rigor mortis— still too soon after the death of my relationship with my parents.

There was a hole in my chest, a piece of me missing without them. When I thought about continuing down this path, trying to find my way, the crater grew. I folded my arms across my torso as if that could stop it, but the void swelled and billowed, laughing at me.

But then when I thought about making up with them, the hole in my chest closed as a cavity opened in my brain, a partial lobotomy. I couldn't go through life as a shadow. If I gave in to them, I'd lose myself.

No matter how painful this was, I couldn't go back. But just because I knew that didn't make it any easier.

● ● ●

In the Chinatown supermarket, I dug through vacuum-sealed packages of pork jerky, jelly candies, and seaweed but couldn't locate the dried squid. I had spent thirty minutes on the T, gotten lost twice, and now I couldn't read the obscure characters on the product labels.

I grasped my head with both hands and held back a scream. First the Star Market hadn't stocked the snacks I craved, and now this.

Okay, Universe, I get it. I just want some dried squid, damn it!

My breath rushed in and out of my nostrils noisily, and I focused on it to ebb the rush of emotions.

A voice behind me said, "Mei?" It was more of a question than a statement.

I turned to face a middle-aged Chinese woman I didn't recognize. *"Āyí hǎo."* My greeting was robotic; my mother had so many acquaintances I couldn't remember their faces (and my poor vision didn't help).

"You look just like your mother!"

"I do?"

She touched her hand to my chin. "Yes. Same bone structure and delicacy. Your features are obviously from your father, but your base is so clearly her."

My chest tightened at the mention of my parents. I guess my tale hadn't traveled too far down the grapevine yet.

She lowered her hand, then her eyes. "I was so sorry to hear about, you know."

Guess I spoke too soon. My lips hardened into a line and I acknowledged her condolences with a brusque nod.

"I'm shopping with my sister. You remember her, I'm sure. She used to drive you and Hanwei to Chinese school." She put her hand on the woman beside her, whose back was to us.

Mrs. Pan turned and dropped the vermicelli she was holding. "Mei! Oh! Uh, hello."

I bent down to pick up the noodles at the same time she did, and when our fingers grazed, she snapped her hand back as if my disobedience were contagious. Pretending I didn't notice, I scooped the package up and dropped it in her shopping basket.

"*Āyí hǎo*. How's Hanwei?"

Mrs. Pan flinched when her son's name came out of my mouth. "I'm sorry, Mei, but Hanwei has been spoken for. He has a girl-friend now, a good girl, so you should just forget about him. I'm sorry it didn't work out."

Her pinched lips and cold eyes told me she was lying, and even though I had never wanted Hanwei for a second, disgrace shot through me. They hurried away and left me, my limbs shaking, in the prepackaged food aisle.

I left sans squid. Back on the street, despite the cold, my feet wouldn't listen to me. *Go home*, I told them, but they remained planted. *You have no home*, they reminded me.

I stood on the sidewalk, staring at the Chinatown archway, the gate into this other world. My body was inside, past the entrance, but it felt like the rest of me was outside.

The people around me morphed into a blur, and I eventually stopped registering their shoulder grazes as they pushed past me. They became a sea of black hair. . . .

But then I spotted a familiar shape. Two contrasting bodies—one tall and thick, the other short and petite—walking together yet apart.

I ran toward them, not thinking, not sure what I wanted, but I had to see them. My parents' eyes met mine—my father's hard and distant, my mother's wounded and helpless—and they took a sharp turn into the first store beside them. Silky Fabrics. A store they would never go into otherwise.

I couldn't breathe. I couldn't see. I hadn't realized my heart could break all over again.

• • •

Outside MIT's financial aid office, I let out a breath and watched the water molecules condense before my eyes. As the puff of fog drifted languidly, I wished I could float away with it and leave everything behind.

Seeing my parents had been a wake-up call to get my shit together. And not only were my emotions in pieces, but so were my finances. Because I was under eighteen and there was no "my Chinese parents disowned me" check box on the form, I would have to go to court to become emancipated. My parents would probably contest, it would be a long process, and it "just wasn't a viable option," according to the gray-haired financial-aid lady with coffee-stained teeth.

Xing had offered to help me, but I hoped to keep him out of it. He had enough parental-related burdens without adding mine. And for all I knew, he was still paying our parents back for college and med school.

Instead of secrets, my dumpling was now stuffed with fear and way too much responsibility. And it was already exploding, even without squeezing.

An unfamiliar voice called out my name. I peered up at a handsome male stranger who looked a few years older than me. My eyebrows furrowed. "Sorry, do I know you?"

"I'm Eugene."

Oh, Eugene. My preapproved Taiwanese knight. I shouldn't have been surprised—Harvard and MIT students frequented each other's campuses—but it just never occurred to me that I would one day put a face to the dreaded name.

"Nice to meet you," I said, but despite my best efforts, my tone implied the opposite. "How'd you recognize me?"

"My mom showed me a picture. Of course." He rolled his eyes. "I'm sorry about your parents."

"Oh, you heard?" Maybe I was Ying-Na 2.0 already.

"Yeah. My mom's a bit panicked that your mom will still try to set us up despite everything. Because of your . . . situation . . . she's finally gotten off my back about our meeting. Good for us, right?"

I tried not to be offended since I never had any interest in him either. But it was hard not to be a little stung by his rejection, especially now that we'd met. "Guess I'm not good enough for you anymore," I joked. "I won't be the obedient Chinese wife she wants for you."

He laughed, a little mocking and a lot haughty. "Yeah, I'm not going down that road. She'll learn eventually."

"How can you say that so confidently? Won't she freak out and guilt you or cut you off until you do what they want?"

Eugene squinted at me like I was an alien. "I'm their only son. I'll get my way eventually. I just have to wait them out."

"Lucky," I mumbled.

"It was nice to meet you, Mei. Maybe in another life we could've been friends, but I have different taste in women than my mother."

I watched as he disappeared from view (and my life), thankful I wasn't going to be Mrs. Huang in the future. Or Dr. Huang to his Dr. Huang.

VOICEMAIL FROM YILONG

Mei! You better not go to Xing's wedding. Nǎinai has spent the last four years crying over him, and if you go, you'll break what's left of her heart. Then it will be that much harder to fix this mess you've created. Stop diving into the fire pit headfirst!

CHAPTER 21

The End

Wedding Day.

I showered first since that seemed like the normal thing to do before a date, especially for a sweat-prone individual. I snuck some of Nicolette's fancy soap, which smelled like flirtation, laughing to myself that she could borrow my fifty-cent soap bar anytime. I'd make it up to her later somehow.

Then I combed through my closet. Too frayed. Too tight. Too loose. Too bedazzled. The mountain of clothes on my bed grew with each rejection, but I eventually found a rose-colored dress I didn't hate. And despite the storm of emotions brewing in my chest, today was a celebration; red was the appropriate color.

I stared at the mirror, trying to see past the fingerprints Nicolette had left behind. Instead of the frustration (and fear of chlamydia) I used to feel, the smudges now made me smile (and it wasn't just because I was pretty sure she was cured). I could picture her leaning one palm against the mirror for leverage as she plucked her eyebrows, put on eyeliner, checked out her own *pìgu*. She didn't give two shits (or even one) *what* I saw her doing, usually turning to me and asking, "See anything you like?"

I sat down to tackle the last item on my list: my face. I was an expert at stage makeup but knew I couldn't show up decked out in false eyelashes, bright red lipstick, and fuchsia blush. I did my best with the carnival colors I had, trying to mix bronzer into my blush to darken it, but ended up staring at a clown. Blue eyeshadow was hard to pull off. I tried to cover it with more eyeliner. Now I looked like a panda. Fan-freaking-tastic. I folded my arms on the desk and buried my mess of a face.

"Aurgghhh!" My body muffled my yell, decreasing the satisfaction.

In my head, I could hear my mother laughing at me. She had refused to buy me normal makeup, not until I was ready to meet Eugene. *Can't have you attract the wrong boy, now, can we?* The horror. Well, congratulations, Mămá. You won.

Nicolette hip-checked her way into our room, and my head snapped up when the door banged against the wall. When she saw my pitiful face, she screamed and dropped the books in her hands.

Now my cheeks were fuchsia, both naturally and cosmetically. "Jesus, a little dramatic, are we?" I scrubbed my face with makeup remover.

"You don't need all that crap. Haven't you heard? Less is more, especially for nice guys who like you for who you are on the inside," she said with a wink. "And you smell nice for a change. But you owe me a coffee, one for each time you use my soap. That shit's expensive!"

I nodded, making a mental note to get her a coffee *and* a hot chocolate. Maybe I could convert her. "Thanks, Nicolette."

"My friends call me Nic," she said with a soft smile.

After I fixed my face (just mascara and bronzer this time), I received a butt pat from Nicolette, along with a *Go get him, tiger; you look hot as fuck.* As I clicked down the stairs in uncharacteristic heels, I laughed to myself wondering whether Nic knew I was a tiger on the Chinese zodiac. *No better time to start living up to your inner animal*, I told myself as my steps gained confidence.

I paused at the door to the lobby. Through the narrow window, I stole a glance at my handsome date, whose back was to me. How did he get his hair to look just messy enough to be sexy?

When I opened the door, Darren turned, revealing his orange tie, white dress shirt, and navy suit—all beneath a black dress coat. And . . . *drumroll* . . . two cups of hot chocolate. Good thing I hadn't surprise jumped into his arms like I'd wanted.

He froze when he saw me. "You look beautiful. *Kawaii.*" I tilted my head at him, questioning. "It's Japanese for cute. I, uh, learned it for you."

Could he be any more *kawaii*? My goodness.

I did a *relevé*, rising on my tiptoes to peck his cheek. But unused to my heels, I overshot to his temple, which I kissed anyway before my lips found their way to his cheekbone. His grin grew wider with each peck, and as I stared at his slightly crooked lower canine, I thought, *Maybe I should've just grabbed his face with both hands and kissed him all over his gorgeous,* kawaii *face like I'd wanted to.*

"You look quite *kawaii* yourself, *shuài gē*," I said as I took one of the cups. Mmm. Extra whipped cream, just the way I liked it. Definitely worth it despite the whipped-cream mustache it always left behind. Just as my tongue swept over the errant foam, Darren ran his thumb over my lip.

"Oh God, sorry!" His thumb tasted like soap. Not the most appetizing, but there was nothing hotter than a man who washed his hands regularly.

"Let's try that again," he said softly. He gently lifted my chin with his finger, then closed the distance between us and kissed me where the whipped cream had been. If I were more ladylike, my weakened knees would have wobbled.

Darren stuck an elbow out, and after looping my hand in comfortably, I followed outside to the waiting taxi. He waved the exhaust away, opened the door, and gestured grandly as if the dirty, beat-up cab were a horse-drawn carriage.

"Excited?" he asked as he slid in next to me.

"Sure," I said, which was a step above what I was really thinking—how my attendance today was a giant leap forward on the rebellion road. I couldn't stop replaying Yilong's voicemail in my head, squeaky voice and all.

I leaned my head on his shoulder and he held my hand, stroking my thumb the entire ride.

The church we pulled up to had red lanterns, balloons, and double happiness symbols lining the entrance. Yup, we were in the right place, all right. There was even a red carpet—shaggy and stained, but a red carpet nonetheless.

The sanctuary was already half full. The guests mingled, introducing themselves and asking one another how they knew the bride or groom. Did they know what today meant? That in a few hours, Xing would cross the Lu-family bridge and burn it?

The laughter and chatter bubbled up around me, increasing in volume as time ticked on.

No one knew.

It's a celebration, I scolded myself. I hated that I needed the reminder. I tried to focus on the red streamers lining the pews, the *rè'nào* buzz of the room, and the handsome man beside me.

Xing entered, and his face lit up when he saw me. We hugged, less awkward than the last few times, and I introduced Darren. Xing gave him a brotherly glower but skipped the protective speech (thank God).

On our way to the front, Xing leaned down and whispered in my ear, "Thanks for everything, Mei-ball—your support, your wisdom. You helped me through an impossible time, and in some ways, you helped me get to this day. I can't tell you what having you here means to me."

It was the most he'd ever expressed, and I widened my eyes, hoping to dry the tears before they fell. I wasn't sure if they were there because I was happy for him or sad at what this day meant. I wasn't even sure how I felt about the role I'd played.

Xing ushered Darren and me into the front pew, labeled LU FAMILY. The rest of the empty bench screamed *Mom and Dad aren't coming!*

Across the aisle stood a man and a woman, both rigid as a board, who I presumed were Esther's parents. They made their way over with tight-lipped smiles on their lined faces, and Xing bowed to his future in-laws before making proper introductions.

I mimicked his bow for no reason. Maybe I felt the need to make up for my parents' treatment of Esther. I could hear my mother yelling in my head about how Mr. and Mrs. Wong owed her a dowry—a huge one since Esther was so flawed. *Practically a man.*

"Mrs. Wong, what a beautiful dress you're wearing," Darren said.

She straightened her dark silver gown. "It was difficult to find Chinese formalwear without black flowers, which of course is forbidden since it brings bad luck."

I took a quick survey, locating five black-flowered dresses within ten seconds.

Mrs. Wong's gaze followed mine. "Oh, no, it's okay for others. It's forbidden only for the bride's mother."

I forced a smile and nodded, then turned to Esther's father. "Mr. Wong, shouldn't you go back and get ready to walk Esther down the aisle?"

He stiffened, then said through pursed lips, "It's tradition for the most blessed and fortunate woman in the neighborhood to walk the bride down the aisle. Elder Wu will have that honor.

She has one son and one daughter, both of whom are successful. A CEO and a doctor. She flew in from Taichung this morning."

I thought I had experienced it all, but in the span of three minutes I had learned two new traditions that blew even my mind. The strangest part was that Xing had led me to believe Esther's parents were more like Helen's. During one of our visits, he had told me, tight-eyed and stiff-jawed, about how Esther's "superchill" parents had let her dye her hair, listen to rap, date. It had only emphasized to him just how strict our parents were, making him resent them more.

But it wasn't so black-and-white, was it? Maybe the only lesson here was that I needed to stop comparing everyone.

When the pastor took his place at the lectern, I bowed to Esther's parents, thankful for the interruption.

In our glaringly unfilled pew, I crossed my legs, hoping to calm the gnawing in my stomach. The numbness that prickled down my calf reminded me of my mother manipulating my limbs into this pose.

I uncrossed, accidentally kicking Darren with the bit of anger that shot out. In a silent apology, I placed my hands on his thigh, landing much higher than intended.

Jesus.

Sensing my inner (and outer) flailing, Darren draped his arm across the back of the bench, his fingers caressing my shoulder. Finally feeling safe, I curled up against him.

Xing stood at the front, dapper in his black suit and red pocket square. He caught my eye and smiled, the kind shared by two people bonded for life. My nose burned the way it always did pre-sentimental tears. I nodded to communicate my understanding, to signal I was here for him, to tell him in one sharp movement what I could never say aloud.

The ring bearer carried a stuffed Doraemon down the aisle, the rings tied to its blue, earless head. The doll was almost the same size as him, and by the end he was dragging it behind his *pìgu* until his mother rushed up to help. The bridesmaids were clones of one another in matching knee-length red dresses and sky-high charcoal heels that made them hobble down the aisle like little girls playing dress-up.

Xing fixated on his bride as soon as she and Elder Wu were visible. Instead of looking at Esther like every other guest, I was drawn to my brother. His eyes glowed as if he had seen an angel.

How could anyone oppose this union? Staring at him in that moment, I couldn't fathom a world in which Xing had chosen our parents over Esther.

I thought about my mom and dad's relationship. A lifetime of arguments, a lack of affection, no communication. Stifled by the predetermined husband, wife, and in-law roles, the unyielding expectations. Xing had escaped that—at a price, but a sacrifice worth making.

Esther's veil was over her face, but her joy shined through the silk as she locked eyes with her soon-to-be husband. The moment was so private, the exchange so intimate, that it felt wrong for the rest of us to be present, watching.

The tulle of Esther's ball gown devoured her, an odd choice for someone so petite—or was that just my mother's influence seeping into my brain? She'd always had an *if-you've-got-a-low-BMI-flaunt-it* attitude.

I glanced at Esther's father, whose pinched face betrayed his true feelings about not walking his daughter down the aisle. I wondered why they followed a custom they so obviously despised. Would it have been so terrible for Mr. Wong to accompany Esther?

Yes, I realized. To them it would have been disastrous. By pushing aside their feelings and bringing Elder Wu, the Wongs believed they were bestowing a lifetime of blessings onto their daughter. They'd made a selfless choice. Ridiculous, maybe, but selfless nonetheless.

At the front, Xing wiped his eyes with the back of his hand before lifting the veil. Esther bowed to Elder Wu and an usher led the hunchbacked woman to an empty seat. Holding one finger up to Xing and flashing him a playful smile, Esther dashed to her parents and embraced them. I watched them hug with total abandon, her parents squeezing with their eyes closed. *None of the Lus know how to do that*, I thought.

But then Xing stepped forward to hug the Wongs as well. No awkwardness. Only warmth. As if it were the hundredth time. Mr. Wong whispered something in Xing's ear, then patted him on the back.

Tradition dictated that women leave their families to join the male's in marriage, but the opposite had happened today as a result of tradition. How ironic.

My breath hitched as I wondered whether my parents would

be present when (if?) I walked down the aisle. Would I have to ask Xing to take their place, as I was doing for him? Could they really let a moment like this pass?

My gaze fell to the empty space on my right.

The pastor raised his arms and the guests rose.

"I will magnify You . . . I will glorify You . . . ," everyone sang.

Well, everyone *else* sang. I wasn't familiar with the Christian praise song. Xing and I had been raised Buddhist, with idols around the house and yearly visits to the temples. I was glad my parents weren't present to storm out in protest.

Once the guests were seated again, the pastor began his monologue. In Mandarin. I peeked over at Darren, but his lips were curved slightly and he appeared to be appreciating the beauty of the language. I wondered what it sounded like to his ears. He heard sounds, while I heard words, sentences, meaning.

His serene face relaxed my own, and I directed my attention up front. I was finally ready to be a part of today. Ready to enjoy my brother's happiness. Ready to accept whatever repercussions arose from my attendance.

Pastor [in Chinese]: Marriage is a huge step. The men have to learn how to listen to the wife nagging and the wives have to get used to their dirty husbands.

<Chuckle, chuckle, chuckle>

Bridesmaid [translating to English]: Marriage can be terrible. The women nag and the men are dir—

Pastor [in Chinese]: I'd like to share a story with you.

I wondered if the pastor didn't speak English or was just impatient.

Suddenly, the sanctuary doors burst open and Aunt Yilong marched in, a warrior storming a castle.

With an accusatory finger at Xing and Esther, Yilong filled the chapel with her hoarse yells, which were amplified by the silence. "You murdered Nǎinai! And her ghost will haunt your marriage forever."

CHAPTER 22

Murderers

Everyone was silent, like no one knew
what to make of the clusterfuck that was still unfolding.

Yilong looked through everyone with unfocused eyes. Her voice was almost too calm as she said, "Anyone here in support of this marriage will have three years of bad luck."

Panic struck many faces.

I wanted to stand and announce it was just a ruse to stop the wedding. That this wasn't even the first time Yilong had accused a family member of murdering one of her parents. To this day she blamed Yéye's death on my mother because Xing was named after him—an honor to many, but a death sentence to the Lus.

My mother, who hadn't heard of this tradition, had no idea that her in-laws would believe Xing had to take Yéye's place to equilibrate the universe. Never mind that Yéye had been dying from emphysema prior to Xing's conception. No, Yilong treated my mother as if she had forced Yéye to smoke unfiltered cigarettes for thirty years.

Xing's voice cut through the strained silence. "Is Năinai really dead?"

I held my breath as my pulse accelerated, the two combining into a dizzy spell. No. The answer had to be no.

"Yes. You all murdered her. She died this morning because you disrespected us"—Yilong pointed at me—"rebelled"—Xing—"and deprived her of grandsons"—Esther.

My heart pounded in my ears.

"Năinai died because she was ninety," Xing said, his words confident but his voice thin.

"Năinai died from heartbreak! She was as strong as an ox, her zodiac sign, and would've outlived us all. But no, dead overnight. Because of you! How could you do this after she gave you everything? She loved you the most, Xing! For the last four years, her days were spent staring at your pictures, crying. She didn't shed a single tear over Yéye, but for you—a river. Was *she* worth it?" The pain in Yilong's eyes turned to anger as she scoffed at Esther.

Mrs. Wong's heels banged an angry rhythm as she marched down the aisle, followed by the wedding line. It took all five groomsmen to usher Yilong out, her wails somehow increasing in volume as she disappeared down the hall.

Darren placed a reassuring hand on the small of my back, but I barely noticed. He said something, which registered only because I saw his mouth move in blurry slow motion. I was too far removed. My mind had shut down to protect me. The background commotion buzzed faintly as if everyone were at one end of a tunnel, and I, alone, at the other.

Darren's hand stroking mine eventually returned me to unwelcome reality. I surveyed my surroundings. Xing and Esther were nowhere in sight, and people were conversing in hushed whispers, a frantic burble enveloping the room. Some guests, mostly from the bride's side, glowered at me. I didn't blame them.

Xing and Esther reappeared to a round of applause. They returned to their places by the lectern, Esther's three-foot train held by her maid of honor (the longer the train, the more good fortune).

I barely heard Xing's vows. He slipped a tiny band onto Esther's finger, and a tear escaped, sliding down his face like a kid at a waterpark. During Esther's vows, I stared at the resolve in Xing's eyes. He was completely sure, not an iota of doubt.

As they leaned forward to seal their vows with a kiss, I clutched my seat, not breathing. In that moment, it would be done, the bond between my parents and Xing completely severed. How could something this significant happen so quickly?

Their lips met.

Cheers and whistles exploded from the guests, everyone celebrating. Everyone except me. My eyes flooded, the only sad tears in the building.

I followed the other guests in a haze, trudging through three blocks of snow to the Chinatown reception.

"That was a pretty church," Darren said. "I love the mosaic windows."

He was trying so hard I could see his effort, but I could only manage a rumble in my throat that vaguely sounded like *mm-hmm*.

He halted, pulling me to a stop beside him. "Mei, I'm really sorry about your grandma. Do you want to talk about anything?"

Yes. Everything. I would never make up with Nǎinai, who died thinking Xing and I were terrible. Xing would never make up with her, and he didn't care. There was too much, so I just shook my head.

The restaurant was even redder than the church, decorated with wall scrolls, paper umbrellas, and lanterns. A red wall displaying golden phoenix and dragon statues served as the backdrop, and in front, on a dais, sat a sweetheart table for the bride and groom, most likely to downplay my parents' absence.

I retreated to my table with Darren close behind. In the center, between candles, a paper snake and rabbit—Xing and Esther's zodiac animals, respectively—stared back at me. I hadn't realized Esther was two years older than Xing. Yet another thing my parents would disapprove of.

The newlyweds entered the reception hall to a round of whistling and feet stamping. Esther had changed into a traditional red *qípáo* with gold stitching, but the conventionally skintight dress appeared a size too big, allowing her a larger range of motion. Maybe it was so she could dance. I smiled with hope that I would get along with my new sister-in-law.

On top of the embroidered silk, Esther was weighed down by chain after chain—the more gold, the more *miànzi* for her family. Not enough prestige and the groom's family won the right to bully the bride. Not so much an issue here—the bullying was already at a maximum, and I was the only Lu present anyway—but perhaps the tradition had evolved beyond its meaning, like how American brides wore white regardless of their sexual history.

I watched numbly as Xing and Esther kneeled, their hands over their bowed heads to serve *hóngzǎo guìyuán chá* to the Wongs. The idea of my future tea ceremony with Mr. and Mrs. Wong's smug expressions on my own parents' faces made me choke on my shark fin soup. Except . . . we wouldn't even make it that far.

I barely noticed the first four courses. But since it was the typical Chinese wedding banquet with ten rounds of the most elaborate, expensive delicacies (again, it was all about that *miànzi*), I had six more to get myself together.

I recognized the next course, swift nest soup, from stories I'd heard from Nǎinai. Her point had always been how delicious and rare the dish was, but all I ever heard was how the nests were made of solidified bird saliva.

I shoved it aside with a pinky (for minimal contact), then pushed Darren's away as well. Under the table, I broke out my hand sanitizer.

He tilted his head at me. "What is this? Do you not like it?"

I shook my head at him and mouthed, *Just trust me.* Who knew what kinds of diseases were floating around in there?

The elderly guest next to me leaned uncomfortably close,

shaking a judgmental finger. "That's the most expensive dish. Don't be rude."

"We're allergic," I lied.

Her face brightened as she reached over my arm to swipe my bowl.

The next course wasn't much better: sea cucumber. As I pushed the luxurious booger around my plate, the guests clinked glasses amid laughter and chatter. So *rè'nào*. But all I could do was imagine Yilong here, screaming, *How can you all celebrate after Nǎinai just died? Murderers!*

Xing and Esther began making the rounds, coming to our table first. I stood so fast my chair almost tipped over, but I caught it in time. Esther smiled hesitantly at me, and it made me feel better to know she felt the same anxiousness that was making my palms sweat. I pulled her into a hug, partly because my hands were clammy and disgusting, but also because it felt like the right thing to do.

Her gold necklaces felt cold against my warm cheek, and her flowery perfume overwhelmed my nose. Jasmine. My mother's favorite. How ironic.

"I'm sorry about everything," she whispered in my ear.

I squeezed harder and felt some of the tension leave her body.

"You must have ginormous expectations of me, the girl Xing left his family for," she said. "Those are pretty big shoes my size-six feet can't fill."

I laughed into her hair, and our bodies shook together in relief, pain, and celebration.

When Esther and I separated, Xing's eyes met mine, and we just stared at each other for what felt like forever. I could see the pain and weariness in his eyes, but there was no remorse. He placed a hand on my shoulder, squeezing, and I nodded once to signal my love, my solidarity, and so much more I didn't even comprehend yet. Somehow, the exchange felt even more intimate than a hug.

The moment broke when the swift nest hoarder pulled Xing away to congratulate him.

Darren and I loaded up on abalone in black bean sauce, stir-fried lobster, and pork fried rice—the safest options. Despite the mound of food on my plate and my Lu blood, I only stomached a few bites.

I swallowed hard, my fifth spoonful of rice catching in my dry throat. "Darren, I think I'm going to head home."

"Right now? But we haven't danced yet."

I couldn't dance here, in public, to celebratory music. I needed Mr. Porter. I needed to scream, punch, and stomp. Xing would understand.

I collected my things and stood. "Thanks for coming with me. I'm sorry it was such a disaster."

"Mei, wait! Don't be ridiculous. I'll take you home."

I nodded, then scurried out the door, assuming he was close behind. The cab ride was silent—awkward this time—with Darren sneaking worried glances at me as I pretended not to notice.

As we neared campus, I finally spoke—to my lap, because I was unable to look at him. "I'm really sorry about today."

He grabbed my limp hand. "I'm here for you, Mei. You're not alone."

"How can you even want to be in the same car as me after seeing my aunt?"

He puffed out a breath, the fog disappearing as quickly as my happiness had. But before he could say anything—I didn't think I could take it, whatever it was—I slipped my palm from his, reluctant but determined.

"I don't think we should see each other anymore." I forced my gaze to meet his. "I'm doing this for you, so you don't have to go through what Esther did. I think it'd just be easier. For your sake. For both our sakes."

"When are you going to stop fighting who you are? What you want?" He shook his head over and over. "Don't do this."

We pulled up to Burton Conner. "I'm really sorry."

I exited the car before he could stop me, and before I could change my mind.

Voicemail from my mother

Mei? It's your mǔqīn. Bǎbá doesn't want you to come. <pause>
I'm not the one who told you this, but . . . the Chuang Funeral
Home. In Chinatown. Saturday at noon. Come late and sneak in
so he doesn't see you.

CHAPTER 23

Good-Bye

I took my mother's advice and went to
the funeral late so I could slip in with the crowd, hopefully unseen
by my father and aunt. In what screwed-up world did the granddaughter have to sneak into her grandmother's funeral to hide
from her family? But today wasn't about all that crap. It was about
saying good-bye to Năinai.

"What are you?" the cabdriver asked me in an Eastern European
accent. "Like, as in, ethnicity."

"Chinese."

"No, you can't be. You much too big to be Chinese."

"Well, you're too rude to deserve a tip." Why did everyone

think anything above size zero was obese for Asians? I glared at him, hoping he would see in the rearview mirror.

Fifty dollars later, I arrived at the funeral home. I was too spent to argue with the jerk about driving ten miles out of the way. I threw cash in the front seat as I exited, no tip as promised.

Outside the funeral home, I paused. The pagoda-shaped entrance was from one of my two worlds, the one in which I didn't belong.

I looked at the buildings across the street, outside Chinatown. Tufts Medical Center. The W Hotel. McDonald's. I didn't belong in that world, either.

Roommate number one's harsh words echoed in my mind, reverberating louder and louder. Even my grandparents hadn't belonged anywhere, driven out of China by the Communists, yet foreigners in Taiwan. Maybe I was destined to be lost, just like them.

My legs numbly carried me inside. The funeral home was dark and I relaxed slightly. The dimness matched my mood and masked my presence, almost as if I were a bystander, watching instead of partaking. I felt like an intruder.

The memorial service had begun, and the small space was filled with vaguely familiar faces. Despite the cold, the door was propped open so Năinai's spirit could come in. The guests chanted amid the chiming of bells, and the discordant sounds mixed to become, somehow, concordant. Cloaked by the darkness, I slipped through the sea of black to the back corner. Sticky-sweet smoke filled the room and my lungs as guests approached the casket one by one to bow and light their incense. Before rejoining the crowd, they jumped over a fire and ate a peanut to cleanse their soul.

These traditions—they were about respect. Devised to mean something, like how an engagement ring symbolized commitment and a wedding ring, love. The more traditions you were willing to go out of your way to do, the more you respected the deceased. For a family who didn't stress affection or communication, maybe this was the only way to convey emotion. They believed Năinai's soul was here, watching, so in death they were finally ready to show how much they cared. I would've felt so much better if I *could* believe Năinai to be here, listening, so I could have one last chance to make amends. But to me she was gone.

Someone wailed in Chinese, "*Huílái ba,*" over and over, trying to guide Năinai's soul home. The dissonant phrase, louder, longer, and more urgent than the chanting, broke through my thoughts and returned me to the present.

The room hushed, and the guests filed out the open door into the courtyard to burn paper clothes, mansions, and furniture for Năinai to have in the afterlife. If an insufficient amount was burned, Năinai's impecunious soul would haunt her family and friends' dreams in revenge, complaining of hunger and cold.

I remained in my hiding spot until the room emptied. And finally, I took a step out of the darkness into the candlelight.

Năinai's abandoned walker was parked beside the open casket, a single black bow looped around the handles. A lump formed in my throat.

The altar on the far wall was filled with ceremonial bowls, incense, and Năinai's favorite snacks—oranges, mooncakes, and red bean *bāo*s. Between the food, there appeared to be trash, and I wondered why no one had cleaned it up. I crept over to clear the litter and add my offering to the rest.

Upon closer inspection, the scraps of paper and worn trinkets weren't garbage—they were memories. A crumpled picture of Năinai, clearly well loved and often looked at through the years. A receipt from a dinner for two. Figurines of oxen, Năinai's zodiac year and therefore her favorite animal. Maybe Yilong's hoarding was more than met the eye—it was a way for her to express herself. Similar to how my father showed his love by demanding Năinai's funeral be here, close to the joint cemetery plot he had purchased years ago after Yéye's death.

I placed the bottle of multivitamins at the front of the altar and whispered, "Eat your vitamins," to Năinai one last time.

Clasping my hands in front, I stepped onto the raised platform. Then I stopped breathing.

It was Năinai but not. The cadaver's skin sagged, signaling she was gone. The makeup was caked on, but instead of hiding the lack of life, it drew more attention to it. A tear trailed off my chin onto her cheek.

"Năinai," I whispered, so softly I could barely hear myself. "I'm so sorry."

My words caught in my throat. I lifted a shaky palm but pulled back before it left my side. We rarely touched before, and now it was too late. The body before me wasn't her anymore.

"I wish it didn't end like this. I wish you could hear me right now. I wish you could've seen me for who I was—a loving daughter and granddaughter who just wanted to be heard. Wanted to be happy. I wish you could've understood, but we're from two different worlds. Good-bye, Nǎinai. Rest in peace."

Footsteps. Behind me.

I whirled around. The sight of my mother made the lump in my throat swell. I longed to go to her, but she felt like a stranger.

I held her gaze and she stared back, the moment stretching. My breath blew out hot in the silence.

"You have to go," she said finally, her face tight with worry. "He'll know I told you. About the funeral. I wasn't supposed to."

That was it? I shook my head in disappointment. "Nǎinai's gone, you have no children, and that's the first thing you think of? You know, I used to think that one day you'd learn to stand up for yourself. Then, when I realized you wouldn't, I thought—hoped—maybe you'd at least stand up for me. Or Xing. But I've finally accepted that it will never happen. Bǎbá is all you have now. And Yilong. I hope you're happy with the people you've chosen."

More footsteps, heavy and angry this time. My mother's eyes widened in fear. I didn't need to turn around to know that I should brace myself for—

"Get out!" Yilong screamed. "You're not allowed here! You murdered her!"

My father's face twisted into a deep scowl—brows furrowed, eyes narrowed, and jaw tensed. I glanced at my mother, hoping she had internalized my words, but she merely opened her mouth, no sounds coming out.

Three deep breaths. I concentrated on my chest rising and falling, imagining my lungs filling and emptying of air. I had to calm down before I said something I could never take back.

Yilong grabbed my arm and yanked, causing me to stumble over the step. I fell, catching myself on Năinai's walker.

"Don't touch that!" Yilong screeched.

I let go, not because she had ordered me to, but because touching the walker felt like touching Năinai's ghost.

I turned to my parents. "Isn't Năinai's death enough? Can't we compromise now? I'll never be able to make up with her—don't you want better for us?"

My father's voice was more gravelly than usual. "This isn't a negotiation. If you want to make up, you know what it takes."

Air rushed in through my mouth, scratching my sandpaper throat. I said nothing.

He turned his back to me. "Leave. I don't want you here. Năinai doesn't want you here."

Something snapped inside me. I found my voice, and I spoke clearly while staring straight into my father's eyes. "Can't you see a piece of me dies every time I ignore what I want and just do what you say? I wish you could accept me the way I am."

In a gust of wind, Xing and Esther walked through the door.

I shouldn't have been surprised—I was the one who had told them where and when the funeral was—but I had hoped they would disappear into the crowd like I had, not show up at the worst possible moment.

"Get out! *Gǔn!*" Yilong yelled. "How dare you bring Nǎinai's murderer here to rub her dead nose in!"

Xing remained calm, but his eye twitched—a flash of anger I knew to look for. "I want to say good-bye to Nǎinai."

Yilong turned in a semicircle, pointing first at Xing, then Esther, then me. "None of you belong here. You're not family." She clenched her fists, then took a step toward Esther. "This is all your fault!"

Esther instinctively covered her belly with her hand. It was only a second before her arm dropped back to her side, but I noticed. So did my mother, whose eyes were so wide they were about to pop out of their sockets.

Xing's gaze met my mother's, and unspoken understanding flickered between them. Joy filled her face, completely out of place in the dim funeral home.

My mother turned to Esther and spoke to her for the first time. Like she was human. "Are you pregnant?"

Even the crickets didn't chirp. They left the room as fast as they could to avoid the inevitable Lu-suvius eruption.

Suddenly, Esther's billowy wedding dress, the loose *qípáo*, Xing's comment about how his salary was more important now than ever . . . it all made sense.

Xing stepped between Esther and my parents. "None of you will be in his life. You made damn sure of that."

"*His* life?" My father's eyes were glued to the baby bump. "How is this possible? You said she couldn't get pregnant."

Xing shook his head. "I never said that. I just said she may have some trouble."

I threw my hands in the air. "So is this all over now? She's pregnant. Your one objection is moot. And it's even a boy. The Lu family line will indeed carry on."

My father turned away. "Xing still disobeyed us."

"So did I. I guess that's it for us, then. No redemption." I turned to my mother, my last hope. Her eyes were downcast, shoulders slumped.

My voice dropped to a whisper. "Look at all of you, pushing away every relative you have for no good reason. Maybe I should ask myself if I even want to be a part of a family like this. I'm open to reconciliation if we can learn to talk like adults, but until then I'm going to stop trying so hard. Let me know when you're ready to have a real, open conversation."

Xing glanced at Esther. "We've discussed it and we're open to reconciliation as well if you apologize."

I held my breath. He'd finally done it. He'd made the first step. My father had to acknowledge that, be moved enough to take a step forward too, right?

But he just folded his arms across his chest and shook his head.

Xing shrugged as if they were discussing where to have lunch. "Then we're done here too."

"This is so ironic," I said, some spit flying out. "Bǎbá, you disown Xing for disobeying you, not providing grandchildren—which isn't even true anymore—yet that's what you've done too, since according to you, you have no kids. How can you stand in front of Năinai like this? You failed."

My father's tears proved I had struck his Achilles' heel. The rare sight filled me with guilt, but I couldn't back down now. I fled, Xing and Esther close behind.

We crammed onto a park bench, Esther in the middle. It was silent for some time as we processed.

"Do you think they'll ever come around?" I asked quietly.

"I don't care." Xing's words sent chills down my spine.

VOICEMAIL FROM MY MOTHER

Mei? I, um . . . <pause> Can we . . . ? <pause> Please call me.
It's . . . your mǔqīn.

CHAPTER 24

Affair

After my 5.111 lecture, I walked home along the Charles, wondering why I didn't take Memorial Drive more often. The air was nippy but also invigorating, much fresher than the stale Infinite Corridor air breathed in and out by so many passing students. Every fifty feet sat a bench, clones of the one I had shared with Darren. Each of them sent both a thrill and a pang through me.

My phone rang exactly five minutes after the end of class. Only one person knew my schedule that well.

My mother's picture filled the screen. God, that moment felt like a lifetime ago. Before picking up, I paused to take in the bright pink MIT MOM shirt and the hint of pride at the edge of her eyes.

The line was silent, and I stilled, exhaling only when I heard my mother's sharp intake of breath—an indication the call was intended, not a butt dial.

Her voice was choppy. "Can we meet? At Bertucci's?" The Italian restaurant marked the farthest she was willing to drive herself.

I nodded, then realized (duh) she couldn't see me. "Okay." I hung up first so she wouldn't hear the tremors in my voice.

I arrived first and waited outside, rocking back and forth on my heels atop the brick sidewalk. I crossed my arms, worried I looked too aggressive, then forced them down by my sides.

My mother's sea-green minivan pulled up, identifiable by its two dents, one on each bumper. She didn't notice me on account of her laser focus on the road. The front seat—or *death seat*, as she called it—was piled so high with Chinese newspapers I could see them from where I was standing.

She pulled the van across three parking spaces, braking every few feet so the car appeared to be breakdancing (more accurately, brake-dancing, heh . . . at least I crack myself up). Aware of her poor parking job, she readjusted but ended up in the same position as before. Drive-reverse-drive-reverse. Eventually, she managed to straddle just two spaces.

The familiarity of it all made me hug her when she got close enough. I didn't know what I was expecting, but when she patted my back with a cupped hand, I realized I had been expecting nothing. Maybe even rejection. Encouraged, I reached an arm out to put around her shoulder, but she ducked under and maintained a few feet between us as we walked.

Inside, my mother scoured the restaurant like a spy. An incompetent, nearsighted spy too vain to wear glasses.

I grabbed her arm and pulled her away from the unsuspecting patrons. "What's wrong with you?"

She clucked her tongue. "If you had done this when you went to dim sum with Xing, Bǎbá and I would've never found out. Use your head!"

"I doubt any of your friends are here."

"Still . . ." She asked the hostess for a booth in the back corner, beside the bathrooms.

We settled in, my mother sitting with her back to the entrance as an extra precaution. Then she handed me her cell phone.

"Can you erase my call to you in case Bǎbá looks? Now I just have to practice my story for what I did today. Or erase the tire tracks from the lawn."

"Or not drive over the lawn when you're backing out of the driveway."

She ignored me. "I don't even know what he would do if he knew I was here." She shuddered, and pity surged through me.

"But I'm *your* daughter too. You should get to decide for yourself whether or not you want a relationship with me, regardless of what he thinks."

She shook her head. I couldn't tell if it was because she couldn't comprehend what I was saying, or because she did want to make her own decisions but didn't know how to get there.

"Whether we have a relationship is up to *you*, Mei. Not me. We're disowning you to get you back on track. You cannot become Ying-Na. Not just for my sake but yours. That's no life to live."

"You don't even know what Ying-Na is doing. Everything you hear is a rumor. For all you know, she could be a neurosurgeon married to a billionaire tech god." *Or maybe she's struggling but happy*. I kept this thought to myself since my mother wouldn't understand the value of that life.

My all-knowing mǔqīn shook her head confidently. "No. I'm sure Ying-Na's still taking off her clothes for money. I just heard it from Mrs. Ahn yesterday. That's your future unless you come to your senses. Just try biology. Meet Eugene. Stop seeing Xing. How will you pay for college, food, a place to live? You need us."

I made a mental note to find Ying-Na, not just to prove my mother wrong, but also to get a glimpse of what post-disownment life was like. If she had survived, maybe I would too.

"You're trying to use money to control me. Forcing me to do what you want with threats isn't healthy. Can't we talk? Don't you want to know how I feel?"

"That's why I'm here." She fanned her flushed cheeks. "But I feel like I'm having an affair. This is so stressful. How does anyone else do this?"

I dug my nails into my palms. I closed my eyes, and when I spoke, my voice was serrated. "You feel like seeing me, your own daughter, is the same as cheating on your husband? This is so messed up. All of this. Your relationship with Bǎbá needs to change. You don't have to do everything he says. How do you feel when he orders you around? Don't you *want* to stand up for yourself?" I mimicked my father's booming voice, supposedly made deep from all the raw eggs he was forced to swallow growing up. "Old woman, fetch me my tea. Cook ten dishes for me to eat the second I come home, not too cold and not too hot."

My mother winced, her shoulders slumping so much her spine curved. "It's my place. That's how it is."

"Just because you were born with one more X chromosome than him?"

"When the daughter marries, she joins the male's family. She becomes theirs." Her monotone voice made her sound like a Stepford wife.

I shuddered. "People aren't property, not anymore. Are you expecting to pay a dowry when I get married?"

"Yes. Because your husband will be accepting the responsibility of having you."

"Because I'm such a burden."

"You will be if you're jobless and broke!" *Cluck*. "You're too young to understand all this."

I shook my head. "No, *you're* the naive one. You're in denial about your relationship. Bǎbá should treat you better—appreciate you, be nicer."

"He *is* nice to me! He's changed! Now after he yells at me, he tells me he's sorry."

I raised an eyebrow. "He says the word 'sorry'?"

"Well, no, but he shows me. He ends the silent treatment, then says something sweet, like how I'm not as bad of a cook as I used to be."

"That's not sweet."

"How would you know? You've never had a boyfriend."

I clenched my teeth, forcing my secret—Darren, or whatever we were right now, anyway—back inside. We needed to step back and reboot. Lu-suvius was bubbling ominously, and I didn't want to boil over before we could actually talk about anything substantial.

In the ensuing silence, the waiter approached.

"She'll have a side salad, extra vegetables," my mother ordered for me.

I slammed my menu shut. "I'd like a Coke and the meat lover's pizza, extra cheese." Meat lover's didn't even sound good to me, but it was the unhealthiest option I could think of.

My mother whipped out her credit card. "I'm paying. If you want a tip, she'll have water and the side salad."

"If you want to support freedom, Coke and pizza. I have money too." I pulled out my wallet. He didn't have to know there was only a five-dollar bill in there.

The poor waiter took a step back, looked between the two of us, then rushed off with a mumbled excuse, not even returning to bring bread—he sent someone else. I snatched a roll and dodged my mother's hand swat in one swift motion.

Cluck, cluck. How I hated that tongue.

"I risk everything to come see you, and you act like this? Have you not learned your lesson? Maybe I should leave."

"I'm just hungry. And it's not like I'm a fugitive. I'm your daughter."

"To Bǎbá, you're nobody. He changed our will. Yilong will get everything now."

The words brought tears to my eyes, but I blinked rapidly, refusing to let her see. "You have no kids left. What does that tell you about your parenting style? You raised us. If we're so terrible, aren't you to blame?"

My mother clutched her chest, signaling that I had hit the nail square on the head, straight into her heart.

I continued, hoping to break through before the opening closed again. "Xing and Esther are happy. Are you really going to be absent from your grandson's life because of something so outdated? They're married. It's done. Not to mention, you don't believe in divorces. And she's even giving you the grandson you wanted so bad! Isn't it time to move on? I don't think you even feel that strongly about all this. I think it's more Bǎbá."

I talked slower, wanting my words to sink in. "Mǎmá, ask yourself what *you* want. Bǎbá's way isn't the only option. You could have a say, and you *should*. You should get to decide your own opinions, your own actions."

My mother's face contorted as if she were tasting a lemon. Before, I would have backpedaled, pulled out the Mandarin to wipe the disapproval away, but now I merely sighed, then looked at her with empathy. "You need time, and that's okay. I'll be here when you're ready. I just hope we'll be on the same page some-day. Think about what I said. There isn't just one way to parent, one way to live. We all have options. *You* have options."

She shook her head as if shaking my ideas out. "There are no other options. Not with Bǎbá. There's just his way. Please, Mei, it's up to you now. Do what he wants so we can be a family again. He only wants the best for you. Win-win, right?"

"I believe he wants the best for me, but he doesn't know me well enough to know what that is."

My mother was silent. When her phone rang, she jumped, spilling the winter gear beside her onto the gross, sticky floor. "It has to be Bǎbá. No one else calls my cell phone. I have to get back. He doesn't want me here."

"When will it be what *you* want?"

Her muscles stiffened only for a second, but she heard me.

LATEST ON YING-NA THROUGH THE GRAPEVINE

Ying-Na had sex once and got herpes. Now she can't nab a rich husband to support her.

Even Ying-Na's jobless boyfriend who majored in art history dumped her because her eggs are getting old.

Ying-Na said if she could go back in time, she would not have sex, not drink, and be premed.

Ying-Na can only make money by demeaning herself for laughs.

CHAPTER 25

Future Mei 2.0

I sipped my Coke, which had absurdly cost five dollars. The flyer on my table at the comedy club read: CHRISTINE CHU, ONE NIGHT ONLY. LEAVE YOUR ANCESTORS AT HOME.

I had tracked down Ying-Na. It wasn't easy—she no longer went by Ying-Na; she was Christine now—but Xing knew someone who knew someone who was still friends with her. I was simultaneously excited and terrified to see future Mei 2.0.

An abstract picture of Ying-Na was artfully splashed across the flyer. Her features were blurred such that the focus was on her red, skintight *qípáo* and the slashes cut into the chest, stomach, and sides.

Slicing my *qípáo* or the goddamn sweaterdress would be so therapeutic, I thought. I wondered if Ying-Na had cut hers in anger or for the flyer.

I leaned back in my seat. Even though most of the chairs were filled, the club was so tiny there couldn't have been more than forty people. I appeared to be the only unaccompanied spectator, but for once I didn't feel alone. Part of the group, but separate enough to sit back and watch—a peaceful change from the recent norm.

The lights dimmed, and I sat up straighter. A male announcer in a collared shirt took the stage.

"Welcome, everyone, and please, give it up for the fabulous, hilarious, and ballsy Christeeeeen Chu!"

The way he dragged her name made me think, *She's the real deal!*

Amid the applause and whistles, Ying-Na clicked onto the stage in four-inch heels. Her slashed *qípáo* hugged her body perfectly, and the waist-length hair I remembered from childhood was lobbed into a stylish pixie. Her baby fat was gone and her body had developed curves, but the most striking difference was her confidence, which radiated from every pore.

She moseyed to the microphone and detached it with experienced hands, like it was a daily routine. Then she jutted a hip out. "So what's the deal with Panda Express?"

Pause. She relaxed her stance. "Just kidding. It's not going to be that kind of show."

She smiled at the audience in a way that made me feel like the grin was just for me. "Thanks for the warm welcome, everyone.

I knew you'd be a great crowd. I begged The Laugh Den for tonight's slot because my Chinese Farmer's Calendar told me that today would be a funny day for Chinese zodiac mice, which I am. I just wish it would also tell me when my period would actually come, and which cycles would be an uber-bitch." She pretended to flip through a calendar. "December nineteenth, female mice beware. Your ovaries will try to kill you today. Stay home from work no matter how uncomfortable your male boss is with menstrual cramps."

My man-laugh burst from my lips, louder than the rest of the audience, but I didn't care.

Ying-Na grasped the mic with both hands. "As most of you know, this is a pretty diverse show. Because there's just too much in Asian culture to make fun of." She smiled. "In all seriousness, I think we need more Asian comedians out there. But it makes sense why there aren't that many of us. Humor isn't valued. Every time I made a joke, my father would ask, 'How's that going to help you get a husband?' Because, of course, a docile, quiet, obedient woman is easier to marry off than a funny one full of personality.

"My tiger parents weren't proud of me, but nothing was worse than when I told them I wanted to be a stand-up comedian. They asked if I was being blackmailed, and if so, was it a Chinese single male willing to marry me?"

Pause. "Just kidding. Their actual response was to throw me on the street with one box of *bāo*s to hold me over until I came to my senses. Those *bāo*s lasted me until I found a minimum-wage job and this club. Contrary to what the Asian grapevine is saying, I did not also find herpes or a boyfriend who majored in English. Yes, those are equally bad in my parents' eyes."

She strolled as she spoke, as if she were speaking about buying groceries, not the worst day of her life (the way I still viewed my disownment day).

"I turned into the local Chinese community's cautionary tale: whore, spinster, homeless, whatever that Asian parent's biggest fear was. Since I don't go by my Chinese name, I often hear these stories from other Asians who don't realize they're telling me about my own sexcapades and failures. Did you know I was giving head in the public-school bathroom yesterday at the same time I was peddling heroin on the other side of town? And all because I tried one sip of alcohol."

A link formed between Ying-Na and me. We weren't all that different, using humor as a coping mechanism.

"The only thing these rumors got right was that I don't give a shit about dishonoring my ancestors. But I see it as being honest. And so far I haven't been struck down, although I guess getting struck with a hundred cases of proverbial STDs might count."

As I bent forward in laughter, my eyes locked with my neighbor, an Asian girl approximately my age. We nodded to each other as we snickered, bonded by a shared sense of humor.

Ying-Na turned and strolled in the other direction.

"So I went on this date the other day. To my mother's dismay, he wasn't Taiwanese, but he did have yellow fever, which is the only way I get dates now. I guess most men are turned off by my hooded eyes, snub nose, and pan face." She circled her face with her hand. "It's like I was the tragic victim of God's whack-a-mole game. I didn't have a chance being a hundred percent Chinese, the one race that selected on obedience, not looks."

While the audience laughed, my girl crush on her grew. I hoped my confidence could be as high as hers one day.

"So anyways, this guy, my date, tells me he's going to give me an education in Chinese food because he's a quote-on-quote 'expert.'" She made air quotes with her free hand. "Well, of course, he took me for chow mein, General Gao's chicken, and moo goo gai pan."

No one else laughed, which amplified mine. I stopped short, embarrassed. Wait, why weren't the other Asians laughing? Were their families not as judgy as *Lu Pàng* about Americanized Chinese food?

Ying-Na gestured to me. "Thank you, *jiějie*! My Asian sister!"

She smiled, and I wondered if she could make out my features from stage. Would she remember me?

"For the rest of you, that's not Chinese food. And for the record, I'm also not related to every other Chu out there."

She sipped her water as we laughed. I thought of how in high school, everyone had assumed Ping Lu was my cousin, but no one assumed Ally Jones and Mike Jones were related.

"So halfway through our date, this guy tells me he has ESP. He thought he was part of a government experiment." She paused to push her lips into a straight line and stared at us with wary eyes. "This is a true story, guys. He told me that he exclusively dates Asians because we're the only ones who can understand since we also have superpowers—math, obedience, and DDR, of course. Naturally, I stayed. I only have two check boxes on my list." She held up one finger. "Not chosen by my mother and"—another finger—"doesn't like my mother."

Pause. "Just kidding. I actually chucked five rolls at him, then yelled, 'Use your fucking ESP' when they all hit him in the face."

The audience cheered. Some whistled, some *woo*-ed, and others chanted "Chu! Chu! Chu!" which blended with the *woo*s concordantly.

"Now, after my date with Racist Man, Boston's newest superhero, my checklist also includes no yellow fever . . . which means I will be single forever. Unless I let my mother help me. The last time she tried to set me up, she brought three brothers over and told me to choose one. I started haggling with them, thinking she'd be impressed by how much I'd learned during our last trip to China."

In a Chinese accent, she mimicked, "Two dollar, how about two dollar for you to leave me alone?"

She reverted to her American accent. "By the end of it, I was out fifty bucks and my mother was probably out another hundred bucks just to get them there in the first place."

She smiled while the crowd chuckled. The mic still in her hand, she grabbed the stand with the other and froze for a second, thinking.

"You know, that's a lucrative business there—matchmaker for the mothers, bouncer for the daughters. Anyone out there interested in investing?"

She placed a hand over her eyes to shield the spotlight and looked left, then right. Several hands went in the air.

"Two dollar?" she asked in a Chinese accent. "Two dollar going once, twice . . ."

Everyone roared. I glanced around at the bodies rocking back and forth, the knee slaps, the clapping hands. Closing my eyes, I focused on the laughter wrapping around me, basking in Ying-Na's hard-earned success. She hadn't just survived; she was on her way up, and all by herself.

"So for those of you who aren't familiar—and to those, I ask, what Big Dig rubble have you been living under?—boys are the desired babies in Chinese culture. When my brother was born, my parents snapped hundreds of photos of him daily, get this—with no pants. They got their firstborn son, and damn it, the world had better see the teeny-tiny proof. Good thing they didn't have Instagram in those days. His penis would have been immortalized, the Confucius of penises."

Ying-Na's aura was on fire. She was so clearly meant for this. If only her parents could see her now. If only the entire community could see her. Although then she'd lose her source material. I chuckled, thinking about how she had won. She had turned their punishment into her success, the ultimate revenge.

"Have any of you noticed how a lot of Chinese proverbs revolve around bathroom humor? Anyone got one for me?" Ying-Na held a hand up to her ear and waved encouragement with the other.

"*Búyào tuō kùzi fàngpì!*" I bellowed.

Ying-Na clapped her hands, the sound amplified by the mic.

"Yes, thank you! Don't take your pants off to fart!"

The audience laughed. How amusing—the idiom was hilarious enough to be a joke in itself.

"*Chī shǐ dōu jiē bú dào rè de!*" an elderly woman yelled from the front row to a wave of groans.

Ying-Na snapped her head back in shock. "You're so slow you can't even eat the shit while it's still hot," she translated. "Damn, that's extreme, even for stinky tofu lovers!"

She stopped gesturing to the audience and grasped the mic with both hands again. "Along those lines is one of my favorites: *Gǒu gǎibùliǎo chī shǐ.* It's kind of like 'a leopard can't change its spots,' but directly translated, it's 'a dog can't help but eat shit.'"

My nose burned. That had been Nǎinai's second favorite phrase. Who would've guessed dog shit could stir up such nostalgia? It was so ludicrous I laughed through the grief. Best medicine, better than acupuncture or the cow's hoof.

"Why did they have to go with something so crude?" Ying-Na continued. "There were so many other options. . . . A panda is still a bear beneath the cuddliness, scallion pancakes will always give you diarrhea, a woman can't run in her *qípáo*. . . ." She flashed the slit up her left side, revealing her leg, Angelina Jolie–style. "Unless she's an American girl who knows how to use a knife!"

She raised her voice to shout over the thundering crowd. "You've all been so wonderful. Thank you so much! Remember, none of this was racist because I have Asian immunity! *Zàijiàn!*"

The spectators whistled, screamed, and stomped their good-byes. Their enthusiasm mirrored mine, and even though I barely knew her, I felt proud of Ying-Na. She wasn't the cautionary tale; she was the hero. The dreamer. The fighter.

As the audience stretched before the next act, I downed my Coke, then collected my things. Should I try to get backstage? I hadn't realized Ying-Na was so popular. Now she felt like a celebrity, not an old friend.

A club employee tapped me on the shoulder. "Miss Chu would like to extend an invitation backstage."

I followed his broad bouncer shoulders, weaving through chairs and feeling like a bit of a celebrity myself. The dressing room was merely a coat closet with a stained armchair on one side and a stool on the other. A smudged mirror leaned against the wall, threatening to topple at any moment.

Ying-Na's face brightened when she saw me. I stuck a hand out, but she pulled me into a hug. Her sweaty skin stuck to mine, and I held back a cringe.

Now that we were in close proximity, memories flashed through my mind. Ying-Na, age six, yelling out her mother's mahjong hand to the rest of the table. Everyone had been amused except her mother, which now, in retrospect, had probably been her motivation—getting some laughs, but more important, annoying her ultra-tiger mom. Ying-Na, age eight, grabbing the stuffed animals to put on a show for the younger kids, cartoon voices and jokes galore. I remembered keeling over with laughter, my stomach hurting, just like tonight. Ying-Na, age twelve, reading us kissing scenes from her romance book, telling us she'd teach us how to kiss since our Chinese mothers never would. She had grabbed stacks of oranges for us to French with. I had eaten mine.

I pulled away first. "Ying-Na, I mean Christine, I can't believe you remember me!"

"Of course! And I still have an ear to one last grapevine leaf. I heard about what happened with your parents. I'm really sorry."

I sat on the armchair, folding one leg beneath me. "Figures. Disownments usually make the mahjong-table gossip."

Ying-Na laughed, and I filled with pride that *I* had made *her* laugh.

She sat on the stool, able to cross her legs because of the slits running up to her thigh. "You're becoming quite the tale yourself. Kicked out of MIT, possibly pregnant, dating a bad biker dude"—I snorted at that one—"and the kicker, that you had Romeo-and-Juliet-ed yourself into the Charles River."

"Jesus, I had no idea."

"Don't worry. You're immortalized now, just like Ying-Kan's penis. And me."

I chuckled. "What an honor."

"I tried to spread a rumor like, 'Ying-Na is a stand-up comedian, and she's actually funny. Go watch her!' But nobody bit on that one."

I laughed. "Your show was fantastic. And I love the slashed *qípáo*—brilliant."

"Slashing down nonsensical traditions one at a time." She flashed her stage-worthy smile.

"I'm really happy you're doing so well. You're a celebrity!"

She sighed. "Not really. Cultural humor is tough. A lot of

Asians don't like it if your material doesn't match their experience, and non-Asians sometimes just don't get the joke. I'm lucky to have enough fans in the area to fill this tiny club—and don't get me wrong, I'm thankful for that—but I'm still struggling. This road isn't easy, but at least it's getting better. The beginning was the hardest. I wasn't used to being alone. . . . I was busing tables . . . working odd jobs here and there. I knew my parents would be so ashamed that I was washing dishes, but after about three months, I stopped caring. Actually, they'd still be ashamed of me now, doing this, but . . . " She shrugged and meant it.

"God, I'm so glad I'm past that," she continued. "Now I have regular work with an improv group, I teach some comedy classes at the local community college, and I bartend at this club the nights I'm not onstage. The checks are infrequent and pretty small, but it's enough to get me by. I don't need much—just a roof over my head and distance from my mother."

"I'm sorry it's been so hard for you."

She gave me an appreciative nod. "Thanks. You know, it's cliché, but you really can't put a price on happiness. And don't worry—it won't be as hard for you as it was for me. I know you have plenty of options—more than I did. You were always the one my mother compared me to. . . ." She mimicked her mother's heavy accent. "Mei got straight As last semester. Mei is in all honors classes. Mei poops golden nuggets."

I cringed. I remembered Mrs. Chu and her stern face with perpetually pursed lips, like she was always constipated. Out of all my mother's friends, she had scared me the most. "Sorry about that."

Ying-Na shook her head. "It's not your fault. I will never be good enough for her. It took me nineteen years to realize that, but once I did, things got easier. It sucks—I mean, she's my *mother*—but once I stopped trying so damn hard to be someone else, I started to enjoy life. Being alone was hard, but better than feeling shitty about myself all the time."

"That's the eventual goal—to enjoy life."

Her face turned down with empathy. "Do you need anything? A job?"

"I actually have one. I'm teaching dance, just two classes for now, but I'm hoping to add on a few." It wasn't enough, but that plus the financial aid that would kick in when I turned eighteen would hopefully get me through.

Ying-Na clapped her hands together in excitement. "I'm totally there! Save a spot for me!"

"Maybe I can fill my class with sympathetic Asians who want to get me off the streets."

She laughed. "I'll spread the word. We Asian-Americans need to stick together. No one else understands the shit we have to deal with."

She pulled me into another hug. She felt like my *jiějie*. A dirtier, foul-mouthed older sister.

VOICEMAIL FROM MY MOTHER

Mei? It's me. Can we meet at Bertucci's? We need to talk.

CHAPTER 26

Affair 2.0

My mother stared at the scratches on the Bertucci's table. There hadn't been any sleuthing for friends today. From the moment I saw her in the parking lot, I knew something was different. She radiated sadness. I drummed my fingers on my lap, anxious for her to tell me what was going on.

She took a breath. "Bǎbá saw on the GPS that I went to Bertucci's. We fought."

Meaning he yelled and you cowered in a corner, I thought to myself.

"I fought back." My mother's strong voice shocked me as much as her words. "I stood up for you, Mei. I told him I still wanted a relationship with you. I had to. I didn't want things to end like with you and Nǎinai. With Xing and Nǎinai. And now"—she took another breath—"Bǎbá's not talking to me anymore."

"Thank you, Māmá." My voice came out a husky whisper. I sniffed, very unladylike, but she didn't reprimand me. She was busy muffling her own sniffle.

"Mei, I raised you how I was raised because I thought it was the only way. But your words the last time we met"—she patted the spot over her heart—"I heard them. I ask myself, what if things could be different? I never considered it before. Then I thought about my childhood. I hated when my mǎmá—your wàipó—gave away my toys. Or told the neighbor her daughter was better than me. Or scolded me no matter how good of a grade I got. It was what every parent did so I didn't question it, but I hated it. Of course you hated it too. We believe a stern hand is the way to produce moral, hardworking children, but . . ." Her voice trailed off.

Now I couldn't keep the tears from falling, but for once I didn't try to hide them. "Thank you for saying that. I know this hasn't been easy for you. Any of it. As a child, I could tell you didn't want me. And now you standing up for me . . . well, I feel like you want me."

She looked up, her eyes transparent for the first time. "Of course I want you. Maybe I wasn't . . . ready . . . when you were little. I'm sorry you could tell. You weren't planned. Actually, I found out I was pregnant with you at my appointment to get my tubes tied. Counting doesn't work, even if your period is regular."

I wanted her to add, *just kidding*, but I knew she was telling the truth. It explained why Xing and I were nine years apart in age.

Deep down I had known that I was an accident, but I could never admit it to myself. I couldn't handle my parents not wanting me before *and* after my birth.

"I want you now." She placed a hand on mine, but as soon as contact was made, she lifted and pulled back. "Xing was such a handful—he ran off at airports, colored the carpet with marker—and I had him before I was ready."

She took a few moments to collect herself, then locked eyes with me. "Your yéye was dying when Bǎbá and I met. Emphysema. He only had a few months. Bǎbá was the only other Taiwanese student in Missouri, where we were in graduate school, and I was already twenty-seven. Past marrying age. My eggs were going to be dinosaurs soon!"

I groaned but let her continue.

"We married after three months. I didn't love him. How could I when I barely knew him? I hoped the feelings would grow with time. But I didn't know he couldn't communicate. That he was so angry underneath."

Her eyes left my face, as if she couldn't look at my reaction as she told me the rest of her story. "As you already know, Bǎbá is the eldest and only son. He had to carry on the family name. The moment we married, Yéye demanded a grandson. If it was a girl, Yéye didn't want her. Girls don't matter. For Yéye's generation, only the boys count. He used to say he has three siblings when he actually had eleven—three brothers and eight sisters."

I knew the culture was largely to blame, but I couldn't help loathing him a little. "Well, good job, you had a boy."

"I ate nothing but tofu, lettuce, and oats for a month."

"What does that have to do with anything?" I felt like we were speaking different languages.

"Those foods increase your body's pH, which helps you have a boy." The usual lecture quality to her tone was missing. In its place, regret. "As soon as Xing was born, Năinai and Yilong took him from me to Taiwan. To Yéye."

I thought of the pile of photographs in the back of the hall closet that I had stumbled upon when I was too young to understand. Hundreds of photos of Xing's first year of life—all of him with Năinai, Yilong, and Yéye. The only photo of Xing with my mother from that year was in the hospital, right after he was born. I had never guessed the truth—it was too preposterous, too horrifying. But now, hearing it straight from my mother, it made complete sense, and I wondered why I had given my dad's family so much credit that they had never earned.

Her voice became stripped, raw, breaking between sentences. "I didn't see Xing for the first year of his life. I couldn't afford to go with him. I was still in school. We were living in a trailer home. No health or auto insurance."

Part of me wanted to say, *How could you let them take him?* But I knew there was no way I could understand what it had been like for her. And hadn't I also felt trapped? Hadn't I done things I normally wouldn't have because I felt I had no choice?

She dabbed at her eyes with a napkin. "When Yéye died, they sent Xing back. Suddenly I had to figure out how to become a mother on my own. Băbá didn't help at all. I became bitter at everyone. I couldn't take it out on Năinai or Băbá, so I took it out on Xing. Then, when you came along, I took it out on you. I'm so sorry."

I felt like I had been dragged under by a wave, overwhelming me in the moment but washing me clean in the process. For the first time, she had been honest. And for the first time, I saw her. "I'm sorry it was so terrible for you."

She planted her palms on the table and closed her eyes in shame. "I want to redo it. I want to shove you back in"—she pointed to her womb—"and start over. When I think about all the things I did to you that I hated when I was in your *xiézi*, I feel so sorry. I regret it. Please forgive me."

She reached for my wrist but stopped before contact, her hand hovering. I grabbed it and squeezed.

"I'm trying to make Băbá come around," she said. "He's just so difficult. But he needs me. He can't cook or clean or do laundry. I have some leverage. One time he brushed his teeth with Preparation H, then blamed me! Can you believe it? He said I shouldn't have left it so close to his toothbrush."

"Yeah, Mămá, how could you do that to him?" I let out a laugh, mostly from picturing my father brushing with hemorrhoid cream.

She joined in, and we laughed together for a few minutes. A first.

She stared at our hands, still adjoined. "I'm sorry it took me so long to see, especially when I suffered in similar ways. I *do* want you to be happy. That's all I've ever wanted for you. But now I see—your idea of happiness doesn't match mine. Mei, I want more for you than me. I always have."

"Are you not happy?" I leaned forward, trying to read her eyes.

She ignored my question. "I had a cousin whose parents wanted him to be a doctor. He went to medical school, of course—no one would even think about disobeying their parents back then—but he hated it. On his medical school graduation day, he handed his parents his diploma, then drowned himself in the river."

I gasped and pulled my hand from hers. How could she have pushed me so much after witnessing that?

"He'd always been in the back of my mind. Haunting me. I was hoping maybe when you tried medicine, you would fall in love with it. . . ." She grabbed my hand again. "But I don't want to risk your happiness. If you say you won't like it, I trust you."

My response was a breath of a whisper, quieted by my welling emotions. "Thank you, Mămá."

"I trust you to decide your own major and your own track"—she paused—"as long as you don't become an artist or musician." Her curved lip implied she was joking.

My mother! Cracking a joke! I grinned, a welcome reaction instead of the usual frustration.

She slid a red envelope across the table, shielding it with her hand as if it were contraband. "Take it. It's all I could scrape away for now, but I'll try to get you more. I'll do what I can. I don't want you to worry."

I accepted the tiny red packet of love with a shaky hand. "So you want to see me again?"

"Of course." No hesitation.

Outside the restaurant, I wrapped my arms around her. Beneath her winter layers, she relaxed, and then finally, what I had been waiting for, for far too long, she reciprocated. Two petite arms wrapped around my back. Squeezing. Because she wanted me.

VOICEMAIL FROM MY MOTHER

I watched some of the videos you sent of Ying-Na. I didn't laugh, but at least she's not taking off her clothes. The audience seems to like her. Hunh. Who would've guessed?

CHAPTER 27

Hacking

"Are we doing this or what?" Nic jumped up and down and threw a few jabs. "Get pumped, Mei!"

"I am, I am," I said in my best tough-chick voice. I wasn't used to being up in the middle of the night, and Nic was right—I needed to circulate some adrenaline. Rocking back and forth on the balls of my feet, I returned a few punches.

"More! Not because we're going to have fun, but because it'll be really fucking cold and we need to get our blood pumping."

I burst into laughter.

"That'll work too, I guess." She grabbed my chin. "Good, your cheeks are flushed." She circled a finger in the air like a lasso. "Let's move out!"

Nic and I were dressed like cat burglars—matching black turtlenecks, spandex leggings, and beanies. Our outfits weren't all that visible beneath our coats, scarves, and mittens, but *we* knew what was underneath.

We swept through the empty hallways quickly, communicating with only hand gestures and looks.

It's a roommate thing, I thought excitedly.

We snuck past the lone security guard whistling down the corridor, then crept through Barker Library, up the endless staircase, and past the locked door Nic picked with ease. Once we were on the roof, I let out the breath I didn't know I'd been holding. It fogged immediately as the wind cut through my down coat, numbing my body.

Nicolette leaned a ladder against the little dome's platform and motioned for me to go first. No six-foot-something companion to help me up this time. As I climbed, my shivers threatened to topple us. If it weren't for Nic beneath me, pushing me on (sometimes literally head-butting my *pìgu*), I might have turned back.

On top of the little dome, I tried to take a moment to reminisce about Darren and my first kiss, but thinking about him poked at the remorseful bubble that had been floating around inside me since the night of the wedding. At least it motivated me to push through the cold. Grand gestures weren't normally my thing, but turns out, trying to find the right words to express yourself was really freaking hard.

I turned on my flashlight with shivering fingers.

"Okay, quickly now," Nic shouted over the wind. "Work fast so we can get the fuck outta here."

I gritted my chattering teeth and we moved swiftly and in sync, just as we had practiced in our room. Because of the wintry weather, we had opted for a simple design, just a few sheets of cardboard that were easy to carry and required minimal assembly.

The final piece. We were almost there. Just had to tie down one last corner . . . and . . . oops. I lost my footing.

The wind whistled past my ears as I careened down the side of the dome. I clutched the rope in my hands. My lifeline. My feet smacked against the limestone repeatedly. I gripped the rope until my hands hurt. A burst of pain exploded in my leg. Finally, the line went taut and I was jolted to a stop. My arms burned at the resulting tug, but it was nothing compared to what I felt in my thigh.

I bit my lip to keep from screaming—I knew it would be a five-hundred-dollar fine if we were caught up here. Nic tied off the last bit of rope, finishing our hack, then helped me inside.

As we huddled for warmth, she shined the flashlight onto my leg. My pants were torn, my Hello Kitty underwear on full display, and a trickle of bright red blood dribbled from my inner thigh down to my knee. The sight flipped my stomach upside down.

"Shit," Nic said between chattering teeth. "You must've caught a jagged edge of limestone on your way down."

I used my hand to shield the blood from view. "If you make a joke about my underwear, I swear to God I'll find a way to grow real claws."

Nic forced a smile. No laugh. Crap. It must be pretty bad.

"Let's get you downstairs before the numbness from the cold wears off," she said in a tight voice.

"Great, so we'll just leave my DNA all over the crime scene."

"We didn't commit any crimes. . . . Well, not really. And it's supposed to snow later anyway."

I looped an arm around her shoulder. Her wavy hair was frozen with wayward icicles, and they snapped at my biceps like Medusa's snakes.

"Mei, I think you need stitches. I'll call Student Health. EMS can give us a ride."

"No! They're the worst! They're going to do more harm than good!"

Nic rolled her eyes. "They can't be so incompetent they don't know how to give you stitches."

"Oh yes they can! Trust me."

"Well, where else are we supposed to go? You don't want to just bleed all over our room all night, do you?"

Annoyingly, she had a point. I wanted to ask her if she would come with me, but her tight grip around my waist answered my question. I reluctantly agreed.

Ten minutes later, at the entrance of the Infinite, flashing lights appeared. The student EMT exploded from the back of the ambulance like a firefighter. I shrank down in embarrassment. No burning building or children to save—just sad little ol' me with a scratch on my thigh. I grabbed the flap of my torn pants to cover Hello Kitty.

When the EMT was close enough for me to make out his features, my jaw dropped. "You?"

"At least you have underwear on this time?" He forced a laugh. "Glad your rash cleared up."

I wanted to disappear.

Nic stared at me with wide eyes. "What haven't you told me?"

"Oh my God, it's not what you think. He walked in on me in the bathroom once."

He leaned down toward my crotch. "Let me take a look."

I inched backward, and a sharp pain shot down my leg. I winced. The numbness was wearing off.

He looked at me warily. "I've already seen you naked. And I'm a medical professional."

I sighed and gave in, dropping the flap and flashing Hello Kitty.

He pushed the fabric aside and blotted with gauze. "So how did this happen?"

"Dancing," I said at the same time Nic said, "Rock climbing."

He raised an eyebrow at us. "It could be medically relevant. What were you doing?"

"She was trying to dance while on the rock wall, okay? You got to peek at her goods again, you perv, so congratulations. Now can you get her to the *real* medical professional?"

He blushed as red as my old rash (and maybe I did too).

We loaded into the ambulance and tore away, sirens screaming. I felt like they were announcing to the world, *Here's the biggest baby! She can't handle a little blood!*

At MIT Medical, we settled into the waiting room. One student beside me held a bag of frozen peas against his ankle while another held a carton of Ben and Jerry's to his temple.

My gaze met theirs and the ice-cream man said, "Chair surfing."

Nicolette nodded in approval.

"We've been here for three hours," Pea Boy added.

Nic looked right, then left, and seeing no employees, she darted down the Urgent Care corridor. I yelled after her, but she either didn't hear or didn't care. Probably the latter.

Twenty minutes later she returned with a wheelchair and carted me off to an examination room, where Dr. Chang was waiting.

With a sour look on her face, Dr. Chang took a deliberate step to distance herself from Nicolette.

"I'll wait for you outside," Nic said with an eye roll. As she walked away, I heard her mumble, "Jesus, and she knows I don't fucking have chlamydia anymore."

Thank. God.

Dr. Chang prepared the anesthetic for the stitches that she had determined were needed. Trying to distract myself from the twenty-two gauge that would be in my leg soon, I asked her, "Fish anything out of the toilet lately?"

To my surprise, she laughed, which shocked me so much I didn't even feel the pinch.

• • •

Around ten the next morning, I fought my exhaustion and dragged myself to 77 Mass Ave. Nic's friend had to hack—

traditional definition—to get Darren's schedule, and this was the only time he'd be crossing in front of the little dome.

The ground was dusted with a white layer that crunched beneath my UGG knockoffs. Luckily, there wasn't enough snow to cover our hack, but there *was* enough to cover my DNA on the roof, as Nic had promised.

The passersby pointed at what Nic and I had added atop the dome's apex, but I barely registered their reactions. Instead, I was scanning for that spiky hair that made my heart beat faster.

I stamped my feet to stay warm. Then, finally, the jagged outline. The class-to-class traffic thinned, leaving just the two of us amid a couple stragglers. When the recognition dawned on his face, he stopped in his tracks, staring with so much intensity he didn't notice me sidling up.

"Think there's whipped cream in there?" I asked.

He tore his eyes away from the three-dimensional hot chocolate cup strapped to the dome. The words "thinking of you" were scrawled across in red script. I had considered writing it in Japanese, but Darren wouldn't have understood and according to Google Translate, it was twice as long. Beside the words was a picture of two nuts—I think they were almonds? Pecans? Whatever. I had printed the first non-X-rated image I'd found online.

He gaped at me with his mouth slightly open. "I can't believe you did that."

"It cost me a chunk of leg, too." I gestured to my right thigh, thick with bandages beneath my sweatpants.

"Are you okay?"

I nodded, then took one of his hands in mine. "I'm sorry about what I said after the wedding. The thought of you having to jump through hoops for me was just . . . I care about you too much. But being apart made me realize it didn't make sense to throw away what we have because of other people and beliefs I don't agree with." *I'm ready to fight for you*, I thought but couldn't say aloud. I hoped the hack said it for me.

He took a step closer. "Is this your way of asking me to be your boyfriend?"

"Um, sure."

He stuck his lower lip out. (I wanted to kiss it so bad.) "Not too emphatic there. That's it? No speech?"

"All right, fine, but no laughs because it's too cheesy or whatever." I closed the gap between us. "I like you, Darren, Lord Pecan, Sir Almond, and I want to date you, and just you. Like normal MIT students. I want to awkwardly hold your hand, share bowls of liquid nitrogen ice cream, and drop metallic sodium in the Charles."

His face was inches from mine, and when he spoke, I felt his warm breath on my cheek. "I like you too. And I think there's plenty more hot chocolate in our future."

His lips fell on mine hungrily, the sudden heat made more intense by its contrast to the cold.

Gone was the lost, lonely girl who had looked at her pale, blond classmates and wished she weren't so different. Who had recited "just is frog" instead of "justice for all" to a flag for three years because she didn't know the Pledge of Allegiance and was too scared to ask.

For once, I was at peace.

• • •

I swirled across the linoleum floor in a series of turns, leaps, and waltzes, my shadow dancing on the wall with me, brought to life by the myriad of burning candles lining the perimeter. My gash was still tender, but nothing could keep me from Mr. Porter. A Chinese jazz piece sang from my phone—*dízi*, *pípa*, and stringed instruments mixing into a lovely, smooth blend. At the crescendo, I flitted across the floor in a chain of *tour en l'airs*—airborne spins—timed to each flute trill.

I didn't hear Darren come in, but I sensed his presence when I landed, coming out of my turns into a sweeping pose. His shadow was tall and still, as if he were enraptured by my movement. I pushed away the underlying awkwardness and told myself I wasn't showing off; I was letting him in.

I reentered the music and lost myself in my favorite across-the-floor combination: *tombé-pas de bourrée-glissade-changement*. As I glided across the room, my arms and legs brushing and kicking, I finally snuck a peek at him. His face glowed in the candlelight, illuminating the wonderment and understanding in his eyes.

Yes, he spoke dance.

I *bourréed* to him on my tiptoes, arms outstretched. He took my hands, hesitantly, clearly more used to watching than dancing. I shepherded him to the center of the room, then gently guided his upper body into proper ballroom frame. Without speaking, I showed him a basic step-ball-change. After a few missteps, he caught on, and I led him around the room.

When the music lulled, I dragged him to a stop, spinning into his arms and landing with my lips on his.

No words needed.

VOICEMAIL FROM MY MOTHER

Mei? <pause> I'm sorry. I tried, but Bǎbá won't be joining us this weekend. <pause> Maybe next time. <pause> Don't give up.

CHAPTER 28

May

6 MONTHS LATER

Nicolette plucked a Taboo word from the bowl, then delivered her hint with confidence. "It's the opposite of integration."

She had dragged me, literally, almost pulling my arm out of its socket, to the common room to "see if there was anyone on our floor worth our time."

"Differentiation!" I yelled in unison with my teammates, three sophomores whom I'd nodded *hello* to all year but hadn't learned their names until thirty minutes ago.

Valerie huffed. "That was too easy."

Every time she spoke, I wanted to throw my shoe at her. I took some satisfaction in the fact that she hadn't been able to meet my eye once. I kept her cheesy secret in my back pocket, and it inched toward daylight with every snide comment.

Nic stuck a hand on her hip. "No, not differentiation. The opposite of *integration*."

"I spoke too soon," Valerie said. Another inch.

Everyone including me was dumbfounded. It was a mathematical definition: The opposite of finding the derivative of a function (differentiation) was to integrate it (integration).

Valerie thrust the beeping stopwatch into the air. "Time's up!"

Nicolette wadded the paper and flicked the tiny ball across the room toward Valerie. "Segregation. The opposite of integration is segregation."

After a five-second delay, everyone burst out laughing. I couldn't help a chuckle either. MIT had shut off the right side of my brain except for the sliver I used for dance.

Valerie's laugh was especially loud. (No surprise there.) "What high school did you go to, Nicolette? You're gonna be our Course Eleven"—urban planning—"burnout, aren't you? The rest of us are *real* MIT students. Of course we were only going to think of math."

Nicolette beat me to the punch. "Suck my beaver, Valerie."

Even though Nic didn't need me to, I added, "I wouldn't be so quick to throw the first stone if I were you." Valerie squirmed, just as planned.

"Oh my God, Mei, what do you know?" Nicolette asked.

Instead of answering her (or telling Valerie that I haven't eaten cheese in months), I waved my hand. "Come on, Nic, we don't need this."

In the hallway, Nicolette grabbed my elbow. "Spill it!"

I shook my head as if I could shake the memory away. "It's not my place to tell."

"But we're roomies! C'mon, Hello Kitty, pleeease! I'm so embarrassed, and this would make me feel soooo much better." She threw a hand over her heart dramatically.

I rolled my eyes at her exaggerated pout. "You're not fooling anyone."

"You're no fun at all." She pulled her lip back in and crossed her arms over her chest—a stance that would've intimidated me in the past but now made me laugh.

"At least you can rest assured I won't be spilling your secrets to the floor the first time you piss me off."

Nicolette's fists shifted to her hips. "I should've taken a picture of you with your clown makeup on."

I swatted her arm and we laughed.

As we made our way back to our room, I asked, "Hey, I've been wondering . . . what would you have called your ex-roommate if her name had been Gwendolyn?"

"Chatty Patty," Nic answered without missing a beat.

I should have known.

• • •

I knocked on Xing and Esther's door, a bouquet of flowers in one hand and a stuffed Doraemon in the other for the new baby.

Angry staccato footsteps approached, and the door was flung open with exasperation. Esther's mother wasn't surprised to see me, but I did a double take.

Xing had told me in private that they had kept the pregnancy a secret to keep the Wongs from knowing they had—gasp—slept together (probably many, many times) before marriage. They'd worried that Mrs. Wong would make them elope immediately, preventing Esther from having the wedding she wanted. Because, you know, it was all about the *miànzi* and not losing face in front of friends.

I greeted Mrs. Wong enthusiastically, offering congratulations. She merely gave me a cold stare before marching off, her flyaway hairs dancing and drawing attention to her lopsided bun.

She was still such a question mark to me. Super chill about some things, as Xing had said, but extreme about others. I'd since labeled her a wild card and tucked her away, unfiled.

I closed the door behind me and hastened up two flights of stairs to the nursery, following my nose as well as Mrs. Wong. It smelled like baby—diaper wipes and talcum powder with a hint of poop.

Xing was too busy cooing to his mini-me to notice my entrance. I put the presents in a corner, then hovered awkwardly before clearing my throat. When he finally noticed me, a megawatt smile took over his face, and he bounced over with his *bǎobèi* cradled in his arms.

I waved at the baby even though he was asleep. His short mop of hair stuck straight up, and his chubby, rosy cheeks were so large they took up most of his face. And, ah, lucky him—he had inherited that blessed and cursed Lu nose.

His eyes flapped open suddenly, and I let out a gasp, simultaneously fascinated and terrified by the tiny bundle of responsibility.

Xing extended his arms slightly, though it seemed to pain him to do so, not physically but emotionally. "Do you want to hold him?"

"Oh, no, that's okay," I sputtered, shaking my head and waving my hand.

Xing placed Jonathan in my arms anyway, and my elbows bent into awkward angles as I tried to support every part of him. Sweat pooled in my pits, but so far he was still alive.

Then he came to life, squirming with little baby jerks. I tightened every muscle, trying to keep him from popping out of my arms. "Okay. Okay. I think you should take him back now."

Once Jonathan was safely returned to Xing's waiting arms, I retreated to the corner, from where I asked, "So Esther's mom obviously knows. How'd all that play out?"

"We told her after the wedding. Since we were already married, it wasn't as big of a deal, and once Jonathan came, it wasn't a thing at all."

Well, that was simple. Guess that was the "chill" part coming through. My mom, on the other hand, was still going on about how of *course* Xing and Esther had been having "the sex" since (1) they had been living together (the horror!) and (2) reproductive issues = lower chance of pregnancy = more sex (and yes, she used actual equal signs in conversation).

I ignored my inkling of jealousy (I was so tired of hearing "the sex" come out of my mother's mouth) and asked, "Where's Esther? How's she doing?"

Xing sighed. "Oh, she's fine. She's, uh, doing the *zuò yuèzi* thing."

I widened my eyes until they felt dry from the air. "The sitting month? She hasn't showered since giving birth?"

Ugh, their bedroom must smell disgusting. I had thought the ancient Chinese postpartum tradition had died away, but I guess I shouldn't have been surprised given that my own mother carried a cow's hoof comb in her purse.

If Esther was doing the sitting month, then Mrs. Wong's stern look at the door was explained (though not justified) since visitors were not allowed.

Xing answered the question in my head without my asking. "*Yuèzi* was her mom's idea, but she agreed to it because she thought she'd be pampered for a month. Turns out, it sucks pretty bad, and her mother is so strict it's ridiculous. Esther didn't know she'd be bedridden."

As if on cue, raised voices trickled down the hallway. Xing winced, and exhaustion lined his face, overshadowing the joy.

"Come on," he mumbled, and we bounced to the master bedroom.

Esther was sitting in bed, unwrapping a long, dirty cloth from her abdomen while her mother tried to simultaneously rewind it. If I hadn't known better, it would have looked like attempted murder.

Esther threw the cloth aside—a third of it still constricting her—and screeched, "Mǎmá! Stop it! No one in America does these things and they're all fine!"

Even though it was sixty degrees outside, Mrs. Wong raised the down comforter and covered her daughter up to the chin. She spoke in Chinese with a Kaohsiung accent.

"American and Chinese bodies are different. Put the bandage back on—it's the only way to flatten your belly. Do you want to be flabby the rest of your life? And do you want to lose your teeth in the future? The baby sucks your calcium out while in the womb. Didn't you learn that in dental school? Your yin and yang are unbalanced. If you don't restore it, you'll have joint problems and frequent illnesses in the future."

"That's not scientifically correct! And I'm disgusting! I'm going to take a shower." Esther threw the blanket aside, then ripped wool socks off her feet and threw them across the room.

Mrs. Wong batted the air with her hand. "You'll be taking a shower over my dead body. If you came to Taichung like I asked, then you would be in a confinement center. We would have splurged for you. Two hundred dollars a day for one month is worth a lifetime of health, is it not? Do you want arthritis?"

When Esther rose out of bed, Mrs. Wong pulled out the big guns. "You owe me this. You got pregnant on a random day *and* you refused the C-section. You deprived my grandson of good fortune. Such a terrible mother before he was even born. He could have been famous, rich, but no! You refused!"

So Mrs. Wong believed in Chinese fortune-telling, better

known as *suànmìng*—which, literally translated, means to "calculate fate." A common practice was to use the parents' birthdays, the current year, and other arbitrary details to calculate the ideal day and time to give birth so that the child would have good luck. Obviously, to follow this practice, a C-section was needed.

Xing finally jumped in, telling his mother-in-law, "We don't believe in any of that stuff. You're here because we invited you. Don't make me kick you out."

Mrs. Wong turned to Xing. "So you don't love my daughter? You're depriving her of good health so what, you can run off with another woman when she dies young?"

Despite my intrusion into the private affair, I was frozen in place. *Wild card.*

Esther faced her mother, her expression calmer, probably because she was no longer lying in a pool of sweat. "This month is all about rest, right? I can't rest when I'm hot and dirty. And arguing like this is raising my blood pressure through the roof. So with that in mind, let's negotiate some new rules, okay?"

With a sigh of relief, Xing tiptoed out of the room. I followed.

"That's my wife, smartest person around."

Or . . . master manipulator? Maybe I could learn a few tricks.

Back in the nursery, with Jonathan swaddled in his crib, the tension ebbed, leaving just the poopy scent in the air.

"You did it," I said. "You're happy. Congratulations on everything."

"You're almost there. Business classes—"

"Actually, I just declared my major yesterday as business." I had grand jetéd through my marketing and optimization classes this past spring, and I had especially loved that the latter involved math. Now, not only did I have a bunch of career options in front of me, but the degree could help if I decided to open a dance studio in the future.

Xing nodded his approval, then amended his previous statement. "Business *major*, teaching dance, loving boyfriend . . ." He peered at me. "Are you ready for your dinner with Mom and Darren?"

I nodded. "Ready to release the beast. I can take whatever comes."

Xing laughed. "I wasn't worried about you. Or Mom. I was worried about Darren."

"Worry about Esther. Isn't Mom coming over to meet Jonathan next week?"

Xing nodded, his face twisting with anxiety (and probably mirroring mine). "Touché."

• • •

I had held off on talking to my mom about Darren for months. She had changed, but this was asking a dog to stop eating shit.

As I stood in front of Bertucci's with my heart in my larynx choking me, I regretted making the first move. Well, actually, I hadn't. My mother had, last week, by asking me how the "flip-flop wearer" was doing. A fight had ensued. . . . *Stop being racist, Māmá. Don't forget they slaughtered your family, Mei.* . . . But eventually, after I had reminded her of her issues with my father, we made headway. She didn't apologize, but she promised to try harder, then asked to meet Darren. I had been so relieved at her sincere smile and repentant eyes that I had agreed, only realizing after that it would be a crap-storm.

I wrung my hands. Darren gently pulled them apart. "Mei, stop worrying so much."

"Did you forget everything I told you?" I had tried to prepare him as best as I could, but how do you describe the tiny, formidable hurricane that is Mǎmá Lu?

"You know I've met her already, right?"

It took me a moment to remember. That day seemed like a parallel life.

"Well, that was different. You were a stranger then." And still she had been a stubborn ox. (Sometimes I wished she didn't take her zodiac sign so literally.) "Now you're *Darren*." I gulped. "Oh God, this was a mistake. You're going to break up with me after this."

"Calm down. That won't happen." He took both my hands in his and turned me to face him. "I love you, Mei." My entire body froze. "I started falling for you when I first heard you talk about Horny, and then when we moved on to beavers and nuts and magicians . . ." He placed a hand over his heart.

"I love you too," I said, no hesitation. "Ever since you told me you wanted to try stinky tofu *because* it smells so bad."

He wrapped his hand around the small of my back and pulled me to his lips.

Enjoy this moment. Stop worrying if Mǎmá is pulling up this instant. Don't let her ruin this for you.

And then it was just us.

I sank into him. Melted into his kiss. Snaked my hands around his neck and pulled him closer. I breathed in the sandalwood, then ran my hands through his already-disheveled hair.

When we reluctantly pulled apart, I no longer cared how the rest of today went.

Just in time, too. Moments later, the sea-green minivan (with a brand-new bumper dent) pulled across two parking spaces.

We sat in a corner booth, Darren and me on one side, my mother on the other. I could tell she was trying. She had a plastic smile pasted on, and even though it was all teeth, no lips, and creepy as hell, it was better than the vengeful scowl that usually surfaced in Japanese company.

"We should be meeting for Chinese food," she said. "But you probably were scared out of Chow Chow by the stinky tofu, right, Darren?" Her tone implied *I'm always right*.

"Stop being mean," I said at the same time Darren said, "I love Chow Chow. I actually tried the stinky tofu on one of my visits. To be honest, I didn't like it—the smell was too overpowering— but I love the rest of Chow Chow's food."

My mother leaned back, impressed, her chin pressing into her neck. "You tried it? Even Mei won't try it."

Darren shrugged. "I figured I wasn't allowed to say I didn't like it without giving it a taste."

"That's exactly how I feel!" my mother exclaimed. Her fake smile dissolved and was replaced by a slight curve, no teeth showing—her genuine smile.

"Well, I haven't tried poop and I'm confident saying I don't like it," I said.

Darren laughed, and my mother turned to him in surprise. Was that wonderment in her eyes? Confusion?

She shook off whatever had come over her with a head jerk. "Darren, I didn't know you were interested in our culture. Mei, you should have told me."

You couldn't hear anything about him once you knew his ethnicity, I wanted to say but instead managed a tight-lipped smile.

Below the table, Darren placed a comforting hand on my knee. He squeezed once, and I knew he was telling me to hang in there.

The rolls arrived. When I grabbed one, my mother's hand didn't twitch—a reminder of how far she'd come—and my shoulders relaxed.

It's going well, I reminded myself. No racial slurs, no murder accusations, and Darren had somehow impressed the unimpressible.

My mother broke her bread apart and dabbed the tiniest piece in olive oil. "What are your career plans, Darren?"

Maybe I'd spoken too soon. I braced myself.

"I'm interested in biology—"

"Are you going to be a doc-tor?" Her eyes lit up, and I wished I could extinguish them now before Darren had to.

"That's an option," he said, buttering a roll calmly as if his reputation didn't balance on a tightrope. "Right now I'm leaning toward research."

"Research is for people who can't get into medical school!" my mother huffed, her eyes darkening.

I jumped in. "He doesn't mean being an RA to spruce up his med school application. He wants to be a professor. At a university."

The light returned to her eyes. "A professor. Respectable. Good. And with a biology degree, you will still have the option to be a doctor in case you change your mind later."

I had assumed she was serious, but her mouth was ticked up. A joke attempt? I forced a laugh even though it wasn't funny. Points for effort.

The waitress served our pizza, pasta, and salad all at once to be eaten family-style. Asian-style.

My mother reached for the food first. "I love pizza. It's like an oyster pancake, but with the chee-se." She separated the word "cheese" into two syllables, the way it's pronounced in Mandarin. "I wish Bǎbá liked it as much as I did. Then I wouldn't have to wait until our meetings to get it."

I knew her use of the word "meeting" was the result of the language barrier and that she hadn't meant to refer to our bonding sessions like a business gathering. But still, I needed a deep breath. I reminded myself how her voice rose in pitch when we made plans and how her face always brightened when she saw me.

"How's Bǎbá?" I asked. I hadn't seen him since the funeral, and not for lack of trying, mostly on my mother's end. I had sent a few emails and left one voicemail, all unanswered. On the outside, I pretended my infrequent tries were because I didn't care, but it was really because the rejection was too hard. I tried to focus on the positive, how he no longer objected to my mother's relationship with me. I hoped that one day we'd be a family again. Some days it felt like a matter of time, but others it felt like a delusional dream I was clinging to for survival.

Like today. Before my mother had even responded, I knew the answer to my question. Lines had appeared on her face, a handful of new wrinkles since our last get-together that said, *Your father hasn't changed.*

Yet, I tried to remind myself.

My mother tore off a piece of crust, and without looking up, she said, "He's the same. Mopey. He misses you and Xing but won't admit it. I don't know why he can't just give a little."

"Cognitive dissonance perhaps?" I suggested.

My mom raised an eyebrow in question.

"Bǎbá sacrificed so much because of these traditions, and if he gives a little, it would mean his hardships were unnecessary," I explained. "So in a way, he *can't* give in because he can't accept that he suffered for no reason."

"My daughter, so smart," my mother said with a proud smile. I waited for the faux part of the brag, perhaps something about how I never used my intelligence for anything useful, but nothing came.

Suddenly my food tasted better despite my nose burning. I smiled at her, a cheek-straining, unadulterated smile I haven't given her since I was a little kid.

When only a few sausage balls remained on the pizza pan, Darren excused himself to the bathroom.

My mother cupped a hand over her mouth and whispered, "He's cute, like a young Takeshi Kaneshiro. He has the same jaw-line and nose."

"Ew, Mămá, please don't make me throw up my shrimp Rossini." I made a mental note to Google Takeshi Kaneshiro later.

Her face and voice grew serious, and I leaned forward instinctively.

"He likes you. He didn't care how loud you laughed or how fast you ate. How is this possible?" Her voice was tinged with jealousy.

My heart sank with the realization that she was ladylike for my father, fighting her natural instincts in fear of being cast aside. She looked exhausted from a lifetime of acting.

I placed a hand over hers. "You don't have to pretend. You can be yourself."

She turned her palm up and squeezed. "I'm learning from you. My smart girl. My American panda." Then she said the words I'd waited seventeen years to hear. "I'm proud of you."

I sucked a noisy breath in through my nose, unable to do anything else.

She slipped her hand away, reached into her purse, then tucked a red envelope into my palm, as she did every time we met.

"Thank you, Mămá," I breathed, referring to both the money and her words.

Darren was weaving his way back to us.

"Hang on to him, Mei. No one else will love your manly laugh."

I grinned. "So will I never hear the name 'Eugene Huang' again?"

"Of course you won't! Didn't you hear? He didn't get into medical school!"

Then we laughed. Together.

• • •

"And a five, six, seven, eight!"

The studio came to life with thirty tiny feet stomping, leaping, and trotting. At first I hadn't guessed those stubby legs could create such vibration, but now I was used to it. Rose arm-flapped right up to me, her red ballet skirt flowing, and she arched her neck to stick her giant smile in my face. Well, more like my stomach. I leaned down and flapped my arms in sync with her. She shrieked, then ran away to join her posse (of which she was queen, of course).

The pop music transitioned into Dunhuang bells and lutes, and I yelled, "Switch!"

Fifteen heads bobbed side to side in Xinjiang fashion as they rose to their tiptoes, *bourrée*-ing around the room amid giggles. I glanced around, taking in their energetic movements and gummy smiles.

If my heart hadn't been contained within my rib cage, it might have burst from happiness.

Once the little munchkins were gone, my adult students streamed in.

I clapped my hands to signal the start of class and switched on Beyoncé. I took my place at the front of the studio and eased into our warm-up routine, starting with isolations. As my head turned right-center-left-center, I glanced at the students in my peripheral vision. I couldn't make out their features but knew each of them by the way they moved.

Ying-Na was a hip-hop queen, each hip jut, body roll, and knee pop as natural as having a microphone in her hand. From the second she entered the studio to the last beat, she gave it everything, as if her movements could keep the ancestors away.

The first class, Tina (no longer Dr. Chang to me) had stood still in the corner. Just watched the others with wide mooncake eyes and slumped shoulders. But she returned week after week, and the fifth class, she took her first step. First stomp. First punch.

I looked at her now. Squared shoulders, wide smile, and bright eyes not focused on the others. Not focused on anything. She was feeling the music, throwing herself into each head turn. When we moved on to hip isolations, her pops were stiff and small, but she no longer flushed while doing them.

And when she walked, she no longer disappeared. Just like me.

I breathed dance every second of my life but spoke it to others twice a week. It seemed unfair to get paid to do something I loved so much. And in addition to getting a paycheck every month, I also got to take free classes.

After the students were gone, I took a moment to stare at the empty studio. My second home. Dance was where I had learned to be myself, but I no longer hid there. I danced everywhere I went, a little *pas de bourrée* slipping in here, a *tombé* there.

Always myself—noodle slurper, face toucher, and all.

Author's Note

Dearest Reader,

I wrote *American Panda* because it was the book I needed in high school and the book I needed when I decided to put my dental career aside to try writing, which I had no experience in. (I'll let you use your imagination to picture how my parents reacted to that.)

This novel is steeped in truth either from my own life or from friends. Some parts are from people I've met in passing who trusted me with their stories. It is based on experiences, but it has been fictionalized, and no characters or situations are exactly as they unfolded in reality.

I worked hard to keep Mei's experience authentic, but it is just one Taiwanese-American experience. I hope there will be more and more Chinese-American books to help represent the wide range of experiences out there.

I can't thank you enough for picking up this book, and I hope knowing Mei's story (and mine) will give you something I didn't have: the gift of knowing others share your experience, that it's okay not to feel wholly one thing or another, and it can get better.

You are not alone. You shouldn't have to hide to be accepted. You deserve to be appreciated and loved no matter who you are.

Find your inner *měi* and own it!

Gloria Chao

Acknowledgments

Thank you, first off, to you, dear reader, for picking up this book and sharing in Mei's story. I hope I was able to show some of you that you're not alone.

Kathleen Rushall, literary agent extraordinaire: Thank you for your wisdom, hard work, and endless optimism. Thank you for your spot-on revision notes, for taking risks with me, and for prioritizing my desire to keep this book authentic to my experiences. I feel like I can do anything with you on my side!

Jen Ung, my exceptional, *zuì yōuxiù* editor: You are such a perfect fit for me and this book, I sometimes think I wished you into existence. Thank you for bringing out the best in these characters, for championing this and other diverse books with so much heart, for being a dream to work with.

Thank you to the Simon Pulse team for your enthusiastic response from day one. I knew immediately that my book had found not just a publishing house but its home. Mara Anastas, thank you for your passion, your brilliance, and for everything you've done for this book. I am so grateful to the sales, marketing, and publicity teams. Special thanks to Liesa Abrams, Jodie Hockensmith, Nicole Russo, Vanessa DeJesus, Catherine Hayden, Lauren Hoffman, Amy Hendricks, Chelsea Morgan, Penina Lopez, Stacey Sakal, Kayley Hoffman, Christina Pecorale, Emily Hutton, Michelle Leo, Anthony Parisi, Amy Beaudoin, Janine Perez, and Anna Jarzab.

Sarah Creech, brilliant designer: Thank you for creating a cover that makes me smile and feel fuzzies every time I look at it. It captures Mei and the book better than I could have dreamed! And thank you, Tom Daly, for the gorgeous interior design!

Kim Yau, fantabulous TV/film agent: Thank you for believing in this story and for your passion. I'm so excited to work with you!

Thank you to the wonderful friends who made this book possible and who have left their footprints in these pages: Susan Blumberg-Kason, for your advice, endless support, and all your help with this manuscript. I'm so glad I picked up your book and reached out on Twitter. At the time, I had no idea I'd be making a lifelong friend. Lauren Lykke, for being my first writer friend and critique partner, and for squealing with me, dancing with me, and being one of my favorites. Rachel Lynn Solomon, for being my Simon Pulse sister, for our brainstorming sessions, your spot-on feedback, your constant support, and all the laughs! Meredith Ireland, for riding this out with me and for your editorial eye. Eva Chen, Melissa Ong, and Michele Margolis, you're the best beta readers and friends I could ask for! Lizzie Cooke, Samira Ahmed, Jilly Gagnon, Maddy Colis—you've made Chicago feel even more like home. A special hug to Claribel Ortega for your generosity and support, always. Arielle Eckstut and David Henry Sterry, for being the first two in the industry to believe in me (and Mei) and for your priceless wisdom along the way. A shout-out to Zoraida Córdova, who so kindly helped me with my cover reveal—thank you! Janice Zawodny, for showing me the beauty of dance and making me fall in love with it in a way I never thought possible. Thank you to the friends who supported me when I decided to change careers—you know who you are!

The Electric Eighteens, for your advice and encouragement. Class2K18, for your friendship and promotional help. The Kidlit AOC group, for your support and commitment to diversity. The We Need Diverse Books organization, for all the important work you do. Team Krush, you are as supportive as you are talented, and I'm proud to be a part of this loving family. Hugs and Kisses to ChiYA & my Awesome Authors Support Group.

Thank you to the lovely folks who were kind enough to read pages and provide feedback throughout this process, including: Whitley Abell, Christa Heschke, Jen Linnan, Sandy Lu, Myrsini Stephanides, Janine Le, Ella Kennen, Ronni Davis Selzer, Lisa Schunemann, Gracie West, Rachel León, Tamara Mataya, Roselle Lim, Katie McCoach, Naomi Hughes, Kevin Winn, Laura Heffernan, the AYAP Workshop.

Thank you so much, Tong Chen, Youqin Wang, and Jin Zhang, for your help with the pinyin in this novel and for not asking why

Acknowledgments

I had so many phrases about poop. Thank you, Koichiro Ito, for verifying the Japanese.

A huge thank-you to the wonderful librarians, booksellers, bloggers, and teachers out there putting books into the hands of readers who need them. An extra hug to the Chicago indie bookstores who have been so welcoming and supportive! And a special thank-you to Franny Billingsley, who I'm honored to call a friend, and Rachel Strolle, whose love of books is inspiring.

And a loving thank-you to my family: my grandparents, for their love, support, and stories. Dan and Matt, for helping me find the humor in stinky tofu, shrimp oil, and old Chinese songs growing up. Remember how we used to lock ourselves in a room, towels stuffed under the door, whenever Mom and Dad cooked stinky tofu?

Mom and Dad, for supporting my dreams and education. Oh, and thanks for the material. ;) Mom, I'm so grateful this book brought us so close. I don't know what I'd do without your support and love. Thank you for helping me with this book and for sharing your experiences and thoughts. I'm so happy I know you, *really* know you, now.

Anthony, there are no words for me to tell you what you mean to me. Thank you for believing in me before I did. For inspiring me. For reading a thousand drafts. For loving Mei like I do. For loving me more than anyone deserves. And of course, thank you for putting a roof over my head and feeding me and all that other important stuff while I typed-typed-typed into the night. You are my home, my hero, and my better half. *hip-level wave* (It works, people!)

Don't miss the next stunning
novel from Gloria Chao!

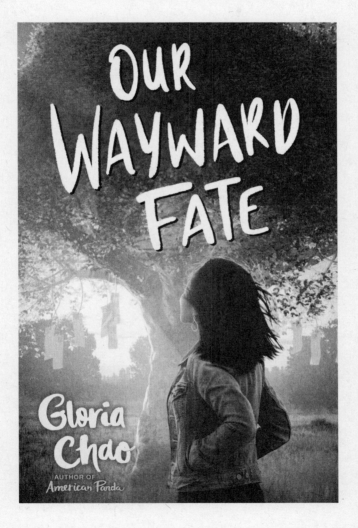

Turn the page for a sneak peek.

CHAPTER I

DRY TOAST

My mom believes in magic penises.

Because at the moment she was saying for the umpteenth time, "If you had been a boy, things would be different." The problem wasn't my genitals—it was my mother's outdated belief that boys were better. Plus, it wasn't *my* fault Dad's X sperm had been faster than the Y.

She waved the crumpled note in my face. It was only a sliver, a tiny corner of the whole with five measly words scrawled in my friend Brenda's loopy handwriting, but it was enough to cause all this.

"I'll ask one more time—what were you doing on the baseball field?"

Brenda was the one who'd rounded second base, and I was the one getting in trouble? It was so backward I wanted to laugh. But I didn't. I just stood there, my MO to the point where I often wondered if this next time would be the one to turn me into Buddha, bird poo on my head and everything.

"So disrespectful!" my mother huffed. What would she have done if I'd laughed? "If you had grown up in Taiwan, you wouldn't be so mù wú zūn zhǎng. And you would know what that phrase means."

Well if you had grown up here, maybe your lifelong dream wouldn't have been to grow a penis inside you.

Again, instead of voicing my thoughts, I stood there. Stared. Just like I had done yesterday when Mrs. Finch had asked if I was related to P. F. Chang, just like I'd done a week ago when Ava had told me I should wear eyeliner to "fix" my eyes, just like, just like, just like always.

"Baseball is too expensive a sport, all that equipment," my mother uncharacteristically continued. "And it's dangerous, and it doesn't stand out on college applications. . . ."

Since she gave me a rare peek inside her head, I returned the favor. "Don't worry, Mǔqīn, I've kept it to first base so far."

"First base, second base, it doesn't matter! No more baseball field, okay?"

My father walked in, not looking at either of us, not caring what was going on—aka his MO.

Since I knew his presence would hollow my mother into a shell,

I escaped our duplex in silence, wishing, for once, that my mother would mutter "mù wú zūn zhǎng" again under her breath, just so that someone would be saying something. Neither of my parents said good-bye, and I was guilty of the same because apple, tree, and all that.

I spent the rest of my free first period walking to my high school, located in the center of town in the sad triangle of "happening" places: the elementary school/middle school/high school, a tiny mom-and-pop grocery store, and a deli/hardware store.

When I arrived in our peeling, pubescent-boy-scented hallways, my friends ran up to me, more excited than anyone in Plainhart, Indiana, ever should be.

"No running, girls!" Mr. Andrews, the social studies teacher, yelled at us. "Hey, Allie," he added, turning to me so he was walking backward. "You'll love class today. We're discussing North Korea, and I can't wait to hear what you have to say!" He followed that doozy with sad, finger-pointing-guns, which was inappropriate on so many levels. I managed a straight-lined, half-assed smile and didn't bother to remind him I was Chinese.

As soon as he turned his attention to his next victim, Ava, Kyle, and Brenda fully encircled me.

"God!" Kyle exclaimed. "Took you long enough to get here."

"Have you seen him yet?" asked blond, perfect, white-as-a-bāo Ava as she grabbed my arm, which meant that whatever it was, it was big enough to make her break my no-touching rule.

I shook her off. "Who?"

"Okay, she hasn't seen," Kyle said in the bossy tone she'd

developed to survive being a girl with a mostly boys' name.

Since they were being so annoyingly cryptic and the only way to spill the gossip beans was to pretend I didn't care, I walked to my locker and started making myself a PB&J for lunch later. I actually hated peanut butter, but better eating that than hearing yet again how my congee looked like bleached vomit.

"Allie, pay attention! This is going to blow your mind!" Brenda said, which made me pause, because the excitement was so out of character for her.

I stared at White, Whitey, and Whiterson, holding my face steady even though I wanted to scream at them to freaking say it already.

But before they could, I saw him. I froze, a deer staring into the Asian headlight of the new student. It was almost as if there were a spotlight from God shining on him to tell me, *Ta-da! Finally, another person in this school who looks like you!*

I found myself taking in his clean-cut khakis, the guāi olive zip-up sweater, his tidy, close-cropped hair. His eyes met mine, but as the whispers around us grew, we both looked away.

Out of the corner of my eye I saw him disappear through the BC Calc classroom door, the same door I'd be slouching through in a moment.

Kyle grabbed my arm and shook it. "Allie, you two should totally become a thing—you go so well together!"

I wanted nothing more than to disappear, but to defuse the situation, I made a joke. "Why? Is it because"—I fake gasped—"we're both . . . nerds?" I gestured toward BC Calc.

Brenda started shaking her head, and I knew she was getting ready to say the obvious—*No, because you're both Asian*—but luckily, Ava cut her off by squealing, "And he's hot!"

That got my attention. "Hot like sriracha or hot like Szechuan food?" They stared at me. Oops. Slip-up. I was off my game suddenly. "I mean, hot like Noah Centineo or hot like *Fight Club* Brad Pitt?"

"Noah Centineo," Brenda and Kyle said just as Ava said, "Brad Pitt."

We all turned to stare at the odd one out as dictated by high school rules. Ava shrugged. "I saw him smoking just now. That's more Brad than Noah."

He smokes? Part of me was turned on, and the other part was just like *Gross* and *What's wrong with him?*

"You all know what's number one on my dream-guy list," I said to the nosy trio. Two words: *not Chinese*.

Kyle cleared her throat. "I hate to say it, Allie, but maybe you should forget that list. I know Jimminy Bob sucks"—Jimminy Bob was our code name for everyone we hated, and we always knew from context which Jimminy it was, in this case my mother—"but you're allowed to date Chinese guys!" More like *only* allowed to date Chinese guys (hence my aversion—I took every opportunity to stick it to my mǔqīn), but my friends were privileged enough not to understand the difference.

Ava leaned toward me. "Think about it, Allie. You'd finally have a hot boyfriend, who's also smart—well, I mean, I assume he is. That sounds like a dream guy to me."

As I went back to my half-built PB&J, I turned their words over in my head, but only for a second, because I refused to fulfill this Podunk town's stereotype. The only two Asians getting together—I could taste some bile just thinking about everyone saying, *Of course, of course, that makes sense; they belong together.* And besides, if my last interaction with another Asian had proved anything, it was that no one understood me, regardless of race.

I broke the end slice of bread into four pieces and rapid-chucked them at each girl, emphasizing a word per hit. "Not. Interested. At. All." Kyle got the extra hit, to the boob.

I made my way to BC Calc, and, of course, as soon as I entered, whispers of "meet-cute" and "so perfect" and "both Asian" filled the small, suffocating room. My fists clenched to keep from hurling chalkboard erasers at every last one of them. I tried to purposefully ignore the giant not-yellow-but-also-not-white spotlight as I walked past, my head in the air, but then—I couldn't help it—I scanned his notebooks, textbooks, papers for his name, and finally, on the corner of the class schedule in front of him, there it was: Chase Yu.

Possibly Chinese, maybe Korean?

"Oooh, checking out the new Asian meat?" someone called to me from the back of the room.

Womp womp. Mission to blend in and be as dry as white toast: failed by my own doing for the first time in years.

I ignored them and slunk into my seat, hunching in the hopes of shrinking the massive bull's-eye on my back. Who knows what

Chase did in response because I was already tuned the F out.

"Settle down, settle down," Mr. Robinson said as he entered, shuffling papers.

But he stopped in his tracks when he saw Chase, apparently also a deer in the Asian headlight. "Oh boy, now there's two of you?" he said, looking from Chase to me. "The rest of the class better watch out for you guys ruining the curve."

Surprise, surprise: Racist Robinson strikes again. Seriously, there wasn't much that could make me hate math, but Mr. Robinson was up there. I folded in on myself even more, keeping my head down as I waited for the naked-in-school dream-turned-reality to pass.

But Chase shot up out of his seat. "Well, by that logic you, Mr. Robinson, must love Dave Matthews, and you probably have a Chinese tattoo on your butt that you think says 'strength' but actually says 'butthole.'"

Hole-y crap. Chase wouldn't last two days here, not when he was being Taiwanese pineapple cake with red New Year's streamers— the opposite of white toast.

Robinson gaped at Chase, then shook off the shock and said with a laugh, "Aren't you Asians supposed to kowtow, especially to authority?" He waved a hand in my direction. "This one certainly does."

Chase looked at me, and even though my blood was hotter than Szechuan food, I gazed out the window. He grabbed his books and stalked out of the room, slamming the door behind him just as Mr. Robinson yelled, "Hey! You better be on your way to the counselor's office!"

A muffled "fuck you!" drifted past the closed door.

Who *was* this clean-cut bad boy?

I lay my head on my folded arms. I knew—*knew*—there had to be a better place than this, where shit like this didn't happen every day. I didn't even know what my inner voice sounded like anymore. (Maybe deep and a bit gruff from constant annoyance?)

When the bell rang, I trudged out of the room, and in the hallway, his back against a locker, was Chase.

Pleeease don't be waiting for me. . . .

"Why didn't you say anything?" he asked as he fell in step with me. "Didn't it bother you?"

I shrugged. "Easier to let it go."

"Doesn't mean it's not worth trying. I couldn't *not* say something."

I shrugged again.

He shook his head at me in disbelief. "Bú xiàng huà," he muttered, so quietly I may not have heard, but I'd been holding my breath.

The Mandarin threw me. Like, threw me across the room and knocked the wind out. I hated that this was the first time I was hearing Mandarin in these desolate hallways, and even more, hated that it created a bond between us. And by hated, I mean I was 100 percent drawn to him. I could practically hear my mother laughing her head off at me. *I'm always right, Ali. This is why you need to be with a Chinese boy.*

"Hope you grow some balls someday, Allie," Chase said as he started to walk away.

My fingernails dug into my palms. I fucking *had* (proverbial) balls. I also had a brain, which was why I hadn't said anything. That was the way to get out of here unscathed ... right? Regardless, I was sick of people accusing me of not having male genitalia. I preferred my vagina, thank you very much, not that anyone in my life cared to ask.

I don't know why—maybe it was because my blood was past boiling—but I called after him, "It's Ali, jackass." And for the first time, my name rolled off my tongue the way it was supposed to: Āh-lěe, after the mountain in Taiwan, my mother's favorite place in the world. I'd never said it that way before, with beauty. With meaning. With pride. It had always been Allie, the dry-toast way, at first because it was easier, and then for survival.

Chase turned back to me. "That's a start."

A smile lifted the corner of his lip. It made me want to smile too, but I shrugged instead. He chuckled with a shake of his head before jogging down the hallway.

"Hey, wait!" I yelled after him. "How'd you know my name?" When he didn't respond, I embarrassingly yelled, "Chase?"

Which, since I technically shouldn't have known his name yet either, was the opposite of dry toast.

CHAPTER 2

BROKEN EGG ROLLS

That evening, while my mother swished her spatula rhythmically against the wok, I hovered near her, setting the table with chopsticks, white rice, napkins, and lots o' bowls (we didn't own plates). I'd be eating alone later because I had kung fu soon, but I was waiting for my opening like a Putt-Putt ball trying to clear the windmill. As usual, my mother was oblivious to my inner unrest.

Chase's abracadabra appearance out of nowhere had torn through the school like that gonorrhea outbreak last year, and as much as I'd wanted to escape him, he had shown up in every single class of mine today. Everywhere he followed, so did the "yes, yes, they belong together" whispers. Why did he have to be the only other person taking a more-than-full load of honors and APs? God, Chase, you just *had* to give us a bad name. There was only room for one stereotypical Asian in these Podunk hallways, and I had nabbed the title against my will years ago.

When the sizzling from the stove lessened and my mother's movements quieted, I cleared my throat, a signal of how infrequently we talked.

"Hmm?" she said, her eyes never leaving the wok.

"You know how you always tell me that when I date—"

"Only Chinese boys," she said automatically, like it was a programmed response, which, well, at this point, it was.

"Why is that so important to you?"

She poured the now thoroughly stir-fried meat-and-veggie egg-roll filling into a large bowl. The silence stretched so long I wondered whether she'd heard my question.

But I stood my ground, both figuratively and literally.

"You know I want the best for you, right?" she finally said, still not looking at me and instead sitting down to wrap egg rolls. But she pushed the skin and filling toward me, and by inviting me to join her, I knew she was extending a hand and a little love.

I planted my pìgu at the dining room table a little too eagerly. "But what does that even mean, Māmá?" *How can you know what the best is when you don't know me?*

"I've had experience, Ali. Don't you remember? In Chinese culture, we revere the elderly for their wisdom. Just trust me."

There it was, that condescending tone with no explanation,

just instructions and pithy Chinese sayings. I started to ask her to elaborate, but she hastened her folding and I knew the door I'd briefly opened was sealed as tight as her egg roll.

Not wanting to leave just yet, I carefully peeled a thin sheet of egg-roll skin off the stack, irrationally wondering if she would open up more if I impressed her with my wrapping skills. You know, reminded her we were mother and daughter, not strangers.

Her eyes were glued to her hands as she spoke. "Ali, have you thought more about taking the trip to China I suggested?"

This again. I'd been lulled into a false state of security since she hadn't mentioned it in two weeks—actually, now that I thought about it, we hadn't *spoken* in two weeks except for the second-base debacle.

I proceeded carefully. "You said you want me to go there to find my roots, but you're from Taiwan."

"Yes, but before me, our family was from China."

"Doesn't it make more sense for me to visit Taiwan, though?"

She sighed. "Aiyah, Ali, you always have to make everything so difficult. I'm trying to do a nice thing."

"We don't have the money," I stated, a simple truth.

She didn't disagree with me. After a brief pause she started to say something, but at that very moment the front door opened and closed.

No "Honey, I'm home" for this household, in either language. My mother stiffened, her fingers flying as her jaw set in its clenched position (I often worried about her teeth and whether she had ground them down to the pulp yet).

My father passed through the kitchen because he had to, and as usual he nodded at each of us with a forced smile.

How was your day? and *What did you have for lunch?* and *Will you please talk to Mamá?* all floated through my head and danced on my tongue before dissolving in the graveyard where the other hundred thousand questions were buried.

My mother didn't even look up. Was it improvement or regression that she hadn't bothered to glare at him? If experience showed anything, it was the latter. The worst step had been when they'd stopped fighting, when they'd chosen to ignore each other instead of trying.

My dad disappeared into the bedroom and my mother's shoulders relaxed again. Just like hers, my fingers tackled the egg roll with desperation, as if that were somehow the solution.

Filling—corner—corner—tuck and roll. Like riding a bike. I stacked my finished egg roll next to hers, and it looked almost identical, only a smidge looser. No longer was I the child making egg rolls that spilled meat and veggies out one or both ends or through an accidental hole made by a clumsy fingernail.

My hand froze, and for a moment I pretended it was years ago, before we had moved here, before my parents had become the ghosts they were today. I used to be so disappointed that, unlike my mother's perfectly jǐn and tidy egg rolls, mine were fat and luànqībāzāo, like a drunk, sloppy Santa on December 26. But my mother would always tell child Ali, *Patience. One day, if all goes as planned, you'll do better than me. In everything. Qīng chū yú lán.*

But it hadn't gone as planned. My father had been denied

tenure at Boston University, and then he'd accepted a job against my mother's wishes at a tiny, "not prestigious" liberal arts school. To my mother, rankings were everything, to the point that she learned how to use the internet just to stay up to date with *U.S. News & World Report*'s college rankings. She chose to put all her trust in those numbered lists and didn't care that everyone else in town seemed to be impressed by my father's job at the "local gem," Frank College. For the record, I didn't care either, but it was because, as with everything, there was a sprinkle of racism on top: *Of course he's an intellect—he's Asian, so smart.*

After my father moved us here to our own little microaggression hell, the Chu family fell apart faster than shaved ice in hot pot. At the time, I hadn't understood how something so small could have such a huge ripple, but then—hello cornfields and lower pay—I learned way too young that it's harder to be happy when you're ostracized and worried about the roof over your head.

When I aligned my second egg roll—this one as tight as hers—with the others, I noticed my mother had tears in her downcast eyes.

Was it because of my egg roll? Or because of what had just happened with my father?

Seeing a crack in her wall, I reached a hand out and placed it on hers, which was mid-wrap.

How it played out in my head: she grasps it back, tells me she loves me, then apologizes for being so distant the past eleven years.

Okay, maybe that was a bit too cheesy and unrealistic, but I definitely didn't expect it to play out as horribly as it did.

About the Author

Gloria Chao is an MIT grad turned dentist turned writer. She currently lives in Chicago with her ever-supportive husband, for whom she became a nine-hole golfer (sometimes seven). She is always up for cooperative board games, Dance Dance Revolution, or soup dumplings. She was also once a black belt in kung fu and a competitive dancer, but that side of her was drilled and suctioned out. Visit her tea-and-book-filled world at gloriachao.wordpress.com.

RIVETED

BY *simon teen* ♥

BELIEVE IN YOUR SHELF

Visit RivetedLit.com & connect with us on social to:

DISCOVER NEW YA READS

READ BOOKS FOR FREE

DISCUSS YOUR FAVORITES

SHARE YOUR IDEAS

ENTER SWEEPSTAKES FOR THE CHANCE TO WIN BOOKS

Follow @SimonTeen on

to stay up to date with all things Riveted!